KALEIDOSCOPE hearts
VOL. 2

NINE MORE CHANCES TO FALL IN LOVE

GINA ARDITO	LINDA BOULANGER	LAURA HERN
GRACE AUGUSTINE	EDWARD BUATOIS	ANDI LAWRENCOVNA
CJ BATY	JENNIFER DANIELS	M.M. ROETHIG

KALEIDOSCOPE HEARTS

Vol. 2
Nine More Chances to Fall in Love

Gina Ardito, Grace Augustine, CJ Baty, Linda Boulanger, Edward Buatois, Jennifer Daniels, Laura Hern, Andi Lawrencovna, & M.M. Roethig

Copyright © at Gina Ardito, Grace Augustine, CJ Baty, Linda Boulanger, Edward Buatois, Jennifer Daniels, Laura Hern, Andi Lawrencovna, & M.M. Roethig, 2020

All rights reserved. Printed in the United States.
Front Cover art from: Linda Boulanger, Tell Tale Book Covers.

First Edition: February, 2020
BISAC: Fiction / Romance / General

10 9 8 7 6 5 4 3 2 1

The novels created in this compilation are works of fiction. The characters, incidents, and dialogues are the creation of each author's imagination and are not to be construed as real. Any resemblance to actual events, or persons, living or dead, is completely coincidental.

The author of each novel is solely responsible for the content of their work.

All rights to all stories included in this collection are retained by the individual author. No part of this book may be reproduced or transmitted, including photocopying, recording, or by any information storage and retrieval system, without written permission from the individual author except in the case of brief quotations embodied in critical articles or review. The unauthorized reproduction, sharing, or distribution of this copyrighted work is illegal. Criminal copyright infringement, including infringement without monetary gain, is investigated by the FBI and is punishable by up to five years in federal prison and a fine of $250,000.

Some of the novels in this anthology contain romantic situations that may be inappropriate for audiences under the age of 18.

Dedication

THIS BOOK IS dedicated to everyone. Love is a part of everything around us. Families, friends, lovers, companions – these are all just words representing the different types of love in our lives. Never take for granted the smallest kindness from someone who cares, because these are the most important expressions of love we can receive.

Table of Contents

Dedication III
Letter from the Authors VI
Play-Action Pass 11
The Magic of Sapphire Creek 57
Second Chances 103
Surrender to The Storm 115
A Love Full of Colors 129
Whispers of Fate 147
Roommates 183
The Nightingale 221
Two Hearts 251
About the Authors 271

Letter from the Authors

Dear Readers,

We are delighted you have chosen to read and enjoy Kaleidoscope Hearts vol. 2! The stories within are crafted with love, and we hope that you find a little of the same within these pages.

It is our greatest wish that you fall in love with the characters in our stories and with the authors who wrote them.

From all of us to you,
The Kaleidoscope Hearts

KALEIDOSCOPE hearts

VOL. 2

Play-Action Pass
Gina Ardito

Chapter One

"Not again."

Cameron Delgado entered the front office to find roses erupting from her receptionist's desk.

"*Three* dozen this time," Val replied from behind the blazing forest of ivory-frosted crimson blooms. "The delivery boy said they're called 'fire and ice' roses, because they're red on the inside and white on the outside, instead of just basic red." Her blond head popped up from behind the garden like a prairie dog's. "Nice, don't you think?"

Nice? Not particularly. Even before she pulled the florist's envelope from the plastic stick, Cam knew who'd sent the Overkill Bouquet.

"Toss them." She waved a hand, noticed her ragged nails, and shoved her fists—with the florist's card still clutched between her fingers—into her jacket pockets. "But not here. Take them out to the hallway trash. Anywhere in here, and they'll make the whole office smell like a funeral parlor."

An odor she'd rather not relive in the coming few days.

"Umm..."

Val's unusual hesitancy ruffled Cam's already frazzled interior. Rising on tiptoes to stretch to full-force-intimidation-six-foot-height, Cam peered over the flowers. Her normally staid receptionist blushed like a teenager with her first crush.

"Spit it out, Val."

The young woman's teddy bear gaze darted in a dozen directions before landing on the ostentatious blooms. "Can I keep them? I mean...you probably get flowers like these all the time...but...well..."

Cam rolled her eyes. *Oh, I so do not have time for this right now. The awards dinner is in six hours. I still have to shower, change, and now it looks like I need an emergency manicure.*

As if rubbing salt in Cam's bleeding wounds, Val folded perfect cotton candy-painted fingernails into a clasp of prayer. "Please? I bet they cost a fortune. It'd be a shame to just throw them in the trash."

Annoyance sparked, and for a moment Cam considered using the water in the vase to douse her rising ire. Finally, she sighed. "Put them in the kitchen area until you leave today."

While Val reached eager hands to the glass vase, Cam strode into her office and shut out the world. On the other side of the door, she lifted her purse to eye-level in front of her, dangling it from her fingertips by a thin strap. "Delgado lines up for the kick."

A quick drop...

A swing of her right leg...

Contact!

Her bag soared through the miniature goalpost standing sentry on the other side of the room. *Da-thump!* The black canvas clutch landed in a small vinyl storage box sitting directly behind the uprights on the carpeted end zone.

"A perfect extra-pointer," she exclaimed in her best sportscaster voice. "And *that's* the game!"

Exhaling air to imitate the sound of a roaring crowd, she shimmied to her desk in a victory dance. When she sat in her office chair, the ergonomic hiss was a welcome sound in her inner sanctum. She pulled the florist's card from her pocket. The envelope displayed the name of a high-priced Manhattan flower boutique. When she pulled out the cardboard square, the words kinked her stomach in spirals of torment.

Please don't let the past ruin what could be a bright future for hundreds of kids. Your dad wouldn't want that to be his legacy. Call me.

-Jordan

Her gaze strayed to the gilt-framed photo on the corner of her desk. Daddy's smiling face, shadowed by the football helmet askew on his head, stared back. Almost thirty years had passed since that horrible night. Yet, she still heard her mother weeping, still felt that gnawing hunger in her belly, still shivered as icy realization clutched her heart.

The dire words floated through a miasmic sea of memories.

"...storm over Guadalupe..."

"...plane went down..."

"...rain forest..."

"...no survivors..."

The tiny white envelope fluttered to her desktop.

And now Jordan Fawcett, the one man she'd ever dared to let into her private life, the man who'd betrayed her, wanted to do business with her, using her beloved father's memory to goad her into submission. As if nothing had ever happened between them. He actually thought a coupla dozen roses would make up for her heartbreak, for her inability to trust any other man, for the self-doubts that plagued her to this day.

"Sorry, Jordan Fawcett." She tore the card once, twice, a dozen times until pieces of white cardboard confetti littered her scarlet pencil skirt. "Go play on someone else's field. I'll win this game without you."

JORDAN FAWCETT HUDDLED outside the gated alleyway, waiting. The rain, a light drizzle all afternoon, had become a deluge. Sheets of icy water streamed from the black sky, carving a path between the collar of his raincoat and his shirt, dousing his back until fabric stuck to his skin like pilot fish on a shark.

Thunder rumbled overhead and seconds later, a spear of lightning pierced the night. Great. Just what he needed.

He supposed his name and past triumphs would have gained him entry into the honorary dinner tonight. If he'd attended the awards gala, he probably would have found an opportunity to corner her alone in some quiet alcove, instead of here on the street. But there, he'd also have to contend with a host of angry pro football players acting as bodyguards.

The players from the New York Vanguard, both active and retired, considered Cameron Delgado their lucky charm, their mascot, their Little Orphan Annie. The moment the wreckage of Duke's plane was discovered, his daughter became a media magnet. Delgado's teammates immediately went into protective mode, closed ranks, and blocked her from the spotlight.

Fifteen years later, when the foundation held its annual Duke Awards ceremony and fundraiser, there was the fatherless waif, now fully grown and controlling the reins of Duke's massive financial empire. With a shiny new MBA from Wharton and a corral of young and old football players surrounding her, Cameron Delgado claimed her place as the league's princess. And there she remained.

When he made the pros, Jordan focused on his career, and hadn't given much thought to some dead has-been's foundation for children in need around the world. But he'd noticed *her*, and he'd done everything he could think of to get her to notice him. They'd been the perfect couple—until he'd gone for broke and proposed. That was when it all went to shit.

Tires hushed over wet pavement, and a black limousine pulled to a stop outside the sleek, modern building.

Thank God. He pushed himself forward out of the shadows, but remained far enough back that he stayed invisible to anyone standing on the sidewalk.

The green-coated, white-gloved doorman reached for the handle of the passenger door while simultaneously opening a black umbrella. Out stepped a pair of shapely legs, tanned and supple, shod in strappy black shoes. Rhinestone clips near the toes glinted beneath the streetlights.

Time to get this show on the road.

Rushing forward, he held out his hand. "Darling! I'm sorry I'm late. Traffic was brutal."

Cameron Delgado stood on the sidewalk, the car door yawning open behind her. Dammit, he'd forgotten how tall she was, how she still managed to look delicate and lovely in dresses and heels when he knew damn well she was meaner and stronger than a linebacker.

Judging by the disgusted expression that crept over her face, she saw him as a pile of dog crap on the bottom of her shoe.

"You should have called, honey," she purred.

Without missing a beat or disclosing any revulsion in her tone, she leaned close enough to kiss his cheek. Her cologne, lightly floral with a hint of musk, tickled his nostrils and evoked memories of long ago days filled with laughter. A sharp pang of regret pierced his chest. Maybe she had run scared, but he'd screwed the follow-up—badly. If he had stayed with her, had never left for Houston, would they have found their way back together by now? Would he still have a thriving football career?

The doorman, hovering with the umbrella, also leaned closer, and the rainwater flowed over the convex edge directly onto Jordan's head to shock him back to the here and now.

"When you didn't show," Cam added, straightening to her full height again. "I made other plans."

As a final insult, she ruffled his sodden hair through her fingers before turning away, effectively dismissing him. Her familiar laughter, this time filled with derision, rang over the clack of her heels as she strode into the apartment building, the doorman running to keep up with her fabulous, long legs.

Chapter Two

THE ELEVATOR WHOOSHED Cam up to the penthouse suite while she struggled to rein in her soaring temper.

Of all the nerve…

Did he really think he could accost her in the street and she'd simply play along with whatever game he'd devised this time? The door slid open into her living room, and she stumbled to the couch, peeling off her coat along the way. By the time she collapsed into the plush gray cushions, the trembling in her legs had made any further movement impossible. Tears filled her eyes, and she sniffed them back to keep her makeup in place. The Duke Awards, an annual fundraiser and celebration of her father's life, always ripped her emotions apart. Greeting all the most famous names in professional sports who attended exhausted her. The endless reminders of her father and his generosity brought on melancholy. Watching her mother dancing with the man she'd married last year riled her. Everywhere she turned, everything that met her gaze, evoked some kind of physical reaction.

Tonight, though, coming face-to-face with Jordan after all this time, left her an overwrought mess. Yes, she *hated* him, but she couldn't help indulging in a teeny bout of sympathy at how cruelly fate had treated him after their breakup. She hadn't seen him in person since before the injury that ruined his career. She'd seen the game, of course. Two years after he left the Vanguard franchise to sign with the Houston Privateers, a blitz by the defensive line ended with him being sacked, the hit from three players at once so hard it damaged his lower spine.

Despite the hard feelings she'd nursed over his abrupt departure, she had immediately flown to Texas to help him in any way she could, but he refused to let her in. Seeing Paris Redmond glide by the hospital security desk with a smile and a wave in the guard's direction told Cam exactly where she stood, physically and romantically. By putting her on his no admittance list, Jordan had tattooed his ambivalence directly onto her heart. Now, he was back in New York. Was Paris with him? Did it matter? Not really.

On a deep sigh of regret, Cam removed her shoes and flexed her aching toes, then let her body go limp, boneless. She flung one arm over her head to shield her eyes. God, she was a mess tonight! Wired as she was, after the annual homage to her dad, toss in Jordan's sudden appearance in front of her building, and no wonder her skin felt electrically charged and too tight for her frame. She needed a hot bath, an enormous glass of wine, and a friend to talk to.

Problem was, she didn't have the energy to move. She dug into her teeny evening purse to grab her cell. Only one person she could call right now, and she didn't hesitate, regardless of the hour.

The phone on the other end rang once before his cheery voice said, "What took you so long? I've been waiting for details all night."

"Feel like popping over for a while?"

"That bad, huh? Don't worry, sweetheart. I'm on my way."

Cam disconnected the call, dropped her phone on the cushion beside her, and closed her eyes. Without moving, she announced up toward the ceiling, "Call front desk."

A buzz sounded in the room, and the familiar voice of the overnight manager, Tommy, intoned over the loudspeaker hidden in the alcove. "Good evening, Ms. Delgado. How may I help you?"

"Hi, Tommy. Mr. Wallace is coming over. Send him up right away when he arrives."

"Yes, Ms. Delgado."

"Thanks."

"You're very welcome. Enjoy your evening." The speaker clicked off, and Cam was alone with her thoughts again.

After several minutes of blissful silence, the bell dinged, announcing the elevator's arrival on her private floor. Rousing her tired synapses, she pushed herself to her stocking feet. That one action sapped what was left of her dwindling energy, and she remained rooted to the floor.

The steel door whooshed open, and a grizzled bear of a man lumbered inside, arms extended. He reached her in half a dozen strides and swooped her into a hug.

"There's my beautiful lady," he crooned in her ear as he squeezed the breath out of her. "Was it that bad?"

"No worse than usual." She wriggled out of his embrace to restart her respiratory system. "The same people, the same conversations..." On a huff of expelled air, she flounced back onto the sofa. "You know how this shindig plays out."

For several years, until his divorce from her mother, he'd been an active participant like her. After the divorce, vindictive Mom made sure he never again made the guest list—despite his position as Daddy's best friend and head coach of the team they once both carried to so many game wins. He probably could've shown up anyway, the team would have backed him up, but Bertie, the peacemaker, would never publicly humiliate her mother that way.

"Well, something's got you wound up tonight," he remarked. "What is it? Did your mom start in on you again?"

"No. She was too involved with Mr. Ellison to notice me." Mr. Ellison. Husband number...four?...five?...since Daddy died? She couldn't keep track. Only Bertie mattered to her. Husband number two, the man she'd always consider her only stepfather, no matter how many men married her mother in the coming years.

Bertie gave her a meaningful once-over from head to toe and snorted. "Looking as gorgeous as you do in that outfit? How could anyone ignore you?"

Despite her mangled emotions, she mustered a smile. "Ha. Easy, with perfect-size-two Mom in the room."

He skimmed an index finger down her nose, the way he always did when she was an insecure child with a gorgeous mother who judged her too harshly. "There's more to you than a dress size, beautiful. Remember that." He punctuated the reminder with a poke on the tip of her nose.

She wriggled on the couch, folding her arms over her chest to camouflage the bit of bulge at her waistline that no hydraulic underwear could hide.

"Stop that," he growled, pulling her arms apart. "You're perfect, Cam. A real man likes a woman with curves."

A block of tears clogged her throat, and she swallowed them back, then patted the space beside her. Her palm slapped the slender chain of her evening bag, and she wrapped her fingers around the cool silver links before flinging the accessory over the back of the couch. A clink-thud erupted when the purse hit the polished wooden floor.

"Sit," she said, her voice rough as sandpaper. "I need your shoulder."

"Uh-oh." He settled next to her, his bulk sinking the cushion so that she rose a tick—no small feat, considering her own meatiness. She frowned, and Bertie wrapped a brawny arm around her to bring her closer. His every inhale and exhale echoed against her ribcage, a soothing tempo she'd enjoyed since childhood. She let the rhythm calm her frazzled nerve endings, snuggling closer, her ear pressed to his chest until his vibrato broke the spell. "So...what's up?"

On a weighty sigh, she straightened again, mentally scrambling to figure out where to begin. "Okay, so you know how I've been trying to find a new space for the midtown center?"

"Uh-huh..."

One of the many things she loved about Bertie, he never pressed her or interrupted when she needed to talk. He always let her move at her own pace.

"Well, there's a building about five blocks from our current site that looks perfect. Plenty of space for our growing pains, convenient to bus and subway stops, and in our price range."

"But..."

She uttered the statement in one breath, without a pause. "But the leasing agent is Jordan Fawcett."

Bertie gave a curt nod. "Ah."

"Yeah." She grimaced.

She didn't have to say anything more about her feelings. Without additional details, Bertie understood how painful this situation must be for her. After all, he'd been the one to fly to Texas to help gather up her shattered pieces when Jordan rejected her at the hospital. Not her mother—*never* her mother—whose only advice was the constant, "If you'd only lose some weight, you could have your pick of men." Like she could fight the genetics that made her build more like Duke Delgado's instead of the frail-bird-stature of her mother's family.

"Why do I sense you've got more to say?"

Good old astute Bertie. She tangled her hands in the fabric of her skirt. "Because I do. Guess who was waiting for me outside the building when I came home tonight."

His lantern jaw unhinged and hung open. "No."

She nodded.

"How'd he look?"

"Wet," she retorted. "He must have hung outside here for hours, waiting for me."

"Well, that's interesting."

"Ya think? I find it idiotic. He could wind up with pneumonia."

"I'm guessing he really wanted to see you, so he must've thought it worth the risk. I mean, he could've called the corporate office if it was about leasing the property. But, no. He hung around here in the rain. What'd he say when he saw you?"

She didn't bother to mention the multitude of bouquets he'd sent in the past few weeks or her refusal to take any of his calls once she found out he was the agent on that particular locale. But the message on that last card, burned into her memory, came to her lips unbidden. "He said I shouldn't let our ugly history affect Daddy's legacy."

"Hmm..." He scratched his temple. "Not exactly the apology I would've expected from him."

"Why would he apologize? Nothing's changed. I'm still the fat girl he ditched for a beauty queen when he realized dating Duke Delgado's daughter wouldn't propel his career into the stratosphere. Now that he's no longer playing ball, he thinks he can bounce back into my life and use me to up his real estate creds. Like I'm some kind of trampoline."

Bertie shook his head. "I can't believe I was so wrong about him. I always thought better of Jordan."

"So did I—once. Now, I know he's a user and a creep." Her voice cracked on the last word as the pain pierced her heart yet again, as it always did when she thought about the man she'd once loved.

"At least tell me you got the last word with the bum."

"I did."

He gave her shoulder a quick squeeze. "That's my warrior woman. Now, you listen to me. No matter what you decide to do about the midtown center, your dad's legacy is safe in your hands and always has been. If you really like the space, go for it."

She dropped her gaze to her hands, wringing in her lap. "I don't think I relish sitting across a board table from him, Bertie."

"I'll do it if you can't. Frankly, I'd welcome the opportunity to give him a piece of my mind."

"And let him think I'm still so hung up on him that I can't face him over a business deal?" God, wouldn't *that* be humiliating! "No, thanks. I'll handle him and I'll get that property. By the time I'm done with him, he'll wish he'd stayed in Houston. If I have to, I'll kick his ass back there." She mimed dropping a ball and kicking it over the goal posts.

With a low chuckle, Bertie kissed her cheek. "I know you will."

JORDAN HAD PLENTY of time to review the evening's events when he returned home. After a hot shower, a warm towel, and dry clothes, he would've expected sleep to overtake him easily. But, no. In bed, he stared at the ceiling, reviewing the mistakes he'd made in trying to reach Cameron. He'd really underestimated the power of his charms. Why was she so pissed at him anyway?

Okay, so maybe they hadn't parted under the best of circumstances, but he would always live under her father's shadow if he'd remained with the Vanguard. Regardless of his success on the gridiron, the whispers that he only had his position because he was dating Duke's daughter had grown too loud to ignore. So when the Houston Privateers sought a veteran quarterback to provide leadership for a group of young, talented but inexperienced players, Paris pitched him as the perfect candidate. The Privateers bit, and he signed on the dotted line without consulting Cam.

As soon as she heard, she shut down, broke off all communications, and cut him out of his life. He should have realized her loyalty would always remain with the Vanguard. Daddy's girl, Daddy's team.

But God help him, he still wanted her. Seeing her had been a big mistake. Bad enough he'd ceded home court advantage, but then she'd looked down on him from her dressy sky-high heels, making him feel vulnerable and small with one glare. A devastating fall when she was the one person who'd always looked up to him in the past...

Once again, the ifs invaded his thoughts. If he hadn't signed the Houston contract, how would their lives have turned out? Would he have taken the hit that destroyed his pro career from another player during another game? And if he had been injured while still playing for the Vanguard, would she have cared enough to come back to him? Or would she have kept him on her cut list, the way her mother treated Bertie?

He shuddered. Big mistake, going to her apartment building tonight. *Huge*, honking mistake. She was always brittle after the annual awards dinner, primarily because Bertie couldn't attend. He should've remembered that. Why hadn't he?

He spent most of the night mentally kicking himself for his lack of empathy, and sleep refused to give him respite.

The next morning, bleary-eyed and irritable, he limped into his office only to spot his business partner wearing a grin wide enough to eat the Cheshire Cat.

She veered around the desk, a crisp manila folder clutched in one hand. "Congratulations."

"For what?" he grumbled.

"We just got a call from the Delgado Foundation. They want to set up a time to meet and discuss leasing the old Laughlin building."

Hope sparked inside him, and he pointed to the folder she held. "Is that the file?" She nodded and held it out to him. He grabbed the file and flipped it open to the cover sheet with the company's contact information. As the words infiltrated his muddy brain, he looked up at Susan. "That's Cam Delgado's direct line?"

"Uh-huh. She called first thing this morning. I didn't even have my coat off before I was writing down all the particulars. How'd you convince her? Was it the roses? I told you. No woman can resist three dozen red and white roses."

Clutching the folder in one fist, he headed to his office, allowing Susan to prattle on and take credit for their breakthrough. The truth was, he had no idea what made Cam change her mind, but he doubted *a thousand* flowers would have affected the ice princess he saw last night. For God's sake, she'd ruffled his hair—like he was a street urchin in a Dickens Christmas play. Tiny Tim, all grown up and still a lame beggar. A ball of bile rose in his throat, and he swallowed hard while closing his office door. The bitter aftertaste made him grimace. He removed his jacket, hung it on the coat rack in the corner, then made himself comfortable behind his desk, leaving the folder to the side of his keyboard and monitor. As he stared out the window at the traffic on the avenue five stories below him, a sharp rap sounded on his door. Susan swept in with a steaming mug of coffee.

She placed the white ceramic mug on his desk next to the folder.

"I've told you before, you don't have to do that," he said.

Shrugging, she stepped away. "If I'm getting one for me, it's rude to not get one for you at the same time."

He gave her a disgruntled look. "You don't drink coffee."

"Maybe not right now, but I'm trying to acquire a taste for it."

He stifled the urge to shout that he didn't need her pity, but he understood she meant well. She wanted to help without embarrassing him. He couldn't get angry. He'd spent the first six months of his recovery lashing out at everyone who came near with an outstretched hand. Only intense counseling had reminded him that assistance, whether wanted or not, indicated people cared. And he couldn't punish them for caring, or in Cam's case, for *not* caring.

"Thanks, Susan," he said instead.

She smiled. "Anytime."

Once she'd left and closed the door again, he sipped the brew while going through the papers in the folder. When he finally had a handle on what he planned to say, he picked up the phone and called the number on the top of the form. To his surprise, she answered on half a ring.

"Delgado Foundation, this is Cameron."

"You answer your own phone. How...down-to-earth of you." He could've bitten his tongue the second the scathing remark left his lips.

"I also negotiate my own deals," she shot back. "So, when it comes to investing the foundation's money, no matter how large or small a sum, I answer my phone. How are you, Jordan? It was good to see you last night. You should have contacted me earlier. I would have made sure you were on the guest list for the gala. I'd imagine many of your former teammates would've loved to see you again."

Was that a verbal slap? A reminder of the hard feelings he'd engendered when he'd left the Vanguard team so precipitously? He gritted his teeth, biting back a quick retort for the second time in as many minutes. He didn't want to spar with her. He wanted a deal. But a little drawn blood might gain him the upper hand after last night's hair rustling incident.

"How's your mother, Cam?"

Thwap! The ball landed in her court again. A sharp hiss on the other end of the phone told him he'd aced her.

"She's fine. She remarried last year. Andrew Ellison. He's the CEO of Cooper Industries. They make…widgets or something. I don't know."

The tightness in her tone didn't escape Jordan's notice and for a moment, he felt a pang of sympathy. He hadn't heard about the new marriage, and her mention of another wedding for the Delgado widow sliced too close to the bone for comfort.

If Cam was the ice princess, her mother, Laurel, was the fiery dragon who imprisoned her daughter in a tower of insecurity and crippling self-hate. Laurel Delgado Wallace Kiernan Moffit Ellison had spent decades beating down Cam's self-esteem until she never felt good enough for any man's affections. Not even the one who swore he'd love her forever and backed it up with a perfect square-cut solitaire. He still had the ring, tucked in the breast pocket of the suit he'd worn that night and never put on again. Was it any wonder he wanted to put distance between them after that humiliation?

Nowadays, only Bertie built up her confidence, kept her grounded, and gave her the unconditional love she'd missed since Duke's death.

"Be sure to send your mother my congratulations," he said with a tinge of acid charring the words.

"I will."

A heavy silence fell between them. He could almost picture her in her office, pacing the wide open space behind the desk where the wall of windows looked out over the East River. She rarely sat still, even in a good mood, and the topic of Laurel always riled her into frenetic activity.

He struggled to come up with something else to say to her, something that would remove the specter of her mother from their conversation. When they dated, whenever Cam was all wound up after going a few rounds with Laurel over something stupid, he'd take her to their "quiet place." Inwood Hill Park, a forest in the city, had hiking trails and salt marshes and forests, all perfect for burning excess energy, finding peace, or screaming into the void, depending upon her need at the time.

His hands gripped the handles of his desk chair. He would never again be able to indulge her need for that level of physical activity. The damn spinal injury left him incapable of long-distance walking, any kind of climbing, and a quick jog was impossible.

Face it, Jordan. You're useless to her now.

"So..." she said at last. "...that building."

He shook off his self-pity. "Right. Have you seen the property yet?"

"I have. I'll be looking to make some changes, though, to suit our needs. Would it be all right if I brought my construction manager down to go over the particulars?"

"Of course. When would be convenient for you?"

"The sooner the better, honestly. I don't want to waste your time or mine if the site can't be modified within my budget."

"I can meet you there this afternoon or tomorrow. Which do you prefer?"

"Tomorrow would be fine, thanks. Shall we say three o'clock?"

He paused, pretending to check an imaginary calendar. "I'll shuffle a few appointments around to make it work," he lied.

"I'd appreciate that. Thank you."

"You're welcome." God, they sounded so stiff with each other! Hard to believe they'd once been intimate.

"Terrific. I'll see you then. Goodbye."

He said his own goodbye and pressed the disconnect button, but kept the receiver cradled near his ear. How shortsighted of him to not realize she'd be in charge of this deal. He had assumed once he got her okay to move forward, he'd be dealing with her army of lawyers and accountants. He'd forgotten Cam was a hands-on kind of girl, in all aspects of her life. His mind traveled back to days when those hands had touched him, delighted him, relaxed him.

Dammit, how was he supposed to work with her on a regular basis and not let his resentment leech out all over their dealings? He'd need someone to run interference. Before he could chicken out, he dialed a number he never expected to have to call again.

After only two rings, a silky-voiced receptionist answered.

"I'd like to speak to Mr. Wallace, please," he said. "Tell him it's Jordan Fawcett."

He could only pray Bertie would take his call and help him navigate the coming storm.

Chapter Three

Cam took extra care with her appearance the next day. Jordan knew all her ugliest secrets and wouldn't be afraid to use them to throw her off her game. His "fond regards" toward her mom yesterday told her he wasn't above playing dirty. God knew why, but he wanted to bust her chops.

Mom always said, "Your clothes are your armor." *So, okay. Let's see what protective gear I can find in my closet.*

She chose a pair of soft, suede leggings in a fawn hue, spiked leather boots in a darker brown that came just to her knees, and a cream-colored blouse, which she planned to pair with a maroon blazer. Studying her image in the full-length mirror in her bedroom, she tried to draw up a veneer of confidence. On the outside, she might look like a woman in control, but inside, her soft heart had melted to mush and her nerves bristled at the thought of seeing Jordan again.

Face it, honey. You never got over him.

Tears stung her eyes, and she turned away from her reflection before they fell and stained her cheeks. She couldn't do this, couldn't stand beside him and pretend she didn't care. Every emotion she felt for him, all the love she still harbored, would show on her face, no matter what color blazer she wore.

Had he ever loved her? Or was she just his entry into professional football society, easily discarded when she'd served her purpose? If the latter were true, why would he have asked her to marry him?

Her mother's sneering voice echoed in her skull. *You should have accepted his proposal. A girl of your size won't get that many opportunities to get married. You're too big, too masculine. Men like their women small and dainty. Feminine. You can put an evening gown and flawless makeup on a pig, but it's still a pig.*

"Thanks, Mom." She pressed her nose up and snorted.

She didn't regret turning down Jordan's proposal years ago, regardless of her mother's prediction about her looming spinsterhood. She'd simply not been ready to roll those ugly dice, and avoiding long-term loneliness seemed a stupid reason to say yes.

The first teardrop landed on her sleeve, leaving a blot of tinted moisturizer on the cuff. "Dammit!" Now, she'd have to change her outfit *and* redo her makeup. Frustration released the tap, and her tears fell in earnest.

She grabbed a moist wipe from her vanity and proceeded to scrub her face clean. Defeat fell on her shoulders, heavy and debilitating. Legs weak and shaky, Cam collapsed on her bed, prepared to call Bertie to tell him to go to the meeting in her place.

No.

She couldn't give Jordan the satisfaction.

On a deep breath, she unbuttoned and whipped off the shirt, tossing it in the corner. The boots came off next, followed by her socks and her pants. In just her underwear, she strode to the full-length mirror and stared levelly at her reflection. She didn't need clothes to be her armor. *She* was her armor. Her business acumen, her experience, her intelligence, her quick wit, she was the whole package.

Screw her clothes, screw her broad shoulders and her excessive height, and her cellulite thighs and her nowhere-near-flat belly. If any man couldn't handle all of her the way she was, including Jordan, they didn't deserve any of her. She was also tough enough to take advantage of their vulnerability.

Fired up, she headed to her walk-in closet and looked through the garments hanging there. She wouldn't dress for Jordan. She intended to dress for *her*.

An hour later, she stood outside the building she hoped to acquire, her construction supervisor, Antonio Marrone, at her side. She wore a pink-and-green floral flared A dress with a hot pink jacket and pink suede ankle boots. Whenever the breeze picked up, the skirt fluttered around her legs. The ensemble made her feel fun and pretty, and brought a smile to her lips. She wouldn't apologize for eschewing staid business attire for a spot of color to cheer her dreary mood. Nor would she dress to fade into the background or to appear smaller, as her mother and society often demanded. If Antonio had an opinion on her outfit, he was wise enough to keep it to himself.

Jordan, when he arrived at three-fifteen, had no such self-control. He hobbled up the sidewalk, gave her the once-over and exclaimed, "Wow! You look great, Cam. What's the occasion?"

She tossed her hair. "No occasion. You're late."

"Yeah, sorry. Some idiot truck driver used the handicapped space in the back lot as a loading dock. He decided to take a stroll to the bodega down the street for some coffee while the restaurant crew unloaded a month's worth of beef from the back. Took the keys with him, so I had to wait 'til he came back, settled up with the restaurant's manager, and finally moved the truck out of the space before I could pull in and park. It's not easy being handicapped in the city, between the lack of viable options to maneuver around and the inconsiderate buttholes who don't care if they inconvenience others as long as they shave five minutes off their busy schedules."

"So then why live here? You could manage real estate anywhere."

"Wow. Way to minimize my 'little' job, eh? It's not like I run a multi-million dollar foundation, right?"

"I didn't say that. All I meant was—"

"Ahem!" Antonio cut in. "Maybe we could go inside, rather than continuing arguing here on the street?"

Cam clamped her jaws shut. She had to remember why she was here. She and Jordan had to put their personal animosities aside if they hoped to make this deal work. She *wanted* this building, and judging by Jordan's relentless pursuit, he wanted her to acquire it. So, why couldn't they behave around each other long enough to make their one common goal happen? Well, she'd do her part and hope he followed her lead.

"You're right, Antonio. Jordan, I apologize. Shall we?" She waved toward the locked door and stepped aside to give him a wide berth.

He limped closer and held out the key to her. "Would you like to do the honors?"

A flush of shame warmed her cheeks. She hadn't noticed his clumsy gait the other night. Pity pierced her heart. No wonder he was so bitter. Things she took for granted—getting around the city, finding a parking spot, or even dashing onto a subway seconds before the doors closed— were Herculean tasks for him now. A man as physical and independent as Jordan used to be would probably find making such an adjustment devastating.

"Sure." She took the key and inserted it into the lock.

With Antonio's help, she pushed open the heavy steel door.

"Light switch is on your left," Jordan said as they went inside.

Antonio reached over, and with a click, the interior flooded with light. The empty space seemed massive, but Cam imagined the doorways to classrooms, the laughter of children and teens filling the emptiness.

They moved deeper into the vast open area, and Antonio let out a low whistle. "Nice place. Looks like it's a good size, lots of natural light. I'm gonna go check out the wiring." He leaned closer to her to whisper, "You okay down here with him?" Cam nodded, and Antonio looked over at Jordan. "Where's the panelboard?"

Jordan pointed toward the rear doors. "Door back there, marked 'Electrical Service.' To the right of the utility closet."

With a nod, Antonio toddled off, his toolbelt dangling around his hips.

Cam continued to envision how the place could look when it was ready for use for the foundation. Her architect had drawn up preliminary plans for the building, utilizing every bit of available space to its best advantage, including a greenhouse and vegetable garden out back to teach the children about responsibility, hard work, and healthy eating. Despite the vast nothingness, her brain filled in the blanks, and excitement grew. She hurried forward, turning in small circles as she pictured her vision come to life.

Her heels clacked on the floor in rapid succession, the sound thunderous in the cavernous space. Every noise seemed a slap at Jordan, who stopped every few minutes to take a few breaths, leaving him many feet behind her, and she winced at how without meaning to, her very presence emphasized how far he'd fallen from the man she'd once known and loved.

"I'm sorry," she murmured.

He stopped again, this time to stare at her in confusion. "For what? You don't like the building?"

"No. I'm sorry I'm walking so fast."

To her surprise, he laughed. "Don't slow down on my account. And don't apologize either. It's not like I resent everyone around me because they still have two working legs."

"Well, you definitely resent me for *some*thing."

OH, HE HAD plenty of reasons to resent Cameron Delgado. But here and now was not the time nor place for that confrontation. This was a business deal, nothing more. To change the subject, he pointed to the wall of windows that overlooked the busy street outside. "Plenty of space to display the little ones' artworks, and with the sheer number of passersby seeing those colorful handprint turkeys and lacy doily snowflakes, you'll draw a lot of attention. I'd suggest you put the foundation's name on every other window. No better advertising, in my opinion."

She nodded. "I agree. Thank you for calling me when the place became available. It's perfect for our needs."

"I knew that as soon as I saw it. I'm glad you finally considered working with me on acquiring the site. Despite all the water under the bridge between us, I've always believed in the foundation and the work it does."

Her lips tightened into a thin line. He knew that look. She was biting back something she knew she shouldn't say. Nice to see he could still get a rise out of her. Besides, what lies could she possibly spew to justify the fact she'd abandoned him when he needed her most? He swallowed the bitterness before it could overwhelm him.

Whatever the struggle she fought behind those clamped lips, she won the battle to keep to herself. That was a new quality. Instead, she asked, "How long have you been back in New York?"

"A little over a year." He stifled his disappointment that she'd learned how to monitor her words. Like her mother. What other of those off-putting habits had she acquired since he'd been gone? Besides ditching the man she claimed to love when he no longer served her purposes?

"And what made you go into commercial real estate?"

"My major in college was in construction management with a minor in business administration. With my football career over, it was good to have another occupation to fall back on." All facts she already knew, if she'd stopped to think about their shared history. But clearly, when she'd turned down his marriage proposal, she'd not only closed the door on their future, she'd also locked up their past in some dark, unvisited cellar. Now, they were virtual strangers to each other.

Well, if she could so callously toss him aside, he could do the same to her.

"That's smart," she said. "Bertie always tries to convince the younger players being scouted to take their studies seriously. You're a prime example why that counsel is so crucial."

"How *is* Bertie these days?"

"The same." She shrugged and strolled ahead of him, her gaze flitting around the area as she scrutinized every corner. "How's Paris?"

He blinked at the non-sequitur. "The agent or the city?" She turned to glare at him over her shoulder, and it was his turn to shrug. "What? It's not like I've seen either one of them lately."

"She dumped you?"

"I wouldn't exactly put it that way. After all, for her, I'm only as good as my next contract."

"I'm sorry." She walked to the wall of windows. "That sucks."

"It's business."

"There was more than business between you two."

He snorted. "You always hated Paris."

"Hmmph." She tossed her head and perched her bottom atop the rack of radiators, those mile-long legs of hers extended out across the floor, the toes of those ridiculous boots pointed up toward the ceiling. "Turns out, I had good reason."

God, was she still carrying a grudge over his trade to Houston? "Paris only did what I paid her to do: find me a place where I could use my talents for a team that needed me. Let's face it. With the Vanguard, I'd have always been second best. And with you, too."

"What's that supposed to mean?"

"Come off it, Cam. You didn't *need* me. You never did."

She pushed off the radiator and stood in front of him, her complexion pink with undisguised anger. "I may not have needed you, but I *loved* you. Not that you ever cared about love. If you had, you wouldn't have left me for the first better-looking, skinnier woman who made you hard."

"You think I left you for Paris?!" A bitter laugh escaped his mouth. "You are seriously delusional. I hired Paris for her business savvy, not for her looks. And yeah, she's skinny. So what?" Cam's sudden icy expression could freeze a bonfire, and he shook his head. "God, your mother's insecurities have screwed you up so bad. You've always been the most beautiful woman I know—inside and out. But you never see that, do you?" She didn't answer, and her lips tightened again. "And one other thing, sweetheart. For what it's worth, before you and after you, *plenty* of women have made me hard."

"Ahem!" Antonio's sudden intrusion doused the fire crackling between them.

Great. Talk about perfect timing! Jordan reared back to regain some space and perspective. Whatever he and Cam once had, if anything, was long gone.

"Sorry to interrupt," Antonio said, "but I want to talk to Cam alone for a sec."

No problem. He could use the break from her anyway. "Sure. I'll go outside and wait for you there. Take as long as you need."

A hundred years wouldn't be long enough to get Cameron Delgado out of his system.

Chapter Four

Eight days later, Cam sat at the head of the table in the small conference room, her lawyers and financial officers on the right, Jordan and his team to her left. With all the details hammered out at last, she picked up the gold fountain pen her father always used to sign his contracts and put the nib to the first line requiring her authorization. She'd just started the arc in C when the interoffice unit buzzed.

"Cam?" Val's voice broke into the silence of the boardroom. "Sorry to interrupt. I got an emergency call from Regional Hospital. Something's happened to Bertie."

The pen fell from her fingers with a clatter as she shot to her feet. Panic coursed through her veins, tightened her chest, and stole her breath, but she didn't stop her forward momentum. From behind her fleeing figure, she heard CFO Boris Whittaker announce into the speaker, "Val, have Larry bring the car out front."

"Already done," Val replied.

A high-pitched buzz blaring in her head drowned out anything else said in the boardroom. She pushed out the door and raced past the elevator to the stairs. Later, when asked, she wouldn't recall how she made it down the dozen flights, out to the street, or anything she said to her driver before he opened the door again in front of the hospital's entrance. Minor details became a blur in contrast to the news she heard from some unknown emergency room doctor once she passed the gamut of security. Bertie had suffered a massive heart attack on the field at Vanguard Stadium and died before medical personnel could arrive and resuscitate him.

She listened to this stranger's empty condolences, numb with grief. *I'm very sorry. It was sudden and quick. I can assure you, he felt little to no pain.*

Really? How could Dr. Whoever know that? Did Bertie die with a big grin on his face? Were his last words, "Hey, you know what? This isn't half bad."? She clamped her jaws around the retort and reined in her temper with effort. Blasting this poor man for having to deliver the news to her would help no one.

"Can I see him?" she asked instead.

With a solemn nod, he led her to the private room where the shell of Albert "Bertie" Wallace lay, growing colder and more ashen as time elapsed.

He was gone.

She didn't have to touch him to know that the dynamo in perpetual motion, the bear of a man who had bolstered her through some of her darkest days, no longer existed in this realm. She bent to kiss him and stifled a shiver at the waxy cold feel of his flesh against her lips.

"Oh, Bertie! What will I do without you?"

The doctor cleared his throat and dragged a heavy cushioned chair closer to the bedside. "I'll give you some time."

He walked away, closing the door behind him as he left.

God knew how long Cameron sat alone inside the room, weeping softly and recalling all the moments she'd shared with Bertie, good and bad. Had she told him she loved him the last time they'd spoken? She couldn't remember. "I love you," she said now. "I love you, I love you, I love you." She repeated the same three words until her throat ached and a white-haired nurse arrived to escort her from the room.

"We'll take care of him now," she murmured, patting Cam's hand.

Cameron struggled to get up out of the chair, her gaze never leaving her fallen hero.

"Go on," the nurse prompted. "I promise. He's in good hands. He's with the angels now."

A smile quirked Cam's tight lips. Bertie, the atheist, would probably *love* to hear this news.

"There now, see. I bet you hadn't thought of that. Gives you some peace, don't it?"

More like a fit of the giggles, but she left the room nonetheless, and nearly tripped over Jordan hovering in the hallway.

"Cam?"

She didn't have to say a word. Good thing, since she couldn't say it aloud yet. Saying it aloud would confirm the finality in her heart, and she wasn't ready.

"Aw, Cam, I'm sorry. I'm so sorry."

Blinded by tears, she stumbled toward the nearby waiting area and collapsed into a hard plastic chair. Jordan sat beside her, took her icy hand in his warmer one, and squeezed gently. The floodgates on Cam's emotions broke open, and she wept.

"I was too late. I never even got to say goodbye. He was gone before I got here—before *he* got here. I didn't have a chance to tell him how much I loved him, how much he meant to me. He died not knowing he was my hero."

"He knew, sweetheart. He always knew. Just like you've always known how much he loved you. You two had a special bond. That didn't change when he died."

She looked up at him, noted the tenderness in his expression—not pity; he knew she couldn't abide pity. Empathy and...dare she venture...love?...reflected in his steady gaze. Her lips parted of their own accord, and she leaned toward him, hungry for the connection they once shared. He understood her need and met her halfway, his breath growing warmer near her cheek.

Into this soft and touching moment, her stomach made itself known with a growl that would shame a grizzly.

He jerked back. "When's the last time you ate?"

Cheeks flaming, she shook her head. "I don't remember. Sometime yesterday."

He gave her hand another squeeze. "Well, you're going to need lots of protein to keep up your strength for all that's coming. I assume Larry's still downstairs?" At her nod, he whipped out his phone. "Number's still the same?" Another nod, and he scrolled until he found the foundation's driver in his contact list. "Larry, it's Jordan Fawcett." Pause. "Same here." Another pause. "I'm afraid the news isn't good, Larry, but it's not my place to say. Right now, you and I are going to take Ms. Delgado home and get her comfortable. After that, can you take a drive over to the Grille Room and pick up a takeout order? I'll place it enroute, so you'll have some time before it'll be ready." Pause. "Terrific. Thanks."

While she would've liked to argue with him, the truth was, her stomach could use a refill and the next few days were going to be hell. So, why not let him take care of her for a little while? What harm could it do?

"Let's get you home, Cam."

True to his word, he placed a second call in the car to the Grille Room. He never asked for her opinion before he ordered two porterhouse steaks, a side of asparagus spears, two baked potatoes topped with sour cream and chives, and for dessert, a crème brulee and a slice of chocolate ganache cake. He did, however, throw a questioning glance her way before disconnecting, and she responded with an unenthusiastic thumbs-up. She wouldn't change a thing he'd ordered. It was disconcerting to realize he knew all her food weaknesses—all her weaknesses, period.

An hour later, her nutritional needs met, Cam sat at her bistro table on the balcony, cutting the chocolate cake in half while Jordan scooped out one side of the crème brulee.

From inside the apartment, a sharp voice exclaimed, "Oh for God's sake, Cameron, the man's barely cold in the ground and all you can think about is your stomach."

The slab of cake fell off the fork and landed fudgy-frosting-side-down on her cream-colored skirt.

"Jee-zus, you're such a slob!" her mother exclaimed as she stood in the doorway, hands planted on her hips in exasperation.

Cam scrambled to blot the mess on her lap with a fistful of napkins. At least, she'd already had her protein. Jordan was right. She was going to need her strength right now. "How'd you get in here, Mother?"

"Don't blame Scott downstairs. He said he had to announce me, but once I told him about Bertie dying, he understood you needed me right now and agreed to send me right up."

Cam's temper flared, and she forgot about her ruined skirt. Rising to her full height, she faced off against her mother. As usual, skinny, diminutive Mom looked ready for a photoshoot in a navy suit and leather pumps, her long, blond hair frozen into its traditional Grecian curl style, and a sapphire and diamond necklace with matching cuff bracelet adding glitter to the ensemble.

"You told Scott? Why? The foundation planned to release a statement to the press tomorrow morning. Now, I guarantee you the press not only knows, but they're going to be camped out in the lobby within the next fifteen minutes."

Her mother waved her left hand, and the setting sun caught the wedding set on her third finger, nearly blinding Cam with its brilliance. "I can well imagine the press release you're planning. All about Saint Albert Wallace and his holy hands and how no one can ever take his place." She sniffed her disdain, a sound Cam knew well.

"God, you're petty! You just can't stand to let Bertie have the dignified end he deserved, can you? Somehow, you have to make yourself the star of this tragedy, all because he didn't adore you enough when you were married. What'd you tell Scott anyway? How devastated you are? Did you describe in great detail the pain Bertie's death causes *you*?"

"Don't be ridiculous." She wagged a finger toward Cam's nose, and Cam took a step back to avoid any potential contact. "If you didn't have rules in place that I'm not allowed up here without your permission, I wouldn't need to tell anybody down there anything. But, noooo. You want to keep some modicum of power between us by erecting guardrails, as if I mean you harm. You treat me like I'm an axe murderer, for God's sake."

She might as well be, in Cam's opinion. Like an axe murderer, Mom wanted to cut her down every chance she got, blow by careless blow. Cameron tightened her lips until she could control the words coming from her mouth. When she spoke again, she managed to keep her tone even and at a reasonable volume. "I live alone in a place where the elevator opens up into my living room. I don't have a front door I can lock. My security is the guard downstairs. That means I take precautions. *No one* comes up without my being notified first. That's just common sense and standard procedure for anyone who has a place like mine."

"Don't blame me for your poor choices in life. You're thirty-six years old. I haven't been responsible for your marital status, where you live, how you look, or what you put in your mouth for a long time."

Cam's temper would no longer remain tethered. "Get out. Get out of my home, and don't come back. I'm done with you."

"How dare you!"

WHOA. JORDAN STEPPED forward into the fray. "Easy, Cam. You're not thinking clearly right now—"

"Stay out of this, Jordan. This is between me and her." Cam's eyes, blazing with fire, cut to him before returning to the target of her ire. "Bertie always insisted I give you the benefit of the doubt. With him gone, I no longer have to heed that advice. I don't have to respect you because you're my mother, especially when you've gone out of your way to disrespect me and all I've loved my whole life. I'm over it: the drama, the snide comments about my size and looks, and most of all, the insults about Bertie. He was the best thing that ever happened to us after Dad died, but you never appreciated him. The whole time he was alive, I put up with your crap and let you criticize every breath I took because I had his love to fall back on when you made me feel bad about myself. But he's gone now. And any desire to continue fostering this toxic relationship between us died with him."

Cam's voice was whisper-soft, laced with steel. Under normal circumstances, he'd admire the way she kept control of her emotions, particularly because he knew the history she alluded to. Bertie might have died, but the spirit and confidence he'd instilled in Cameron lived on—along with a little too much fight for today.

When Cam's hands curled into fists, the tension in the room ratcheted up a notch. For a scary moment, he wondered if she'd physically pick up her mother to toss her out of the apartment.

Apparently, Laurel shared his fear, because her complexion paled, and she turned on her spiked heels. "Don't bother to show me out. I'm leaving. I'll expect someone to contact me with the details of the memorial service when they're confirmed." She jabbed the button to open the elevator doors and slipped inside, her perfectly made-up face a mask of fury.

The doors slid closed, and Jordan breathed a heavy sigh of relief.

Cam's posture relaxed, and her hands eased at her sides. "I'm sorry you had to see that."

"To be honest, I'm glad I did," he replied with a smirk. "Bertie would be proud of you."

"Ya think?"

He reconsidered. Bertie, the peacemaker, would've preached for continued patience and understanding. Jordan, on the other hand didn't know how Cam had put up with the abuse for nearly four decades. "*I'm proud of you.*"

"Yeah. Thanks. Great." The words came out in a flat monotone. She trudged into the living room, her gaze pinned to the chocolate smearing her skirt. Plucking the sides of the fabric, she added in the same manner, "I should change. And you should probably go. Thanks for the dinner, but I need to be by myself now."

It didn't take a brain surgeon to see she was fragile right now. No wonder, with that scene with her mother coming on the heels of Bertie's death. The toughest warrior would crumble under that kind of pressure.

At the same time, though, he probably wasn't high on the list of people she'd turn to for comfort and solace. Unfortunately, the one she most needed was the one who'd died.

"Will you be all right?" he asked. "Is there somebody I can call to stay with you?"

She shook her head. "I just want a hot bath and some sleep." After giving him a hard stare, she clucked her tongue. "Don't look at me like that. I'm broken but not beaten. I'll survive."

"Glad to hear it." He stared out the window at the Manhattan skyline, where darkness began to drop and lights clicked on in odd patterns in the offices. Clearing his facial expression of any obvious concern took some time—particularly since that last phrase was pure Bertie, and he wondered if she realized she used it.

His gaze traveled back to her in time to see her hands twisting in front of her stomach. "Can I ask a favor though?"

"Sure."

"Will you ride with me to the memorial service? I know it might not be comfortable for you, that there might be some bad blood between you and some of your former teammates, but..." Her voice cracked, and she looked at him through red-rimmed, wet eyes. "I can't do this alone."

He nodded. "If you want me there, I'll be there. No matter what anyone else says."

"No one will *say* anything. I'll make sure of it. Well, except my mom." She picked up a remote control from the glass-topped end table and pointed it at the window. On a low hum, the vertical blinds slid closed, dimming the light in the living room and covering the view of the Manhattan skyline. "Her, I have no control over. She's a damn tornado in an outhouse."

Another Bertie phrase. He had no idea if she was channeling the dead man or if Bertie's spirit had refused to leave its earthly bonds and had taken up residence in Cam. To hell with masking his concern. She needed someone here with her tonight.

"How about I spend the night?" he said, keeping his tone light.

"Get real."

"On the couch," he added. "You won't even know I'm here."

She snorted. "Trust me. I'll know." Taking a few steps toward the bedroom, she tossed over her shoulder, "Go home, Jordan. I'm fine. I don't need a babysitter."

"Definitely not, but I don't think Bertie would want you to be alone tonight, either."

On a quick whirl, she attempted to burn him with the heat of her anger. "Who made you an expert on what Bertie would want? When was the last time you talked to him? Five years ago?"

"This past Thursday, actually."

Her lips tightened into that single line. Hoo-boy. He'd ticked her off big time with that information.

After a brief but heavy pause, she shook her head. "If that were true, he would've told me."

"Not if I asked him not to."

This time, her jaw dropped. "Why?"

"Why did I ask him not to tell you or why did I call him in the first place?"

She planted her fists on her hips. "Both."

"Okay, well, I called him the day you agreed to discuss the leasing of the building."

Her eyebrows rose in questioning arcs. "Before or after you and I spoke?"

"After."

Another curt nod. "Go on."

"I asked him if you were serious about the site." Her posture stiffened in disbelief. "I thought it was some kind of prank, some revenge fantasy you'd nursed for years."

Not true at all, but he would never admit he'd called Bertie to help him deal with his unresolved feelings for her. Not when she'd made it so obvious she didn't give a damn about him anymore.

"A...revenge...fantasy," she repeated, as if chewing each word and digesting it.

"Well, yeah. I sure as hell didn't assume the roses had swayed you." Despite Susan's assurance to the contrary. "I mean, you weren't exactly open to discussing the building the night before."

"You *accosted* me on the street. What did you expect?"

"An invitation to come up for coffee?" There went her lip again. He let her stew for a beat, then upped the charm factor. "I could still go for a cup. Why don't you go change and I'll make coffee? We can split the crème brulee."

"I've got a better idea." She sashayed closer to him and opened her arms. As he entered her embrace, she made a quick sidestep, dropped both hands to his shoulders, and spun him toward the elevator doors. "Go home, Jordan. I want to be alone tonight."

Chapter Five

ALBERT "BERTIE" WALLACE was laid to rest with great fanfare on a cloudy, chilly September afternoon. In keeping with the requests made in his will, his memorial service was held in the place he loved most: Vanguard Stadium. A dais was set up on the fifty-yard line, with seats for the friends and family members he'd asked to speak at the event.

All of New York's sports royalty attended, along with the biggest names in city and state politics, local celebrities, and news crews from every network. As a former player-turned-head-coach of the Vanguard, Bertie had impacted a lot of lives over the years. At the end of the speeches, all the guests were invited to pay their respects to Bertie's former wife and beloved stepdaughter. For what seemed like hours, Cam stood next to her mother, neither speaking a word to the other as they accepted condolences from the multitudes of mourners. Since they were not part of Bertie's immediate family, past or present, Mr. Ellison and Jordan remained in the background—nearby if needed, but out of sight and basically, out of mind.

Despite her flat shoes, or maybe because of them, Cam's feet ached. Faces and murmured messages of sympathy blurred into a collage of colorful buzz words.

So sorry for your loss...
He's in a better place...

He'll be sorely missed...

Her reaction to the wall of sorrow became robotic: a firm handshake, a whispered thank you, a curt nod, then move along to the next person. That all changed when Paris Redmond reached out to clasp Cam's hand.

"I'm so sorry, Cameron. Bertie was a giant in the sports world. We're all devastated that he's gone."

Cam stiffened, but manners and respect for Bertie would not permit a scene—not here, not now. "Thank you, Paris. Thanks for coming today. It's good to see you again."

Paris should have moved on at that point and allowed the next person in line to pay their respects, but she remained on the platform in front of Cam. "Yes, it's been years, hasn't it? When was the last time? The Aquila Bowl, wasn't it?"

"That was the last time we talked, but, of course, we did see each other in passing at the hospital in San Antonio."

Paris waved a hand, sending her signature multitude of bangles tinkling in the air. "Ah, yes, that's right. Well, I'm sorry about the circumstances that brought us together again today."

"Thank you." To her relief, Paris finally moved down the line to offer her regards to Laurel, and Cam relaxed.

But before the next person could extend a hand to her, Jordan cut in front. "When were you in San Antonio?"

All she could do was blink at him. "Huh?"

Jordan repeated the question in bullet points. "When... were... you... in... San... Antonio? When did you run into Paris there?"

"At the hospital. The day after your—" She stopped, swallowed. Even now, she couldn't bring herself to mention the injury. "After that game."

He arched a brow at her. "If that's true, why didn't *I* see you there?"

Really? He wanted to have this discussion *now*? Fine. Let's go. She folded her arms over her chest and poised to do battle. "Well, maybe, if you hadn't put me on your 'Do Not Admit' list, you would have known I was there. But apparently, you worried your Texas fans might discover I used to be your girlfriend. So you made sure I was persona non grata. Only Paris mattered."

"My... 'Do Not...'?" His gaze shot from her to Paris, who colored and slipped away into the crowd on the other side of the platform. "Son of a—" After giving her hand a quick squeeze, he meandered around where she stood. "We're not done discussing this." Without another word, he scrambled down the steel stairs to chase after Paris.

"Uh-huh. Sure. Whatever." As Cam watched his clumsy pursuit, from the corner of her eye, she caught a familiar look of pity on her mother's face, and it froze the blood in her veins. Turning back to the next mourner in line, she told herself she didn't care that Jordan had, once again, publicly ditched her for Paris. To hell with him. And to hell with her mother, too. She'd survive this latest humiliation with her grace and dignity intact. The pain crushing her chest would ease...eventually. Losing Bertie hurt more anyway.

Jordan...well, Jordan had never really loved her to begin with. Right?

Right.

DAMN, PARIS COULD dash through a throng—even in her spiky heels. But Jordan wouldn't be deterred from catching up with her. He scanned the crowd for a friendly and useful face and found one. "Luis!" he called out. "Grab Paris."

Luis Gallo, retired Vanguard fullback, raced into action. He might have left the gridiron a couple of years ago, but he still had the moves that made him a fan favorite. He faked left, ran right, broke from the people around him. Some of those people, upon seeing the bulk of man in a black suit bearing down on them, scrambled out of the way until, at last, Luis had a straight shot to Paris. As he closed in, with mere feet to go, Luis dove forward, grabbed her by both shoulders the way he would a running back, and held on tight.

Assured she couldn't get away, caged as she was by Luis, Jordan slowed his staggered pace to a more sedate limp. When he finally stood face-to-face with his former agent, he thanked Luis and took her by the arm. "Let's take a walk. I think we need to have a conversation."

She must have realized he'd trapped her because she stole a quick glance at Luis, who stood by, prepared to pounce again, then flashed

Jordan a stunning smile. "Of course. Shall we get a bite to eat? It's bad luck to return straight home from a funeral, you know. There's a charming little bistro on Forty-Sixth. My car is in Lot A."

"What I have to say isn't conducive to a meal, Paris." To be honest, depending upon her answers to his questions, he couldn't guarantee he wouldn't cause a scene by lunging for her lying throat. "Let's start by getting away from all these people."

She cast another glance at Luis, and her smile faltered. "All right."

He led her off the field, past the police officers posted around the entrances and exits, to the memorial garden at the side of the stadium. While they walked, he said nothing, but his insides screamed. When they reached the stone benches in front of the marble effigies of former Vanguard players who'd passed on, he could no longer keep a lid on his percolating emotions.

"Tell me how it's possible you saw Cam at the hospital after my injury and not only did I not see her, I never knew she was there."

She shrugged and hitched her handbag strap up higher on her shoulder. "Believe me, I was as shocked then as you are now. I mean, it never occurred to me she'd charter a plane and fly halfway across the country to see you—unless she felt the need to gloat."

What was she talking about now? "Gloat?"

"Well, why else would she show up? You left *her* team and after two seasons in Texas, wound up sustaining an injury that ended your career. Do you think she came to bring you a fruit basket?"

No. But he didn't, for one second, believe she came to gloat, either. Cam was a woman of integrity with a heart as deep as the ocean. And like the ocean, she swept away hurt with waves of forgiveness. It took a lot to get her to the stage she reached with her mother the other night. She might have felt betrayed by his sudden departure, but it wasn't in her nature to revel in anyone else's pain, not even his.

"Did you happen to ask her why she was there?"

A plane flew overhead, engines screeching, and Paris used the distraction to settle herself on one of the benches, arranging her skirt to best show off her wasp waist and lean legs. She then patted the space beside her, but Jordan didn't take her up on the offer.

"I barely saw her," she replied as she opened her handbag and removed a lip balm. "I was racing through the lobby on my way up to see you after your surgery."

"And yet, in all the hours you spent with me, you never once mentioned she was there."

Paris applied the waxy substance to her lips with deliberate care. "She didn't stick around long enough for me to even think about her. Once she realized she wasn't authorized to get beyond the lobby, she must have turned around and flew home the same night." Paris laughed. "There really isn't more for me to say, except maybe 'I told you so.'"

"You told me so."

After replacing the lip balm and zipping up the purse, she tilted her head toward the sky. "Yes. I told you she would try to keep you tied to her, would hold you back from attaining your full potential just so she'd have a good-looking Vanguard man on her arm for social occasions. Look what she did today, making you escort her to the memorial, allowing the press to assume she had gained the upper hand over you again. You're a nice guy, Jordan, too nice for someone like her. Face it. Like her mother, she eats nice guys as an *amuse bouche*. You should be thanking me for keeping her at bay as long as I did."

"You think so?" Feigning admiration, he sat beside her, in the hope he'd get more details from her. "Were there other times she tried to get to me?"

"Oh, God, probably half a dozen or so. She really thought she had her hooks in you for a while there."

"Like how? When else did you have to run interference for me?"

"Well, let me think. It's been a while. The hospital really was the last time I saw her. Before that, it was just minor stuff. I intercepted birthday cards, and once, she sent a wedding invitation."

"A wedding invitation?"

"Yeah. When her mother married that guy...what was his name?" She snapped her fingers, as if trying to light a spark. "Muffin, Waffle..."

"Moffit. Carlton Moffit."

She pointed at him. "That's him. Can you believe it? What was she thinking? That you'd want to be her date?"

Probably. Not that she couldn't have her pick of men, if she asked. Escorting her to public events wasn't about her having a cute guy on her arm, despite what Paris thought. Cam only asked men she trusted implicitly. So few people understood the way Laurel's constant criticism had destroyed Cam's self-esteem over the years. Public events always brought out the worst in Laurel, which brought out Cam's most vulnerable fears. Had he known about the invitation, at the very least, he would've called her to make sure she was okay. Given her a pep talk to get through without him. But, he hadn't even been able to do that much, thanks to Paris.

"So you made sure I didn't see any of this stuff?"

"It's my job to keep my clients focused on the game. If that means I have to remove the little distractions that pop up along the way, I'm not above picking up a thresher." She wriggled her fingers. "I have my spies set up in all aspects of my clients' lives: housekeepers, security personnel, PAs, even a coach or two. It's nothing personal, Jordan. It's good business."

Queasiness washed over him, and he got to his unsteady feet. "You know, Paris, it's too bad you released me from my contract when the surgeons declared my career over. I would have *delighted* in firing your ass right now."

Leaving her sputtering, he limped back to the field where the service continued. He'd always teased Cam about how much she disliked Paris. Turned out, she was right to be suspicious.

He was an idiot. Cam might have turned down his marriage proposal, but she'd never stopped loving him. He would need a big play to win her back.

And he'd need it fast.

Chapter Six

She had no idea how she made it to the very last mourner without breaking into tears. Her own fault, really. Because despite the multitude of reasons she had to hate Jordan, she still loved him and always would. What a pathetic loser she was.

She studied the crowd on the dais and the grounds. How many of these people had noticed how quickly he'd abandoned her when Paris popped up? *Paris*, who'd dumped him when an injury ruined his football career, because he was no longer *useful* to her. Maybe that's where she always went wrong. Instead of kicking him to the curb and letting him rot there, she kept welcoming him back into her life. Maybe men were only interested in the women who treated them like garbage.

Okay, fine. She would let him go. This time, for good. She'd survived his departure before. She could do it again. Even if she didn't have Bertie to fall back on this time. Bertie had given her the tools to live her life with passion. Now it was up to her to follow his phenomenal example.

As the crowd began to disperse, she detoured past her mother and Mr. Ellison to exit the makeshift platform.

"Cam?" Mr. Ellison's voice stopped her at the first step.

She turned and waited for him to approach. "Your mother and I are going to Ruby's for lunch. Would you like to join us?"

Cam looked past him to where her mother stood, hands twisting as she watched their interaction while desperately trying to feign indifference.

"For what it's worth," Mr. Ellison whispered, "she's sorry. She knows she went too far last time."

As big a step as Mom had taken in admitting her mistake, Cam shook her head. "I wish I could say that's good enough for me, but she went too far about a thousand miles ago. Maybe someday, we can mend our issues. But for now, I think we're both better off leaving some distance between us. Thanks for the invitation, though."

He offered her a curt nod, his smile nowhere near happy. "I understand. You can divorce a spouse for lots of reasons, but a parent...?" He shrugged.

She took his hand. "You're a nice man. I wish you and my mother years of happiness together."

Before he could say anything else, she descended the stairs and stood on the field. Here was where both her father and Bertie spent so many of their happiest days. On a whim, she took off her shoes and allowed her bare feet to touch the turf they'd once run upon. When she was a child, her father would bring her here to play two-hand-touch with his teammates' kids. Her memories evoked all of her senses: the sound of children's laughter, the smell of dirt and grass, the rough texture of the football, the indulgent smiles on the grownups' faces, spicy hot dogs covered in mustard washed down with sugary sodas. Her childhood might have been odd, but at times, it had been a lot of fun.

With her flats dangling from her fingertips, she strode toward the end zone, the spiky green blades tickling her soles. She took a deep breath in, tilted her face toward the sun, and let the spirit of the men who'd guided her through her formative years fill the empty places in her heart. She'd go on. She had a foundation to run—and a life to live.

From the loudspeaker, the voice of the Vanguard for more than thirty years, Powell Arris intoned, "Ladies and gentlemen. May I have your attention please?" The milling crowd stopped and stared upward. It always amused Cam that when a voice came over the sound system in any stadium or theater, everyone would look toward the sky, as if the message came from heaven. "I'd like to direct your attention to the jumbotron on the scoreboard for a special announcement."

What the...?

What had her mother done now?

Like the rest of the spectators, she did as Powell directed and stared up at the scoreboard. The photo of Bertie with his name and the year of his birth and death disappeared. The Vanguard logo briefly took its place, then quickly dissolved, and Jordan's face filled the hundred-fifty-foot screen.

What the...? This time, Mom was not the culprit. Jordan, wearing the same suit and tie she'd seen on him all day today captured the attention of everyone inside the stadium. So, whatever this was, it had to be live—or at the very least, filmed today. What the hell was going on?

She cast a quick glance around the field, but everyone seemed to wear the same baffled expression.

"Hey, folks," he said from the screen. "For those of you who don't know, I'm Jordan Fawcett. A while back, I was a quarterback for the Vanguard. I had a couple of pretty good seasons here, made some great friends, and fell in love with a terrific woman. But I wanted more, more money, more playing time, more of what I thought I deserved. Mostly, I wanted more than what that terrific woman was ready to give me. I was arrogant. And greedy. So when the opportunity arose for me to sign with another team, to have a few more seasons in a place where I could help build a winning enterprise, I took it. I left my teammates, I left my friends, I left the woman I loved."

People stirred around her, staring at her with keen interest. She couldn't move. Her feet had embedded invisible roots in the turf. She could barely draw a breath. All she could do was stare at Jordan's face, her chest tight with dread. Had he proposed to Paris? During Bertie's memorial service? *Please, Jordan, please don't break my heart like this. Not today.*

"Cam," Jordan said, and the camera zoomed closer, until all anyone could see on the screen was his face, the intensity of his expression. "You once accused me of leaving you for the first woman who got me hard."

Around her, murmurs of disgust and discontent rose like a foul wind. Her cheeks blazed, and she dropped her head to stare at the ground, silently praying for a giant fault line to open up and swallow her whole.

"You were wrong. Lots of women have made me hard since I hit puberty. You're the only woman who ever made me *weak*: weak in the knees every time you're near, weak in the head so I never know if I'm saying something stupid or clever when I try to talk to you. Even now, I'm probably screwing this up. Cam, I love you. I've always loved you. And I understand why you don't want to get married—at least, not until you're a hundred percent sure. Give me a chance to be the man you need. Let me prove to you we can make it work forever."

FROM HIS CHAIR in the broadcast room, Jordan struggled to figure out what went on in her head now. What if his declaration of love had come too late? What if she couldn't forgive him?

Well, then, he'd do what he'd just promised in front of a thousand strangers. He'd prove to her they could make their love work forever.

Although he'd managed to get a pretty damn good speech together for the moment, the longer he went without an answer from her, the faster his words fled. His tongue grew thick and his brain misfired. He cleared the block in his throat.

"Cam?" he said into the microphone. "Say something please?"

While his heart thundered in his chest, she strode back to the makeshift dais and, on a screech of feedback, turned the mic at the podium on again. She stared straight up at the windows where he sat. "Are you proud of yourself now?"

"That depends. What did you think?"

"That you used a lot of pretty words I've heard from you before." She folded her arms over her chest. "Go back to Paris. I have nothing more to say, Jordan."

"I was never involved with Paris. Not in a romantic way. Did I listen to Paris? Yes. She was my agent. Did I trust her? God help me, I did. And I realize now I shouldn't have. She filtered my mail, Cam. She screened my visitors in the hospital, and I never knew it. But this isn't about her. *I* screwed up. I gave her all that power because it was easier than taking responsibility for my life and facing up to what I did to you, to this team, to everybody who cared about me."

"She filtered your mail?" Cam's tone held a scalpel's edge. "Did she tie up your fingers so you couldn't call, either?"

"I blamed you, Cam. When you turned down my proposal, I thought it was because you didn't care. But that's not why you said no, is it? I get it now. You, of all people, have every right to doubt a marriage leads to happily ever after. It didn't mean you didn't love me because when *you* love someone, you love them forever. I want to shower you with that same kind of love. Give me a chance. Give us a chance. Please."

She met his plea with dead silence. Not a sound came from anywhere in the stadium. Time stood still, and he held his breath until his chest ached.

Just when he thought he'd lost, she shouted into the mic. "Well? What are you waiting for? Get down here and kiss me."

He left the booth and for the millionth time since that damn sack, he cursed his inability to run. With slow and short but determined strides, he made his way back to the woman he'd left behind. If he had to crawl the last few yards to reach her, he would.

He stepped on the turf to deafening cheers, a sound he hadn't heard from a crowd at Vanguard Stadium in a long time. He didn't care. Only one person mattered to him right now. He climbed the stairs to the platform where she stood with her team, her face illuminated with love, her arms wide open. He fell into her embrace.

Capturing her lips with his, he showed her how much he loved her, how much he'd always loved her, and how much he always would. As if on cue, the clouds parted and a strong single beam of sunlight fell on them. He broke away from the kiss with regret, but kept her encircled in his arms. Heat warmed his face, and he stared up at the brightened sky.

"I'd say Bertie's pretty happy right now."

"So am I," she replied. "Blissfully."

the end

the magic of Sapphire Creek

The Magic of Sapphire Creek
Grace Augustine

Chapter One

Bethany McLintock knelt by the counter. She closed her eyes and ran her hand down the back of the golden retriever. Her hand stopped above the dog's left hip. She felt the dog's overwhelming pain and audibly sighed as a tear rolled down her cheek. It was the third dog she'd met this week who was suffering with hip dysplasia.

"C'mon, Goldie. Let's get you to a room."

Bethany nodded to one of her techs to take the dog and its owner into an exam room. She made her way to the sink, washed her hands, and grabbed the patient chart.

"Dee, help me put Goldie up on the exam table, please?"

The owner buried his face in Goldie's neck and reassured her she was going to be okay.

"Goldie, you are such a pretty girl," Bethany began. "I know you're hurting, honey, and we're taking care of that. I promise."

Bethany directed a few general health questions to Mr. Finnigan who answered them without pause. She began a full exam.

"I know how much you love her. She is such a precious thing." Bethany rested her hand on Goldie's painful hip. Knowing how painful it was for Goldie's owner to see his pet in this much pain, Bethany continued, "Mr. Finnigan, if you would please wait in the outer room it will allow Destiny and I to move more freely in here and attend to Goldie. We won't be long. We'll bring her out soon."

The owner did as requested and as soon as the door closed Bethany pulled her rolling stool to the exam table and sat on its high seat.

"Dee, grab the lavender and the bottle next to it, please. Also, bring one of those protein treats."

Sapphire Creek Alternative Pet Medicine Clinic opened three years ago, four months after Bethany graduated with her doctorate in veterinary and alternative pet medicine. She knew she wanted to specialize in treating animals without conventional medications. Her special gift of animal speak and healing allowed her to do that.

Sapphire Creek, Montana was surrounded by ranchers who'd done things the way they'd always been done. Convincing them of alternative methods of healthcare for their animals had been Bethany's project since arriving. She was making some headway, not as much as she'd like, though.

"Goldie, I'm sorry you're hurting so much," Bethany spoke to the dog as her assistant rubbed the affected area with the oil from the bottle in her hand. "Hold still, sweetie."

When Dee was finished, Bethany stroked Goldie's ears and moved her hands down her spine. She closed her eyes and physically saw the bones of the dog in her mind's eye. She saw the deformity that was causing the problem and allowed her hands to linger over the area. Her hands warmed and she felt vertebrae and other bones shift. Goldie relaxed with a sigh and laid on her side, tail wagging.

"See, pretty girl, I told you we'd fix you."

Bethany grabbed Goldie's leash and watched as the dog bounced down the steps that leaned against the exam table. There was no way this dog could have climbed them when she first arrived. Now, she had renewed energy and no pain...both things Bethany was thankful for.

"Mr. Finnigan, here's your girl." She handed the leash and another special treat to him. "She will be just fine. Continue giving her the vitamin complex daily and I'll see her in six months. Dee will schedule your appointment."

THE MAGIC OF SAPPHIRE CREEK

Bethany knelt and placed her hands on either side of Goldie's head. She leaned her head down to the dog's ear. "You'll be just fine." In her soul she heard the animal relay her thanks. It warmed her to know how much Goldie appreciated and loved her. She smiled. "I love you, too."

Walking behind the counter, Bethany signed off on the patient report and placed the file in the done basket. She tidied up the area before turning down the hall to her office.

The bell on the front door tinkled, signaling another visitor to the clinic. Bethany stopped in mid-stride, turned around, and froze in place. She was speechless, audibly anyway.

What is he doing here? I haven't seen him for ten years and now he shows up? I can't deal with this today!

Bethany fisted her hands in the pockets of her lab coat, plastered on a fake smile through the anger she was feeling, and finally managed a greeting.

"Rowdy. What are you doing here?"

The tall, ruggedly handsome man closed the door behind him and advanced to the middle of the waiting room. His chocolate brown, collar length hair was as wild as always and those bourbon colored eyes danced with mischief as he smiled at Bethany.

"Hey, Beth. I heard there was a new vet clinic in town, and I came to check it out. I had no clue you were the new vet." He reached down to pet the Persian cat who was leaving her scent on his jeans-clad leg.

Of course, you wouldn't! You didn't bother to stay in touch with me. You walked away...in the middle of our wedding!

"Dusty! Scat!"

The cat looked up at Bethany, tail crooked in the air, and sauntered casually over to her bed in the front window and began preening.

"You didn't have to do that. She was fine. You know I don't have issues with animals," Rowdy quipped.

"No, only people," Bethany replied quietly.

"Yeah, about that..." He cleared his throat, which was suddenly parched, and ran a hand around his neck. He thought better of continuing with that line of conversation and took a different path. "I have a Bernese about to give birth. I didn't know if the new vet made house calls. Hence, my reason for being here. I was in the area and decided to stop by."

"Of course we make house calls," Dee stated, extending her hand. "Hi. I'm Destiny. Everyone calls me Dee. Nice to meet you. And you are?"

"Rowdy Walker," he shook Dee's outstretched hand. "I own the tack and western wear store just down the street."

Bethany rolled her eyes. Another lie, no doubt. Last she'd heard he was still on the rodeo circuit riding his precious bulls.

"So," Rowdy continued, "can you come out and give Lucie a look? She's been acting weird…not eating, whining…not normal at all."

"How has her pregnancy gone? I mean, no blood or discharge?" Bethany asked.

Rowdy shook his head. He hadn't noticed anything like that, only the dog not acting like herself.

"Well, could be she is getting ready to deliver. Is she nesting?"

"I have a bed ready for her. Spends most of her time there."

Bethany looked at her schedule. Mr. Finnigan was her last appointment for the morning. "I can look her over now, if you have time."

"That would be great, Beth. Thank you. Do you want to ride with me?"

Rowdy was sincere when asking, but Beth would have no part of it. After asking if he still lived in the same place, she told him she'd meet him as soon as she gathered her bag.

"If you're sure. The recent weather has made the road a mess. I wouldn't want you getting stuck."

"I'm sure my all-terrain vehicle will be just fine. And, I bet you I'll beat you to your house."

Chapter Two

Bethany grew up in Sapphire Creek and lived there until moving to Bozeman to attend Montana State University for her undergraduate degree in biology. Following graduation, she immediately started the DVM program at Washington State University in Pullman.

When one of the leading veterinary alternative medical professors offered Bethany a fellowship, she jumped at the opportunity. It gave her a chance to use her special gifts, gifts she'd had since a young age.

Bethany had been a sensitive child, aware of her surroundings and the feelings of others, especially animals. At the age of five, her cat spoke to her one night. She kept it a secret, something between her and Lily Bear. Later she learned it was something sacred and not to be shared with those who didn't believe or have the same gift.

Placing her bag in the back of the silver Kia Soul, she slid behind the steering wheel, tuned into her favorite country music channel, and headed north. She passed the new shopping mall and an adjacent hotel. Not too far up the road was another multi-family dwelling unit. They seemed to be popping up all over the valley. Soon they would be down to the creek bed. That was something Bethany didn't want to see. Too many strangers were moving into her space, and she didn't like that one little bit.

Sapphire Creek was special. Always had been. It was a quiet, unique little town where you were safe at night walking the streets. There were dances at the community center, family nights at the movie theatre, and free-swim at the pool in the summers. All of that would change now that the mines were open again. More people would be moving in.

She hummed along with Mac Davis as she turned right to travel up the lane that led to Rowdy's chalet-style A-frame. Her vehicle hit one pothole after another. She shifted into 4-wheel drive as the vehicle jostled her and everything in it.

"Man, he wasn't kidding. He really needs to get some gravel out here...better yet pave this sucker. I'm gonna need an alignment when I get back to town."

Bethany slowed when she spotted the garage in front of her. Rowdy wasn't here yet, or if he was, his vehicle was inside the massive wooden and glass structure. She exited her vehicle, bag in hand, and stared at the beautiful windows that faced Sapphire Valley. From up here on the mountainside, the entire town was visible, even the mines and creek.

"Thought you were gonna beat me, Beth. You're slipping in your old age," a voice yelled from the open patio door.

Rowdy stood, hip leaning against the doorframe, his arms crossed over the ecru cable knit cotton sweater that covered his sculpted chest, and a crooked grin gracing his lips.

Damn! He still looks as good as he did ten years ago.

"Well, maybe if you didn't drive like a bat outta hell..."

His low chuckle turned her inside out.

"C'mon in, Beth. Lucie is in her box downstairs."

Rowdy led them down the seven light tan Berber covered steps. And, just as he'd said, Lucie was panting feverishly in the makeshift nest he'd made.

"Hey, girl. Look who's here. Luce, this is Beth." He sat on the floor by the box and fondled the dog's ears. "She's going to make sure you're doing all right."

Beth fished out her stethoscope and set her bag down some feet away from the box. She slowly approached the pregnant dog, knowing some were aggressive with strangers during pregnancy, even if their owners were by them.

She stopped a few steps away from Lucie and quietly stood, eyes closed. She focused on the beautiful Bernese and smiled. Lucie wasn't happy about being pregnant and out of shape and unable to climb the stairs.

Bethany giggled out loud. "It's okay, Lucie. I will take good care of you and your babies, I promise." She knelt and placed the stethoscope on the dog and moved it in different places. Her hands ran over the dog's bulging abdomen and then lifted her tail to see if there were any signs of whelping. Lucie was dilated and soon the first pup would take its first breath.

"Looks like we got here just in time. She's started. By the looks of things, Puppy Gramps, Number One will make an arrival within the next twenty minutes. If you don't have things ready, I suggest now would be a good time."

"Things?" Rowdy stood. "What things?"

"You didn't read up on this, did you?" Bethany shook her head.

"I didn't know I had to. I thought they did their own thing and if there were issues I'd call the vet and they'd take care of it."

Bethany closed her eyes again, sensing the dog's growing nervousness. She communicated to Lucie that things were going to be fine.

"I need to have some clean towels and some of them need to be warm and moist. I'd say a dozen or so should do."

Rowdy rummaged through the linen closet and gave a stack of towels to Beth. He ran upstairs to the bathroom closet for more and made sure he followed her directions to bring warm, moist ones, too.

"Okay, now what?" he asked.

"You're acting like an expectant father in a hospital waiting room. First of all, you need to chill. Lucie can pick up on your emotions. The quieter and more positive we can be, the better it will go for her. Next, we wait. She is the one doing all the work. I'm just here to make sure things go as they should and help out where they don't."

"Thanks, Beth. I'm glad it's you."

"Yeah, I'm kinda glad it's me, too. Lucie is a pretty special dog."

"She is indeed."

Rowdy walked around the perimeter of the great room and glanced outside. The sky was a dark gray, indicating snow was on the way.

"Looks like a storm's brewing out there."

"We haven't had much snow this winter yet," Bethany led. "We're due for a good dumping of the white stuff."

Chapter Three

Bethany wasn't sure what to say in response to his statement. She wondered if it was something he'd have said ten years ago…that he was glad she was there. He'd left her standing at the altar on their wedding day, telling her that he couldn't commit to a relationship, he couldn't commit to her. He needed time. He broke her heart.

She sighed. A lot had happened in the past ten years to her, and to Rowdy. Of course, she wondered what would have happened had he not run. Would they be in business together? Would he still be bull riding? Would there be children?

A muffled whimper brought Bethany back to the present. Puppy number one was momma-cleaned and puppy number two was on the way. Lucie was delivering faster than expected.

"I know you want to meet these little critters, honey, but you have to slow down," Beth assured Lucie with a loving look. "They're anxious to meet their momma, too."

Reaching into her bag, Bethany grabbed a container with pink and blue ribbons. After picking up the first puppy with one of the dry towels, she made sure the airway was clear and Lucie had done her job. After gently wiping the pup's fur, she tied a pink ribbon around its fat little neck. She looked over at Rowdy who'd not let go of Lucie's paw since sitting down beside her. A tear escaped his eye.

"Well, Gramps, it's a girl." She held up the towel with the sweet little squigglebutt so Rowdy could see. She looked down and Lucie had delivered number two, and three was on the way.

Every twenty minutes after that announcement a new little puppy was born. Six girls and two boys. Beth wondered if Lucie was finished. She checked the momma dog's vitals and abdomen. Something wasn't right. Bethany ran her hands over Lucie's abdomen again and left them on a hot spot. She sensed two struggling pups were being strangled by umbilical cords. Lubricating a gloved hand, Bethany moved to the rear of the dog.

"Talk to her, Rowdy. Nice and slow. Reassure her she and her puppies are going to be okay."

Rowdy switched from sitting to kneeling, and a look of dismay crossed his face.

"What's going on? Everything okay?"

Bethany shook her head. "Two are breech and I need to help her deliver them. She needs to know she is safe so I can do this. It isn't going to be the most comfortable thing for her, but I have to save these puppies...and her."

Rowdy bent his head close to Lucie's ear and whispered assurances to her. It was the sweetest thing Bethany had seen in a long time. Seeing him like this brought back a flood of memories: how he treated her, how special she felt in his arms, how beautiful she felt when he spoke to her and told her how precious she was to him. She sighed. Yeah, right. Then he ran.

Ten minutes passed, then twenty. Finally, one squirming pup was delivered and soon after, the last.

Sure, they're boys! Stubborn little shits. I can already tell they will be getting into everything and giving their mom a hard time!

Bethany carefully changed the bedding in Lucie's box, working one side then with Rowdy's help, moving the mom and babies so she could pull the soiled cloths from under them and smooth out the new ones. Thankfully, ten healthy pups and one very tired momma who was now lying on her side with her babies suckling, hadn't a care in the world.

She walked into the bathroom and cleaned her instruments and herself. She was glad to be here. Had she not, Lucie wouldn't have made it. There was no way she'd have been able to deliver the final puppies on her own. She had no energy in reserve, and with those cords so tightly wrapped around their little necks...well, she didn't want to think of the outcome.

Bethany looked at a beaming Rowdy, a look not unlike that of the father of a newborn.

"Well, Gramps, all is right in Lucie's world," Bethany smiled. "I'll get things together and head back to the office. Final count: six girls, four boys."

They climbed the steps to the landing by the front door. She glanced at the clock. Dark had come with the passing of time. It was well past six. Seven hours seemed like an eye-blink to her It was good being around him again. She'd forgotten how comfortable it was in his presence.

"I'll check in on Lucie in a couple days. She should sleep for a few hours then have her full attention on those babies. If you notice anything strange, don't hesitate to call."

An eerie quiet fell between them. Rowdy put a hand on her shoulder. "Have dinner with me, Beth. The least I can do is feed you. I'll cook a couple steaks and make a salad. Not sure I want you driving in this weather." He nodded to the window.

By the looks of it, snow had been falling for quite some time. The wind was whipping good, too. The last thing Rowdy wanted to do was drive back down the pothole filled lane in a blizzard to dig her and her car out of the ditch. Not knowing the main road condition, it was something that was more likely to happen than not if she left.

Great! Just what I need. This so wasn't in my plans.

"You know, I'm a Montana girl. We don't weather frighten easily."

"I know. But I also know you're tired after doing what you just did and I'm hungry. Stay for dinner. If it doesn't let up by the time we're done, you can sleep in the bedroom downstairs off the great room."

"Just for the record. I'm not staying because of the weather or because you asked or any other reason except that the steak sounds amazing and I am starved."

Chapter Four

It was well after eight o'clock when the dishes were taken care of and they'd moved from the kitchen island into the living room. Rowdy had opened a bottle of chardonnay and carried it, glasses, and a package of chocolate covered cookies to the table by the fireplace.

"Please sit down, Beth. There's no need to act like a caged lion."

Bethany stood at the windows looking out over Sapphire Valley. Lights twinkled here and there as the wind-whipped snow swirled in mini cyclones down the lane and across the lawn. There was no way she was driving in this tonight. It wouldn't be safe. But, would staying here be safe?

That's silly, McLintock. Get a grip. Besides, you will be downstairs with Lucie. What could happen?

Rowdy walked up behind her and offered a glass of wine. He nodded out the window.

"Kinda pretty, huh?"

"It is. When did you come back to Sapphire Creek?"

Rowdy walked over to the fireplace and lowered his six foot three frame to the pile of pillows on the floor. The heat from the flames felt good on his bad hip.

"A few years ago. After that accident in Cheyenne, I knew I had to give up riding." He sipped his wine. "Dad needed help with the store and suggested I come home. I couldn't find a place I liked, so drew up plans for this and here we are."

Bethany joined him in front of the fireplace. Being here was uncomfortable because her heart still stung from his abandonment all those years ago. Yet, being here also brought so many wonderful memories of being together, it felt as though they were picking up where they'd left one another.

"Tell me about the accident."

"Not much to tell. I was the last rider at the Cheyenne Days Rodeo. As the luck of the draw would have it, I drew Barclay, the meanest, largest Charolais at the event. The minute I sat on him, I knew there'd be trouble. I should have listened to my gut, but I didn't.

"Pride is a strange thing, Beth. I thought if I could stay on for that eight seconds...Anyway, I got in position, the buzzer signaled the opening of the gate and after three seconds, Barclay had tossed me on my ass and stomped on my left hip, shattering the ball and socket. They airlifted me to Salt Lake where the doctors rebuilt my hip. A lot of therapy later, here I am." He opened wide his arms.

"I'm sorry. I know that bull riding was your passion. It's tough when something like this takes that dream away."

"Yeah, I was five seconds away from the National Championship. It wasn't meant to be."

Bethany didn't know how to respond. She knew it hurt him today as much as it did then, both emotionally and physically. She'd seen him wince a couple times as he shifted on the pillows. Reaching for the bottle of wine, she topped off her glass and took a generous sip.

"You know, I can help with that." She nodded toward his hip.

Rowdy looked Bethany over from head to toe. A sly smile and raised eyebrow showed his playful side.

"Beth, I'm not some bull you can tranquilize and have your way with..."

"Stop right there, Lesley Walker! I'm good enough to make sure your dog lives through the birthing process, but I'm not good enough to offer suggestions about your pain? I can assure you, if I wanted to have my way with you, I wouldn't need to tranquilize you. You damn betcha, I'd have you whimpering and asking for more!"

Bethany walked quickly to the kitchen, placed her wineglass in the sink, and turned into the brick wall that was Lesley "Rowdy" Walker. She was one of a handful who got away with calling him by his given name. She'd always done it when she was angry. This time it was more to get under his skin than anger.

Rowdy's hands gripped her upper arms. That coupled with the fact he was like a mountain not to be moved, made escape impossible. He held her in place and looked into her bright robin's egg blue eyes, noticing for the first time the golden flecks that danced there. He saw the pain in her eyes that reached to her very soul...the pain he caused. He sighed.

"Beth." His low baritone was barely a whisper. "I'm sorry. I was scared. We were barely twenty. I shoved you away to follow the thrill that ate me alive at that time. It was the biggest mistake I've made. Ever. Please, forgive me. I know I don't deserve it. All these years. All these years, Beth, I've never stopped thinking of you. I've never stopped loving you. Please, can we start over?"

Hot tears stained Bethany's cheeks as she stood in front of the only man she'd ever loved. Holding grudges wasn't normal for her but forging to forgiveness? She wasn't ready for that, yet.

"It's late and I'm exhausted. I'm going to check in on Lucie and get some sleep."

Bethany managed to slip away from him and hurried downstairs. She stopped by Lucie's box and noticed she was awake. Kneeling, she placed a loving hand on top of the dog's head, then slumped to sit. Tears flowed freely as her mind replayed what she'd just heard. Lucie licked Beth's arm.

"I know, Luce. I know. I've never stopped loving him, either."

She positioned herself in front of the box and watched the pile of puppies. Lucie had slowly wandered to her water and food dishes then came back and nudged Bethany with her strong head. She heard the dog urging her to go back upstairs that her time with Rowdy wasn't finished. There was more to say and more to hear.

"Let's get you out for a potty break first, girl." Bethany attached the leash to Lucie's collar and let them out the downstairs door.

The wind was brutal, and the temperatures had dropped into the negatives. It was difficult to see across the backyard. Luckily, Lucie stayed closed to the house and did what she had to before bee-lining it back to the door.

After making sure Lucie was back with her babies, Bethany removed the bands that secured her golden blonde hair in the braid that hung over her left shoulder. She shook it free and ran her fingers through the tangles to smooth them out.

Okay, back upstairs I go.

Bethany lingered at the back of the kitchen as she watched Rowdy's left hand brace himself against the counter. She noticed he'd tossed his head back as he drank from a glass of water, indicating he'd taken some sort of medication.

"You okay?" she asked.

"Yeah. Weather systems get the pain riled up. I'll be fine."

"Will you let me help you? I was serious when I said that I could do something about your pain."

"What? What can you do that thousands of dollars and multiple doctors haven't been able to, huh?"

She sensed the frustration and closed her eyes. She knew if she could get him back on the floor, she could assess the real damage and maybe with acupuncture settle down the pain receptors.

"I'll be right back. If you can, lie down in front of the fireplace."

"Beth.."

"I'm serious. Please, let me try. You have nothing to lose, right? And, I promise, it's not gonna hurt, you big baby."

She heard his laugh and smiled as she hurried down the steps for her medical bag. She pulled out her acupuncture needles, alcohol wipes, a bottle of lavender and a bottle of Comfort, a healing oil. When she walked up the steps she saw him lying down as she'd requested.

"Well, now what?"

The sound of Rowdy's voice made her heart leap, as it always had. There was a hint of sarcasm mixed with the reality of his words, and that brought a smile. It was difficult to put the past behind her, but tonight was about helping him be without pain for a while. After all, that was what she did, use her gifts to help people and animals be pain-free.

Damn him! Why does he have to be so charming? Why does my heart have to love him so much even after he stomped it flat? Well, he certainly isn't going to know my feelings. Not yet anyway.

Bethany sat on the floor next to Rowdy. She closed her eyes and inhaled a deep breath through her nose and exhaled through her mouth. She repeated that several times until she was centered, and her focus was clear.

In several places, she saw the kyphoplasty that knit the fractures together. She saw the metal pins that bone had grown over and she noticed a bone spur that had formed on the femoral head. It no doubt was the culprit. It was pressing against the pelvis.

"Les..." She used his given name, like she'd always done. "I need your bare skin so you're going to have to pull down those jeans. And before you protest, I just need them down so I can see your hip, nothing more."

"Sheesh, you sure know how to deflate a guy's ego."

"Listen, this is strictly professional. Think of me as your doctor."

"Yeah, right."

"Are you going to do this?" She sighed. "Or am I?"

"Fine." He loosened his belt and unzipped the jeans but pulled them down only to expose his hip.

The scar Bethany saw was a good eight inches long. She placed her hand on it and noticed the heat from the inflammation. She cleansed the area and set the acupuncture needles. The process took a half hour and she noticed Rowdy had fallen asleep. She was glad he was comfortable.

The pain he felt, Bethany felt. It was searing, like a blade being stuck into his flesh. She closed her eyes again and held her right hand above the acupuncture needles, making a slow, circular motion several times. Then she began pulling pain with her hand from the circle she'd set. A couple times she heard a moan escape Rowdy, and she pushed the sound from her thoughts, continuing to rid the pain from the nerve endings.

He was in such a deep sleep when she finished removing the needles that she wasn't going to wake him. Grabbing the blanket from the back of the couch, she gently laid it over him, turned out the majority of lights, and glanced out the window again.

More snow. More wind. There was nothing she could do about it. It was Montana, after all.

Chapter Five

Rowdy wasn't quite sure what happened, only that he'd had the best night's sleep in a very long time. Getting up from the floor was easier, his mood was jovial, and he found himself singing lines from an Elton John tune.

The house was blissfully quiet. He looked out at the freshly fallen snow that had accumulated over-night and at the flakes still falling. There was a good chance of another half foot. After coffee, he would tackle the driveway, but not if he didn't get in the kitchen and brew a pot.

It was odd to not be greeted by Lucie. She was usually the first one in the kitchen and anxious to go outside. There wasn't one sound coming from downstairs. She must be asleep or taking care of her new babies.

He smiled. The puppies were so dang cute, each a miniature version of Lucie. Having the house filled with happy puppies running all over the house was something Rowdy enjoyed. This was Lucie's second litter. Thankfully seven of this litter were already spoken for. That was another thing on his to-do list today, contact the prospective new furbaby owners.

Holding the mug of freshly brewed coffee to his nose and savoring the aroma, Rowdy closed his eyes. His thoughts revisited the past twenty-four hours. Never had he imagined seeing Beth again, let alone having her as the new vet, or spending time in his house. The sound of feet on the steps up to the kitchen startled him to reality.

Beth yawned as she climbed the final step into the main part of the house. Still dressed in yesterday's clothes and her disheveled hair framing her sleepy face, she managed a weak smile.

"Well, good morning."

"Coffee..." She held out her hands much as a toddler would when seeing a bottle.

Rowdy chuckled, went to the counter and pulled a mug from the cupboard. When full, he placed it on the counter in front of her.

"Not sure if you like anything in it, but there are some creamers in the refrigerator. I can get one for you, if you'd like."

She shook her head and took a sip of coffee, shivering as the hot liquid made its way down her esophagus to her stomach, which growled in protest.

"Sounds like you're hungry, too. Why don't I fix something to eat? Omelet okay?"

Bethany nodded and took another sip of the coffee. She wasn't used to talking with anyone first thing in the morning. It was her sacred quiet time. Dusty would do the wind-my-body-through-your-legs thing and run off, leaving her owner ready to center for the day. That usually included thirty minutes of yoga, a nutritious breakfast, shower, and then readying for the day.

This morning, however, was different. Her foggy brain revisited the events of last night.

"How'd you sleep?"

"She does speak!"

Bethany raised an eyebrow in his direction and sipped her coffee, an indicator that he was crossing into territory he needed to leave alone.

"I slept well. Did you?"

"Let's say it wasn't a good night. You know...new place, new bed, new noises."

Rowdy was chopping mushrooms and peppers and tossing them into the pan. The aroma was divine. He added eggs he'd whisked and topped with grated cheese and waited for the bubbling to stop before perfectly flipping the omelet with the flick of a wrist.

"Luce keep you up?"

Bethany shook her head.

Either she isn't a morning person or she doesn't want to talk with me.

Rowdy placed a plate in front of her and handed her a fork and napkin.

"Look, Beth, I'll leave you alone. I've got shoveling to do," Rowdy stated, leaving her with her breakfast.

The sound of the backdoor closing allowed her to breathe a sigh of relief. She'd finish her breakfast, which was amazing, check on the pups, do her morning routine in peace and quiet, and be ready to leave as soon as Rowdy cleared the driveway. Easy peasy.

Bethany took a look out the living room windows and watched as Rowdy started the snowblower and slowly made his way through the foot and a half of snow that had fallen. She looked out over the valley and at the snow that still fell. She chewed her lower lip. There may be a chance she wouldn't be able to get out today. Pulling her cell phone from her jeans pocket, she pressed the clinic number.

"Sapphire Creek Alternative Pet Medicine Clinic. How may I help you?"

"Dee, I didn't know if you'd be there yet. Everything going okay?" Bethany inquired.

"Of course. No one is out because of the blizzard. I came in because I wanted to get a jump on month end things. Luckily, we have no inpatients and the town seems relatively quiet. Where are you?"

"I'm at Rowdy Walker's place. Lucie had a bit of trouble with the last two puppies so I intervened. Proud to say momma and ten little squigglebutts are doing well. Dee, they are so adorable! I may have to stake my claim to one of them. They all look like their beautiful momma."

"Why are you still there?"

"The snow trapped me. It was dark when we cleaned up from the birthing, and it wasn't a wise idea for me to be traveling back down the mountain in this weather. So, I bunked next to the new little family."

A long pause caused Bethany to smile. She knew exactly what her best friend was thinking and nothing could be further from the truth.

"Before you start," Bethany began. "There is nothing, and I do mean nothing, between Rowdy and me. He did apologize, though, for being such a jerk on our wedding day. Told me I was the only one he'd ever loved."

"Uh huh."

"You don't believe me?"

"Bethie, it isn't that I don't believe you. I know you too well. When you say nothing happened, nothing happened. However, that doesn't mean that you don't *want* it to. Face it, girlfriend, you've never squelched that flame you've carried for this man even after he left you at the altar."

Dee was right. She did love Rowdy. A part of her always would. He was her first love, after all. But, what was she going to do about it? Nothing. There was nothing she *could* do. What she needed to do was get out of his house, off this mountain, and back to her world, her apartment, her things. It would be much needed space between them so she could think. Being around him made it so she couldn't think rationally. Tongue tied with puppy eyes was not becoming to a strong woman, and that is what she was reduced to every time they were around each other.

"How are the roads?" Bethany asked.

"Not good. The state has issued a tow ban and chains are required. If you don't have to travel, hon, I sure wouldn't."

"Dee, I have to get home. Dusty needs me."

"Feeble excuse. I'll look after kitty. Try again."

Bethany sighed and stomped her foot in angst. She didn't want to be trapped here another night. Maybe if Rowdy had cross country skis she could get back into town. She shook her head. No, that wouldn't work.

"What, Bethie? What is it?"

"I don't want to be stuck here another night."

"With that huge house of his, it's not like you have to be in each other's pocket, you know. You could be on one floor and he could be on another."

"Yeah, yeah, yeah. Call me if anything comes up. And, I do mean anything."

"You know I will."

Bethany remained at the window watching Rowdy and sipping her now cold coffee. Shrugging her shoulders she headed to the counter and cleaned up the breakfast leftovers before heading outside to see if there was anything she could do to help.

Chapter Six

Winter was releasing its icy grip on Sapphire Creek: snow was melting, roads were slushy, temperatures were warming, and attitudes were much more pleasant. As Bethany walked from the coffee shop to her clinic, she smiled at how good it felt to be home. It was nice to occasionally have breakfast with her dad, go shopping with her mom, and see her brother, who lived in Bozeman.

Eight weeks had passed since the puppies were born and Bethany had spent time at Rowdy's house. They'd not seen or spoken with each other since she left the mountain chalet. Today she was to make a house call for the puppies' first shots and a well-check of Lucie.

"Good morning, Dee," Bethany greeted, closing the door behind her.

"Hey!"

"What do we have going on today?"

"Mr. Peterson is bringing in his rottweiler for nail clipping. Donna Jordan wants you to look at Sasha, her Maine Coon. Pete Savatch has a molting parakeet. And Rick is bringing Daisy."

"Sounds like a normal day, huh? Oh, make sure to carve out some time for me to go see those Bernese pups for their first shots. You need to come with me. It will go a lot quicker if we do it together."

"Let's do it around one. Pete will be here around three-thirty."

"Good. Call Rowdy and let him know."

Bethany no more than got those words out of her mouth when the door opened. A tall, regal woman entered--not one silver hair out of place, long, perfectly manicured nails sporting the same shade of burgundy as the Melton-cloth ankle length coat that hung loosely on her gaunt frame. She set the small gray pet carrier on the counter.

"Good morning. I'm Donna Jordan and this is Callie." She nodded toward the cowering cat. "I have a nine o'clock appointment."

"It's nice meeting you, Donna," Bethany greeted. "Please, follow me to one of the exam rooms and we'll take a look at Callie, shall we?"

Bethany opened the door leading to the exam rooms and motioned for the client and patient to enter room two. Without putting her hands on the cat, she knew what was going on. Callie was very communicative with her.

"Okay, little girl, let's get you out of there so I can see you." Bethany removed the cat from the carrier. A beautifully pampered twenty pound Maine Coon emerged. She looked to be around five years old, and very well cared for. "How can I help?"

Donna stood on the other side of the exam table and looked lovingly at Callie. "I'm devastated. I don't have any other choice. I'd like her put to sleep."

Bethany's shock shook her to her toes. There was nothing wrong with this cat. She was a bit overweight, but she was happy and healthy. There had to be more to this story and she was going to find out. She stroked the cat as Donna continued.

"I will be leaving Sapphire Creek for an assisted living center in Kalispell at the end of the week. This particular place doesn't allow pets. I have no choice but to put her down. No one wants her because she is so overweight. I'll pay you whatever the fee is. I must leave now."

"Donna, wait, please. I do not euthanize animals because their owners cannot keep them."

Donna tried taking Callie out of Bethany's arms. "Fine. I'll find a vet who does."

"You will drive a ways. I'm the only vet in a hundred mile radius. I'm sure we can figure something out."

"I didn't want the cat in the first place," Donna admitted. "My son thought I needed someone to keep me company after Donald died. I didn't realize this cat would be so much work. I can't do it. Just take care of it."

Donna made her way to the door. She stopped at the counter and put two one hundred dollar bills down, turned without a word, and left.

"Dee! We have a problem."

Dee rushed into room two where Bethany held a whimpering Callie. "What was that all about?"

"She left the cat. She wanted me to 'put her to sleep' because she couldn't take care of her. It was 'too much work.' People!" Bethany continued assuring Callie things would be all right.

"Now what?" Dee moved the carrier from the exam table.

"Let's do a well-check. I guess we are now the owners of a clinic kitty. Now, on the days I bring Dusty in, she will have a playmate."

While Bethany did the normal checkup on Callie, Dee found a basket and made a space for the cat on the desk. They hadn't had a clinic cat but had talked about it several times. Callie seemed up for the job. She was calm and sweet and loved people, that was obvious.

"Well, sweet girl. Welcome home."

Thank you, Doctor Bethany, for rescuing me from that woman. She wasn't kind. I promise to not cause any problems for you.

"I know you won't, baby."

Bethany led Callie to the front desk and motioned for her to hop onto the counter. She did as commanded and settled into the basket and began preening. It wasn't long before she was asleep.

"The nerve of that woman!"

Dee sterilized room two and led the next client and patient to a room. It seemed she was repeating her routine every twenty minutes. It made the morning fly by. Before she knew it, it was time to load up for the house call.

"Bethie, are we ready to go to Walker's house?"

"Yeah, give me one more minute. Did you get the charts for all of them? I hope Rowdy has them named by now."

"I did. I have treats for mom, too."

It was a beautiful day for a drive up the mountain. In a few weeks the deciduous trees would be leafing and spring would be unwrapping her lovely colors. Streams were bank-full already and Sapphire Falls gracefully flowed over the rocks under her and into Sapphire Creek.

Bethany smiled as she took in her surroundings. She was anxious for better weather so she could start working the barrels with Brindle, her quarter horse. She'd boarded her at her parents' stable when she moved back. There never seemed to be enough time to do all she wanted to do. She was certain, however, she would enter the county fair barrel racing event. It had been way too long.

Turning into the driveway to the mountain chalet, Dee was the first to notice Rowdy. He was repairing fence by the lane. She rolled down her window.

"Hey, Rowdy. How's it goin'?"

Bethany chuckled to herself. She knew Dee had a huge crush on the man and her actions were so obvious it was sickening, yet sweet in an odd sort of way.

"Hi, you two." Rowdy looked directly at Bethany. "It's been awhile. How are you?"

"More importantly, how are those puppies doing?" She dodged his question with one of her own.

"Delightful. Can't wait for you to see them. Luce is doing real well, too. She's a good mother."

"Well, take me to them."

Bethany grabbed her bag and made sure Dee had the folders so she could record weight and other pertinent information, like names she was sure he hadn't thought of.

The puppies were still in the basement, but a baby gate was secured at the bottom of the steps so they couldn't wander freely yet. They'd doubled in size since Bethany last saw them and they were playfully running the room. Lucie greeted her with her normal head-butt to her thigh.

"Hi, Baby Momma. It's good to see you, too!" She bent over and kissed the Bernese on the head. "My gracious, you've been busy with these little squigglebutts."

The puppies rushed the gate when they saw Bethany.

"Settle down, little ones," she giggled. "Hey, Gramps, get in here. We're gonna need your help."

Rowdy stepped over the gate and looked at the puppies as they gathered at his feet.

"Whatcha need?"

"I sure hope you've named these puppies. It will make life a lot easier as we record weights and other health information."

Rowdy smiled. Of course he'd named them. Sometimes her lack of faith in his abilities really riled him. He picked up one of the pups with a blue ribbon. "Here is One."

"Oh seriously? Les, c'mon. You can't be serious," Bethany rolled her eyes.

"Dead serious, Beth. This way the owners can name them what they want." His bourbon eyes danced with mischief."

After all ten puppies were weighed and given their initial shots, Bethany checked Lucie. All were well. This is what she liked. This is how it should be, not like the unfortunate incident a few hours ago.

"Everything all right, Beth?" Rowdy must have picked up on her energy change.

"Yeah. Just a stupid thing at work this morning. We now have a clinic cat because someone didn't want to take care of her. Breaks my heart when things like that happen." She paused. "Then I come here and see how loved and how well taken care of these dogs are and it gives me hope."

"Well, which one is yours?"

Bethany quizzically looked at him. How did he know she wanted one of the puppies? She hadn't mentioned it to him.

"Which what?"

"Which puppy?"

"I haven't given it much thought." Bethany knelt and picked up a couple of them.

"I know differently."

Rowdy walked over to Number Four, one of the females. He'd written a 'B' on the ribbon. He cuddled her close to his neck and kissed her before giving her to Bethany.

"Here. This one is yours."

She was the one Bethany had her eye on from the time she'd dried her off and tied the ribbon around her neck.

"How did you know this is the one I wanted?"

"I watched you when you tended them. This one seemed special in your eyes. I made sure I memorized the markings so I didn't get it wrong." Rowdy chuckled. "I think she's a perfect match for you."

"Thank you."

Those were the only words she could manage as they stared at each other for what seemed an eternity.

"I...I...we have to get back to the clinic. I have other patients this afternoon." She reluctantly gave the puppy back to him, their hands touching and lingering on each other during the transfer.

"I'll take good care of her. You can come over anytime to see her, you know that, right?" He winked and flashed a smile at her that he knew made her knees weak.

Bethany's mouth was as parched as the Sahara. No words came forth, only a nod of her head and a slight smile as she made her way back to her vehicle.

Damn it! Damn man! Why do I freeze like this?

By the end of the day, seven other patients had been cared for and other appointments made for a full schedule for the following day. With the counter clean, a load of laundry transferred to the dryer, and all of the charts updated, Bethany was ready to go home. But, instead of going home, she drove to her parents' ranch. She needed her father's wisdom and Brindle's love.

Chapter Seven

Bethany drove into the circular driveway in front of her parents' home and waited a while before shutting off the engine of her vehicle. She didn't know why she waited so long in between visits.

She noticed her dad backing out of the four stall garage and hurried over to his little red sports car, a gift to himself when he turned sixty.

"Hi, honey," her dad began as he exited his car and hugged her.

Bethany breathed in the all too familiar Old Spice fragrance and smiled. She loved the immediate comfort it brought her. She inhaled deeply and burrowed her face in her father's neck.

"You okay, Beth?"

"I am now." She pulled back and smiled.

"To what do we owe the pleasure of your visit?"

"I wanted to spend some time with you and Mom and see how Brindle's doing. I'm planning to be out here more now that spring is on the way. Gonna be working her toward entering the barrel racing event at the fair this year."

"That's great! I'm glad you're finally making time for yourself and doing what you love."

"Thanks, Dad. Mom inside?"

"She's in town getting her hair fixed. Should be home in an hour or so. I can make us some dinner if you're hungry."

"Nah, that's fine. Looks like you were about ready to go for a spin, too, huh? I'll go down to the stables."

"If you're sure. Gus and the guys want to play cards, but I'll cancel. It's not every day I can spend time with my favorite daughter."

"Your only daughter," Bethany reminded.

They walked arm in arm to the house.

"Your mom has chicken thawing for dinner. I think she's planning on me grilling. You can help me with the other fixings, if you'd like."

When Bethany was ten, Mitchell McLintock had been head chef at one of the more prestigious restaurants in Helena. He'd retired from the Brass Bullet, his own establishment, just last year. Food was an art to him. Each meal a magazine show piece.

"I'd love that."

Mitch set the ingredients on the island and washed the produce before instructing his daughter how to precisely slice the vegetables for the salad. His words made his daughter giggle.

"Hey, you know how I am about what food looks like. The more appealing it appears, the better it tastes."

"I know, Dad."

Mitch knew Bethany well enough to know when her visits were casual in nature. He also knew when her heart was heavy and she needed to talk.

"How's work going?"

"Really well. Although it was crazy today. At least the days are rarely the same and there's always a new adventure waiting for me."

The corners of Mitch's mouth curled upward. He knew what that meant. He knew the animals she treated somehow wove themselves into Bethany's soul.

"Everything else going okay?"

Bethany paused before answering him. She had no idea if things were okay. She knew she was confused and that her heart was longing for the man she'd loved, the man who hurt her. She furrowed her brow and pursed her lips.

"Not sure."

"What's that supposed to mean?"

"Rowdy Walker came into the clinic a few months back. First time we'd seen each other since he left me high and dry."

"I see."

Bethany could see discomfort in her father's features as she continued the line of conversation.

"He had a pregnant dog about ready to give birth and wanted the vet to make a house call to check on her. He didn't know I was the vet."

"Why didn't he just bring in the dog?"

"He couldn't carry her to the truck. She was very pregnant...a Bernese. Anyway, it brought back a lot of memories I thought I'd dealt with."

Mitch sat down on one of the stools at the counter across from his daughter. He poured and offered her a glass of sparkling wine.

"What is there to deal with? The rat left you at the altar. Do I need to contact him? Tell him to leave you be?"

Bethany took a sip from the glass. The last thing she wanted was her father throwing his weight around with Les...Rowdy...whatever he wanted to be called.

"No. I can handle it. He was very kind. Apologized for what happened. The day the dog delivered the pups we had a snowstorm and I was stranded at his place a couple days. He was the perfect gentleman. Other than seeing him during meals, we didn't speak."

"So, what's the problem? Do you still have feelings for the guy?"

"Yeah, I do."

Mitch drained his glass and poured another. He was afraid that was what his daughter was going to say.

"I didn't think I did, but then watching him with Lucie, that's his dog, and those puppies...seeing the emotion when he apologized to me for what he did. It brought it all back. Dad, I realized I never stopped loving him. What am I going to do?"

"You know I can't tell you what to do, Bethany. I will remind you that whenever you've had major decisions to make, you always spent time at Sapphire Creek, walking the banks and sometimes in the creek bed. It has always calmed you, given you answers. Maybe you should do that again."

Bethany had forgotten about the solace she'd found at the creek, and the many sapphires she'd collected over the years. Maybe that was where she'd find answers.

Heels clicking on the Moroccan tile announced the arrival of her mother, Anne.

"Mitch? Whose car is that in front of the house? I thought you were going over to Gus's."

Anne turned the corner into the kitchen and saw her daughter.

"Bethany! How good to see you."

"Good to see you, too, Mom." Bethany air-kissed each of her mother's cheeks, something that they'd done since her parents' return from Italy.

"I'm assuming you're staying for dinner?"

"Dad talked me into helping him, so yes."

"Wonderful! I will change and be right back."

Anne returned in no time and conversation centered around town gossip heard at the beauty shop. It wasn't long, thankfully, until dinner was served and cleaned up.

"Thanks for feeding me. I appreciate it. While I still have a few moments of daylight, I want to check in on Brindle."

Bethany hugged her mom and whispered a heartfelt thank you in her father's ear before making her way to the stables.

"Brin," Bethany hugged the horse's head and gave it a pat. "How ya doin', girl?"

The horse nodded a response.

"I know, I'm glad to see you, too. It's been a hard winter. I'm sorry I've been so busy. I promise we will be seeing a lot of each other starting this weekend. Are you ready to race again?"

The horse nodded again and Bethany pulled out an apple from her pocket.

"I just needed a hug before I take off. I'll be back in a couple days. You be good for Maurice, okay?"

Maurice, the stable manager, poked his head out of his office.

"She's always a good one for me. How's Bethany?"

"I'm good, thanks. Tired, but good. I'll be back this weekend to start working toward racing again. I've missed it so much."

"I'll be here, just in case you need any help."

"Thanks. See you Saturday."

Weary from the day, Bethany slid behind the wheel and headed for her house. She couldn't wait to shower, climb into her pj's, and watch mindless television until she fell asleep.

Chapter Eight

Montana is known for its county fairs and rodeos. People come from across the country to experience the western way of life through the eyes of those who participate.

Bethany was excited. Her life was going well: she'd hired another vet tech and a new veterinarian would be joining her at the end of summer. She'd talked Les into keeping Number Four until after rodeo season, when she could devote more time to her training...and come up with an appropriate name.

She'd trained hard the past six weeks and was confident Brindle was ready to compete at the Sapphire Creek rodeo. Her nerves were in check until she mounted her horse and sat waiting her turn.

"And our next competitor is a hometown girl, Bethany McLintock riding Brindle. Brindle is a six-year old quarter horse who has won a couple medals in the past. Let's welcome them to the ring."

Bethany led Brindle to the ring, tipped her Stetson and readied for the signal to go. Brindle shot off lightning quick. She cut the first barrel too close, but thankfully didn't knock it down. Around the second barrel and across to the third. Bethany kicked Brindle's sides, and she flew down the stretch headed for the finish.

"That's a new best time, folks. Twenty-six point six seconds. Doctor McLintock is in first place with two riders to go."

Cynthia Adams led her Appaloosa to a good time, too, thirty seconds flat. Carlie Fagen cut close on barrel two, knocking it over and adding seconds to her overall time.

"The winner of the Sapphire Creek Barrel Racing Event is our own Doctor Bethany McLintock. She and Brindle have qualified for the state competition in August, which will be held in conjunction with the State Fair in Billings. We know you won't want to miss that."

A WIDE GRIN crossed Rowdy Walker's lips as he cheered Bethany and Brindle to victory. He was so proud of this woman. She was doing what she loved, racing. Seeing her out there made him want to be in the ring. He wanted to feel the thrill of the crowd, the adrenaline rush from sitting on the back of those bulls, but there would never be another time. Never.

He made his way to the winner's circle and waited his turn to congratulate Bethany. She was surrounded by friends and family and clients, all hugging her and wishing her well at the state competition. Finally, he inched his way to her.

"Congratulations. Well done!" He side hugged her just as a photographer snapped a picture.

She removed her Stetson and wiped her brow on the sleeve of her red plaid shirt and replaced the hat. She kicked at the dirt with the toe of one of her Tony Lamas.

"Thanks. I need to make sure Brindle is cooled down and groomed."

Bethany knew her words were friendly, but cold. That's all she could offer right now. She'd shrouded heart against being hurt again by the man she loved. If anything negative happened between them, she'd shut down and there'd never be a chance for anything between them, not that she was looking for that. Thankfully, Les seemed to understand.

"Sounds good. See you soon."

"Yes. See you soon."

Maurice helped Bethany load Brindle and secured the door. He climbed into the club cab and started the engine.

"You comin' or are you gonna stand there gawkin'?"

"All right, already!" She tossed her Stetson on the seat, hauled herself into the truck and secured her seatbelt. "Onward!"

FOLLOWING A HOT shower and comfy clothes, Bethany smiled as she held the newly won trophy and blue ribbon. She placed both on the mantle and folded her arms. She was pleased for her accomplishment today and so proud of Brindle. At least there were several weeks before the state competition. She'd take tomorrow off and start fresh Monday working Brindle. Cutting seconds off their time around those barrels was imperative to a win.

She was so tired, but it was a good tired. She sat on the chaise portion of her sofa and grabbed the MSU tied blanket she'd made several years ago. Her intention was to watch the newest episode of her favorite crime show, instead she leaned back and fell asleep.

Shimmers from the yard light filtered through her front window. It was well after eleven when she took the blanket and padded to her room. Dreams of Les leaving her at the altar prevented quality sleep. Scenes would flip from the past to the present, from standing slack-jawed to smiling at him when he walked through the door of the clinic.

The man continued to haunt Bethany's slumber until she finally tossed the covers, made her way to the kitchen, and heated water for a cup of hot chocolate. She sat on one of the oak chairs at the round matching table, picking at dead leaves on the plant that served as a centerpiece.

"What am I going to do about Mr. Lesley Rowdy Walker, Dusty?" she asked the Persian who'd hopped up in her lap.

The sound of the whistling teakettle startled Dusty. She promptly meowed and ran into the other room, leaving Bethany alone pouring hot water over a peppermint tea bag.

Returning to the table, her thoughts turned once again to the man who'd captured her heart so many years ago.

Les was the most handsome, kindest man she'd met. They laughed at the same things, loved romantic comedies, hated Brussel sprouts, and had shared more than one pint of coffee toffee ice cream in the wee hours of the morning. The latter, along with his hugs, fixed anything that was wrong.

Maybe Dad is right. Maybe I need to spend some time at Sapphire Creek.

Wrapping her hands around her favorite mug, she lingered over the warm beverage until its remnants were cold. She made a mental note to clean out the cooler so she could pack a snack for her trek to the creek later that morning.

Trying to sleep at this point was futile. The sun would rise in less than a half hour, she may as well stay up and get some things done. After dressing and pulling on her boots, she grabbed her keys and headed for the clinic. Even though it was Sunday there were things she could catch up on, most importantly chart notes, which took a backseat when she took time off to train Brindle.

Rowdy finished with the fifty-pound kettle bell and set it back with the other weights. He positioned himself on the elliptical and began pedaling. He wouldn't do much this morning, but he needed to do something. He couldn't stop thinking about Beth. His Beth. Was she *his* Beth? Would she even consider *being* his Beth again? The more he thought of her, the faster he pedaled.

He was a jerk. Plain and simple. It was the only word to describe his actions of ten years ago. He was at his prime. One peak performance after another, he was in line for the National Bull Rider title. He had money. He had a beautiful fiancé. He was living the life he wanted. Then Beth pushed up the wedding.

Sure, he wanted to marry her, just not then. There were other things to achieve, like the title he'd worked so hard climbing the ladder to grab. He couldn't tell her he wanted to put off the wedding until the following year. He didn't want to hurt her. Instead, he walked away because he couldn't face his own insecurities and broke her heart in the process.

"Wise choice, dumb ass!" he chastised himself aloud.

He slowed to a cool-down pace. Ten minutes later he was standing in the shower with the hottest water pelting on his muscles. He placed both hands on the tiled wall and held his head under the water.

How was he going to convince Bethany he wasn't the same person? How was he going to assure her that he would never do anything to hurt her again? He wanted to share his life with her. He'd never stopped loving her and living without her these past few years, especially, tore him up inside.

The water was cooling so Rowdy turned off the faucet. He grabbed a towel and headed for his bedroom, not bothering to dry off. He sat down on his bed and thought again what he could do to win back the only love of his life. He needed a plan, and maybe he needed to start by visiting with her dad.

Even though the store was open today, he would spend minimal time there. He needed to get a deposit ready and pay a few bills, but then he'd carve out the time to formulate a plan. He loved Bethany and this time would not let any of his stupid ideas prevent him from following through to get what he wanted.

Chapter Nine

THE SUN WAS high in the sky by the time Bethany finished updating patient charts. She was glad for the quiet office. It was just her and Callie, who'd turned out to be the best clinic cat she could have ever wanted.

"Callie, watch over things. Everyone will be here tomorrow."

Yes, ma'am. You can count on me.

Bethany kissed the feline. She was thrilled Callie was safe and had a forever home.

I'm thankful you didn't turn me away.

"Never. See you later, baby girl."

She locked the door after pulling it shut and made her way down the block to her parked vehicle. Stopping at the coffee shop, she picked up a turkey sandwich and white mocha latte, since she'd forgotten to pack the cooler. Back in the car, she headed for Sapphire Creek, a ten mile drive.

Traffic was light for a Sunday, for which Bethany was thankful. That meant the park would be pretty much deserted and she could do her thing…walk the banks, walk the empty creek bed, provided the spring run-off hadn't come down this far, and find answers that her heart longed to know. She signaled to turn right at the entrance to Sapphire Creek State Park and continued slowly down the narrow two-lane road until she found the right parking place to her trail.

With her backpack situated on her shoulders and secured around her waist, Bethany grabbed her walking stick, made sure her cell phone and keys were in her front jeans' pocket, and set out on her journey.

The trail was well marked, and she knew not to stray too far off the path. It was carved less than a foot away from Sapphire Creek. Her destination today was the waterfall that bore the same name. Blossoms from huckleberry bushes popped their heads through the lush foliage and ground squirrels chattered as they scampered across her path.

Bethany noticed a change in temperature and elevation the farther she went into the forest. The trail curved to the left and opened to a clearing where picnic tables and grills dotted the grassy area. This seemed like a good time to enjoy her sandwich. She sat at one of the tables and unwrapped her food. Sun streamed through the trees, warming her shoulders. She sighed. This was her favorite place on earth. It was peaceful and peace filled.

She allowed herself to bask in the warmth of her surroundings a while longer before setting back on the path to the falls. She nodded to a young couple she met on the path who were coming from the opposite direction. A few more yards and she saw the wooden rails that served as a barrier to the falls and pool it emptied into. Excitement quickened her pace, and once she reached the fence, Sapphire Falls didn't disappoint.

Water rushed over the granite rock wall and into the pool that flowed into Sapphire Creek. She rested her elbows on the top rail as she watched with fascination the water flow over the rock outcroppings. The mist from water sprayed her face and she turned more into it so she could feel each drop.

Closing her eyes, Bethany tuned into the spirits of the water, of the woods, of those who'd traveled this land and lost their lives. Tears fell freely down her cheeks.

My child, why are you sad? You've come here for years to gain strength, yet today there are tears. Listen to the water as it travels over the rocks, gaining speed as it journeys down river. It is strong, not weak, just as you are strong.

Hearing the spirits of old only brought more tears. Bethany dropped to her knees and wept.

Your soul is wise, Bethany, we made sure of that the day you were born. Wise, kind, beautiful, strong. You are the epitome of your name.

You live it daily. Yet you are in a quandary, unable to decide. Your heart knows what your head does not.

"I love him. I've always loved him, but he hurt me so badly that I'm not sure I can love again."

You are meant to love, as proven in your work.

"Animals are different than people. They love unconditionally."

Yes, as do you, most of the time. If you love him, you will forgive him in your heart and in time your mind will forget the wrong done. It's the universal way. Never hold onto wrongdoings, they only become more pain.

"I don't know what to do."

You know what you want, to be loved in return. This man has loved you from the first time he set eyes on you and you've felt the same way. Your path has not been easy with each other and it won't be in the future, but your love will only become stronger and when two loves unite, the bond is unbreakable. Nothing can shake it if it is what both souls want.

You see, sweet Bethany, it isn't only carnal but spiritual. From long ago you were destined to be together, handpicked, if you will, for the other. You are the other's heart and soul and neither of you will rest easy until you are one.

We are so proud of you, of your work, of the young woman you've become. You are never alone. When you place your healing hands on animals, we are there. When you help those around you in whatever way is needed, we are there. We are your love. We are your kindness. We are the essence of who you are. We will not let you fall. We will not let you fail. There is an army of souls who stand behind you ready to come to your aid when warranted.

"I don't understand any of this. I only know I have to do what I do. I have to heal the animals who need healing. I have to be kind to those around me. I have to love Les because he owns my heart."

Then you know what you need to do, dear child.

Bethany sat with her back to the rails, thinking about what she'd just heard. Yes, she knew what she needed to do. For now, though, she would finish her hike and enjoy her surroundings. Once back in the real world, she'd call Les.

"THANKS FOR MEETING me for coffee, Mitch," Rowdy extended a hand before sitting down.

"I'm not sure what you want, Lesley, or how I can help."

"I know I screwed up ten years ago. I apologized to Beth and I'm apologizing to you right now. What I did was selfish and I wasn't thinking straight. I had cold feet. All I could see was how marriage would take me away from something I loved more than life itself, when what I needed to do was love Beth more than bull riding. Fate has a way of getting her point across. The accident happened and now I have neither."

"Beth and I talked a few months back. I think it'd be best if you talk with her, iron things out. Maybe you can find a common point to begin from. If you really love my daughter as you say you do, you will fight for her."

"I've always loved your daughter. She was my first love. My only love..."

"Other than bull riding," Mitch interjected.

"Yes, but now that is over and done. It's not even on my radar. I want to support her when she races and I want to help with her business. I'm sure I can do something that would make a difference."

"Again, you need to be talking with her, not me." Mitch drained his cup of coffee and motioned for a refill.

"I tried calling her this morning, but it went to voicemail."

"She may be out of cell range. I know she was hiking to Sapphire Falls today. Not sure when, though."

"Maybe I can catch her if I leave..."

"No. Wait for her to return. She has some demons to slay and the only way for her to do that is to wander around that creek. There's something about that place that gets to her. It's always been that way.

"When she was five years old, she fell into Sapphire Creek. Things changed for her after that. We found her talking to her stuffed animals and to her cat and we swore we could hear them answering her. We've heard legends of that area and how spirits inhabit the water and woods. Those who are sensitive can hear them and are gifted with special abilities. I believe that is why she is so good at her job. She understands animals better than anyone I've seen," Mitch shook his head. "Even when we polled or branded, she'd have a way to calm the cattle."

Rowdy nodded. He knew exactly what Mitch was talking about. He saw it firsthand when she worked her magic on his hip. He wouldn't say anything about that, though.

"I want to spend the rest of my life with Beth. I want a second chance."

"You're talking to the wrong person, son. I can't speak for my daughter. I can, however, see the changes in you since your accident and return to Sapphire Creek. And, I like what I see. You've developed a good work ethic and show responsibility with how you run the store. Your dad should be proud."

"Thank you. I want to be the type of man Beth can count on."

"Then I'd say the first part of the battle is won. Now, you need to talk with her." Mitch eyed the clock. "I hate to do this, but Anne and I are leaving in an hour. We are headed to Brazil."

"Brazil?" Rowdy chuckled as he questioned the older man's statement.

"Yeah. Anne thinks she needs to explore the rainforest before it disappears. I'm along for the ride." The older man laughed. "You'll learn. You'll learn." He patted Rowdy's shoulder, tossed a couple bills on the table, and walked out the door.

He now knew what he needed to do. Wait. That was one of the things he hated most. Waiting was not one of his gifts, that was for sure. Maybe if he went back to the store for a couple hours it would help.

Chapter Ten

Bethany arrived home around four o'clock, fed Dusty, put away her hiking gear, and phoned Dee.

"Hey, how's your Sunday?" Bethany asked.

"Not bad. Day's almost over. What's up?"

"Just returned from hiking up to Sapphire Falls."

"Man, you should have called. I'd have gone with you. I haven't been up there in years. Bet it was beautiful."

"Yeah. Weather cooperated and I needed to commune with nature."

Dee laughed. She knew Bethany was a tree-hugger, but she loved her all the same.

"Have I told you how much I appreciate you are on this journey with me? It makes things so much easier at the clinic with you there. You know exactly what to do and when to do it."

"That's what the thousands of dollars paid for when I went to college."

The women laughed and continued the conversation for another twenty minutes, talking about the clinic, clients and their pets, and scheduling the next girls' night out.

"When are you getting your puppy? You know if you don't pick her up soon, she will be a year old and you won't have to do any training!"

"Now that I have a set schedule and more help at the clinic, I'm thinking of getting her this week sometime. And she's only four months old."

"And learning all sorts of bad habits, no doubt," Dee reminded.

"Not anything we can't undo. Maybe she can be a clinic dog."

"Hello? We are talking about a purebred Bernese Mountain dog. She will be bigger than my office space!"

"I was teasing. I'm looking forward to working with her in obedience training and just snuggling her. She is so sweet, Dee. You will love her."

"And what are you naming her?"

"I don't know. I have to spend some time with her, get to know her personality. You know, that kinda thing. I don't want to mis-name her. She is too priceless for that. Hey," Bethany changed the subject. "Can you take care of things in the morning? I have a couple errands I need to run. I promise I'll be in by two."

"That's half the day," Dee teased. "Why don't you take the whole day? There isn't anything I can't handle. Besides, it's a Monday and the only thing on the books is a cat manicure. Callie and I can take care of it."

"You're the best. Gotta run. See you tomorrow."

Bethany ended the call and immediately pushed Rowdy's cell number.

"Hey, Beth. How can I help you?"

"Can you take a few hours away from the store in the morning? I have something I want to show you."

"Yeah, I guess. I usually take off Mondays anyway."

"Okay, good. Bring Lucie and Number Four, too, please. I'm ready for her to be home with me."

"Okay," he hesitantly replied. "Gonna tell me what all this is about?"

"Nah. It's nothing really. As I said, I want to show you something. Oh, you may want to wear waterproof boots."

"Now you have my curiosity piqued."

Bethany laughed and confirmed that he was to be at her house at nine o'clock in the morning then ended the call.

"Well, Dusty, I think it's dinnertime. What do you think?"

The feline sped to the kitchen and began munching away as soon as the food was put in her dish. Beth grabbed an apple, opened a container of strawberry yogurt, and sprinkled granola on top and went back to the den. Favorite crime drama number two was on tonight and it was the conclusion of last week's show she didn't want to miss.

Rowdy, Lucie, and her pup arrived on time, actually a few minutes early. Number Four pranced proudly alongside her momma and Gramps. The pink ribbon around her neck was now a pink bow in her hair.

Bethany knelt and was greeted with puppy kisses and a headbutt by Lucie.

"Hi, girls! Lucie, you are such a wonderful momma. Thank you for taking good care of your babies. Number Four is beautiful, just like you." She ruffled the top of Lucie's head and was met with protective puppy yaps.

"Oh stop. You're fine." Rowdy pulled a bit on Number Four's leash. "You talk to Lucie like she understands you. So, telling me where we're headed?"

"Sapphire Falls. And Lucie and I have a special relationship."

"I guess." He chuckled. "Want me to drive?"

Looking at the size of both dogs, Bethany thought better of packing them in the back of the Kia and agreed to Rowdy driving.

When they reached the hiking trail that led to the falls and were out of the truck, Rowdy handed Bethany the pink leash.

"Here ya go, Fur Baby Mama. She's all yours."

"Fur Baby Mama?" She laughed. "Gee, thanks."

They walked in silence up the trail, enjoying their surroundings. The weather again today was perfect for hiking and the sun even warmer than yesterday.

"It's not much farther, just around the bend."

You can do this, Bethany. Remember what we talked about. Use the strength from your soul. If you love him, nothing will keep you apart.

Bethany secured Number Four's leash to the door handle of the truck and Rowdy did the same with Lucie's. She walked a few paces in front of him until she was at the railing by the falls, again feeling the falls spraying mist on her face.

"Les, I've decided to let the past go. I've held onto it for too long."

Rowdy raked his fingers through his hair, wondering if this was a goodbye John moment not in letter form.

"We..."

He stopped her before she said another word.

"Beth, I've already apologized for my actions. I've already told you that you are the only woman I've ever loved, the only woman I want in my life."

Bethany reached a hand up to his cheek and with tears brimming in her beautiful eyes she continued.

"I love you. I've never stopped loving you. I was caught up in the pain of you leaving me standing there in front of all of our friends and family. I was humiliated. When you walked into the clinic, my heart nearly stopped. I'd not seen you since that day. I didn't know what to think. I couldn't speak. But my soul leapt at the sight of you."

He began to respond and she put a finger to his lips.

"Let me finish now or I may never say what I need to say. Les, I want a second chance with you, with us. I know as sure as I'm standing here that our souls are meant to be together forever, but I don't know what the next step is. I don't know how to get past the past without your help."

Again, the love of her life raked his hand through his hair and this time around the back of his neck. Rowdy wanted to sweep her into his arms, kiss her senseless, and carry her off into the sunset, but he didn't want to seem too eager. He'd play this her way, slowly.

In silence Rowdy walked to the truck, untied both leashes, handed one to Bethany, and led them down the path away from the falls. He stopped next to a very shallow part of Sapphire Creek and linked his fingers with hers. Hand in hand they walked, Lucie and Number Four close behind.

the end

SECOND chances

Second Chances
CJ Baty

It had been thirty years since they had seen each other face to face. Daniel checked his phone for the time, again. There was still an hour until Asa arrived. To say he was nervous was an understatement.

Thirty years. How is that even possible? We met before Asa left for Viet Nam toward the end of the war. I was just a kid, still in high school. The one night we had spent together had stayed in my mind my entire life. But that was a different era. Being gay was not something you talked about in the open. By the time I was old enough to be drafted, the war was over, and the soldiers were coming home. Coming home to a different world than the one they had left behind. My thoughts drifted back over the past thirty years.

Life moved on. I tried to contact Asa, but he didn't return to his Virginia home when he got out. After a year I finally gave up. I went to college, studied hard, and graduated with honors. Went to work for an advertising company in Cincinnati and found my niche.

It was a turbulent time for the LGBTQ community. Riots, arrests, attacks, and AIDS came on the scene. Like many gay men at the time, I hid myself in a very deep closet. Being an out gay man meant losing your job or even worse being bashed. So, I stayed in my closet, pushed those feelings down deep, and married.

Carry was a wonderful girl. She worked in the building where my office was located. We're still very close. If she ever suspected back then that I was different, she never said a word. It was just before our twentieth wedding anniversary that she came to me and explained that she knew I'd never been happy in our marriage. She said I know you love me, but it was more like a best friend.

"I've fallen in love with someone else and I think it's time we went our separate ways," she'd said. "I'm not what you want, Daniel. Find someone to love and be happy."

We divorced, our son went to college, and I struggled with what I wanted. Still in the closet, I knew that bars and multiple partners was not the scene for me. I was in my forties and looked like a middle-aged man. The men who went to gay clubs weren't interested in a monogamous relationship with an older man. It wasn't until my son, wise beyond his years, sat me down for the talk that things changed.

"Dad, no one is upset with you. Being gay is not a crime. Living your life alone… is," Tony said.

"I'm too old for clubs and dating services," I said.

"That's bullshit, but I understand why you feel that way," he answered with a smile. "Was there ever someone who you did feel attracted to?"

"Wow. You really don't mind talking about this do you?" I was shocked by his openness.

"Dad, Mom and I just want you to be happy. To have someone to share your life with," his smile had faded. "Someday I'm going to settle down with my own family and I don't want to think of you being alone."

I realized there was no reason I couldn't talk to him about Asa and my past.

"When I was still in high school, I met a guy a few years older than me. It was the first time I realized I was attracted to guys. He worked on my grandpa's farm and we had a blast together. Riding horses, hiking, working in the barn with the animals and just hanging out. The first time he kissed me, and I feel really strange telling you this, it blew me away. I'd kissed plenty of girls in school, but this was different."

"What happened?" Tony asked.

"Viet Nam happened. He was nineteen and his number came up in the draft during the last six months of the war. I tried to find him later but never did. He could have died in the war for all I know," I said. I had tried very hard not to think of Asa dying in Viet Nam, to say it out loud now, even after all this time, hurt.

"Have you tried social media?"

"What?" I looked at him.

"You know, like Facebook," Tony answered. "It's great for trying to find people you've lost contact with."

"Really?"

"Yes, really. Come on let's go back to your place and we'll set you up and see if we can find him," Tony was excited. And secretly, I was too.

"DAD DON'T YOU ever get on this computer? I mean you haven't gotten anything fun on here," Tony said as he booted the computer to life.

"I only use it for projects, I need to do at home. Computers are for work, not fun," I answered.

He looked at me like I was from outer space but kept on working.

"Okay, your account is all setup. And I set up Skype, so you can face time with him when you find him. Keep the username and password somewhere you can find it, just in case you forget it," Tony suggested. "Do you know his last name?"

"Yes. It's Asa Whitaker," I answered.

"That's good. The search would be harder if it were Smith or Johnson or something more common," he said. "Now type in his name in the search bar there." He pointed to where I should type. "Great. Let's see what comes up."

Took some time to weed through the names that popped up, but finally we opened one profile and there he was. I couldn't believe it.

There was silver in his hair now. His face was a little fuller, but that could have been the beard he was now wearing. The man was even more handsome than the boy I remembered.

"Is that him?" Tony asked. "Dad, he's a fox!"

There were a couple of pictures of him and another man in his photos, but Tony pointed out that his profile said single. His posts that we could see were mostly of him working with horses. He had loved working with the horses back when we were young.

"Maybe he's a vet now or owns a stable," Tony suggested. "And look, he lives in Atlanta. That's not that far away, Dad. Be really easy to meet somewhere in the middle."

"Maybe."

"Do you want to contact him dad?" he asked.

I was transfixed by his picture, I couldn't speak. Maybe he wasn't even gay. Maybe he's seeing someone and just didn't change his profile. Would he even remember me? And, more importantly, why would he want to be with someone like me? While I was musing this all over in my brain, Tony took things into his own hands. He was typing on my computer and sending Asa a message.

"What are you doing?" I yelled out.

"I'm giving you a nudge. I sent him a friend request, and I sent him a private message explaining who you are and asking if he'd like to connect?"

"You did what?"

I jumped up from my seat at the desk, nearly knocking it over. Tony came up behind me and grabbed my shoulders, twisting me to face him.

"DAD! Calm down. He lives in Georgia now and it's late. For all we know he won't see this until tomorrow morning," Tony was trying to reassure me.

PING!

We both looked toward the computer where a message was blinking. I stared at him and he looked back with a huge smile on his face.

"He's accepted your friend request," Tony's face was glowing. "And he's sending you a message. See the little wavy line, that means he's typing."

Returning to the desk, I sat transfixed watching that little wavy line until words popped into the small box at the bottom of the page.

"Is it really you Daniel? After all this time, I never thought I'd see you again."

I couldn't move. I didn't know what to do or say. Tony nudged me.

"Dad don't you want to respond?"
"What do I say," I felt numb all over.
"How about hello?" Tony chuckled.
"*Hello.*"

I WON'T LIE, the first few conversations we had were awkward as hell. It was like being a teenager again and dating. I hated dating when I was in school. Ignored it completely in college and kept my nose in my books. Carry asked me out the first time we went on a date, and we just sort of fell into a routine. But this... this was totally different.

We stuck to the Facebook messaging for the first month. Just little tidbits of information and what we were doing in our everyday life. He kidded me about Tony being the one to help me reconnect with him. I enjoyed the stories about the animals he worked with.

He was a vet, and he owned a stable where he boarded horses for people in the northern Atlanta area. I could tell from the messages he typed just how much he enjoyed working with animals. It reminded me of those days on grandpa's farm.

"I remember those days," he said. *"Very fondly. Your Grandpa was a good man. It was his love of animals that inspired me. And then you came to visit one summer..."*

I waited for him to add more but he let it go and I changed the subject.

Eventually, we decided that the little boxes on messenger were just too hard to look at and too small for our conversations. We switched to Skype where we could type more comfortably.

"Hello," Asa said. His voice deeper with age but it still sent tingles down my spine.

That was the first time he voice-called me on Skype. Again, there was that nervous awkwardness like when we first reconnected. But this time, it didn't last nearly as long. Speaking to each other came naturally to both of us. It was like our friendship had been laying dormant, waiting for us to return and pick up where we left off. Neither of us mentioned what happened between us back then. Everything else just came easy.

I asked what happened to him after Viet Nam. For a while he didn't say anything, and I was afraid I'd messed up. Eventually, he told me that because he was in the later batch of troops to be deployed, he also was in Viet Nam after the conflict had been settled. In all, he was there about a year. He had some PTSD when he returned and spent several years in therapy to get better. Asa admitted, he still had an occasional flash back, but they were few and far between now. Some of the guys he came back with never got over the time they spent there. He visits a local VA hospital in Atlanta once a month to see a couple of veterans. He was a good man.

FOUR MONTHS LATER, I noticed that we were talking at least once a week and sometimes two or three times. I really looked forward to coming home and waiting for him to get online so we could chat. That's when he told me about the man I'd seen in his pictures when I first found him.

Asa said he met Logan at a group meeting for vets with PTSD. He was a little older than Asa and had been deployed to Viet Nam twice. His first unit was attacked by the Viet Cong and more than half of them died or were wounded. Logan had been one of the lucky ones. Came home long enough to get patched up and went right back to the conflict. He was gay, like Asa and they had a lot in common. They fell in love and decided to move in together. Asa went to vet school and Logan worked in a factory. After graduation, they moved to Atlanta and bought the stable where they both worked with the horses. Asa had his practice to bring in regular income and Logan stayed at the stable.

Asa grew quiet, and I knew the rest of the story wasn't going to be a happily ever after.

"He got a cold one winter which turned into pneumonia. When he was admitted to the hospital, they quarantined him with a group of guys that were suffering the same kind of infection as he was. We'd heard about the virus that was attacking gay men, but that was happening in places like New York and San Francisco. Atlanta was as far away as we could be from that scene."

I didn't want to rush him, so I waited.

"He had contracted the virus, and he did have AIDS. It was tough, I won't lie to you. I had to be tested and, before you ask, I'm negative. Even now I get tested regularly because once it happens to someone you love, it doesn't let go of you. I'd understand if you'd like to stop talking…"

"What? That's nuts. I'm not going to let you go after I finally found you again!" The words rushed out of me. I could feel my cheeks flaming. I was glad we weren't on camera. "I've never been tested. But, then I haven't ever... well what I mean to say is... except for you and a very few experiences in college... I've never..."

"Daniel as long as you want to talk to me, I'll be here. I don't want to lose you again either. Logan died after a long illness, and I've been alone for the last three years. Finding you again has been a breath of fresh air that I so needed."

WHEN I FINALLY agreed to do a camera call, I didn't eat for two days. I had admitted to myself, and no one else, that I'd fallen deeply in love with Asa over the last six months. Everything about him excited me. His compassion for animals, his kindness to other vets, the smile in his voice when he said hello, and the desire that bubbled up inside me with every conversation we shared. We were talking every night now. It only made sense to see each other when we talked; it didn't make it any less unnerving.

The screen pinged with the incoming call. I brushed my hand through my hair and adjusted my shirt. I wanted to look good the first time he saw me. I answered the call and there he was.

"Hello," he said and smiled at me. "It's so good to finally see you again."

"Well, I look a lot different than I did the last time you saw me. There's a big difference between seventeen and forty-seven," I said.

"Okay, here's the first ground rule. Daniel Owen is my good friend and you are not allowed to talk down about him. You got that," he said with a smile.

"We've both changed, but what I see is the boy who stole my heart forty years ago. He's now a man I really want to know." He winked at me.

My heart jumped and my pulse raced. Could this beautiful man feel something more for me?

"I just didn't want to disappoint you. Tony says you're a fox and I'm a lucky guy."

His laugh echoed through the screen and the smile grew even wider.

"I'm going to like your son a lot and I owe him for bringing us back together," he said. "So how was your day?"

THE NIGHTLY VIDEO calls became just a part of my life and then one night he asked if I'd like to meet in person. Spend a weekend somewhere and see how it went. He admitted that he'd really like to kiss me again. It was the first time either one of us had mentioned anything physical happening. I was too excited to speak at first, then I remembered what Tony had told me just that afternoon.

"Wait, a minute. Have you been talking to my son about this? Not the kiss, but about us meeting up," I asked

"Well," he hedged, then said. "We have been chatting, and he did have a really good idea. Chattanooga is about half way for each of us. It's a great city with an amazing downtown area. Lots of museums, restaurants, and there's the Aquarium. I looked it up on line and I think we would have a great time there..."

I waited for him to stop. Shaking my head in agreement as he carried on. My face hurt from the smile on my face. *He wanted to be with me.* It was clear in his every word and he was as nervous as I was.

"Asa," I said and waited for him to stop. "I've never had a date with a man but if you're asking me on a date. I'd love to."

"It's more like a long weekend date. How does that sound," he asked?

"Would we share a room," I asked. I was still old-fashioned enough to not be so publicly out there.

"We don't have to," he sounded disappointed.

"You're going to have to be patient with me Asa. I'm not saying I don't want to be with you, because I do, but this is all new to me. Can you do that, be patient?" I asked.

He nodded.

"Then let's share a room with two beds," I suggested with a grin. "And if we only use one, it's nobody's business."

THAT WAS SIX weeks ago and here I sit in the lobby of the Hilton Garden in downtown Chattanooga waiting for him to appear. I'd already checked in and taken my luggage to the room. It was Friday evening, and we had four nights to explore the downtown area and where this relationship was headed. I checked my phone again and ninety minutes had gone by. He was late. Had he changed his mind? I heard a cough and looked up.

"Hello," Asa said. He was grinning wickedly at me. "I think you've been waiting for me. The traffic was lousy getting out of Atlanta."

I stood to my feet. Asa dropped his luggage on the floor and wrapped his arms around me. I didn't even think, I just went with it. When his lips touched mine, it was like the years melted away in an instant. There we were two teenage boys standing in the middle of a barn full of horses and cows tasting each other for the first time. When he pulled away, I was still back there in the past for a little longer. Keeping my eyes closed and remembering.

"I've wanted to do that for months and so much more," he whispered before he let me go completely.

I opened my eyes, and I knew I was looking at my future. I wasn't going to be alone after all.

the end

Surrender to the Storm

SURRENDER TO THE STORM
LINDA BOULANGER

SOMETIMES THE ONLY way you win is to embrace the very thing you fear...

Step into that moment when the new wife of the knight known as The Storm first realizes she's losing her heart to her husband.

Love... sometimes it comes softly and at others, it hits you with the full force of a mighty storm.

KALEIDOSCOPE HEARTS

AUGUST 28, 1376
NORTHUMBERLAND, ENGLAND

BATTLE WEARY, HEZEKIAH Strahm watched his castle materialize on the horizon.

His castle. He liked the sound of that, regardless of the price he'd had to pay. He'd traded his freedom and a position fighting alongside the Prince of Wales for a border castle, a title, and a wife who didn't seem to care.

The brawny knight snorted, wondering if there was a chance in hell she'd be happy to see him or whether she had secretly hoped he'd perished in the border skirmish. Three months, two battles, a move across the country, and he had yet to make her his in every way. That was about to change. He'd had enough of the little princess.

He corrected himself. In reality, he hadn't *had* her at all.

He scanned the stone walls of *his* castle in the distance. *He* was Lord of Caristone, by God. And *she* was going to respect that. He was one of the fiercest knights England had ever seen. Known as The Storm, he fought with passion and purpose. He'd lived by that since the day he'd watched his father die protecting the future of his country and he'd sworn to do the same.

He'd also sworn to protect the woman he'd wed, to provide her a home, and to continue to shelter her true identity. In exchange, she was to perform her wifely duties, to oversee the running of his affairs when he was away, and to bear his children. It didn't matter that she'd had no say in her betrothal. It was the way of things and she had a duty. He was fulfilling his promise. It was her turn to do the same.

Only he didn't want to merely lay with her. He wanted her to respect him enough to welcome him into her bed. He wanted to be her lover, not just a man who produced the seed that would make their children.

Frustrated, he spurred his coal black charger and trotted across the bridge that would take him home.

RESTING HER SLENDER torso against the cool stone of the upper balcony of Caristone Castle, Ivetta leaned farther out to see what had caused a commotion amongst the guardsmen at the gatehouse. A cloud of dust announced an approaching party. Her stomach flipped as she contemplated who it might be, knowing it was most likely her husband returning from yet another battle.

A skirmish, he called them. It was his second time to have to go out in as many months. He'd seemed nonplused by it all, but Ivetta didn't like it. She longed for the quiet of her beloved Woodstock. She longed for a life that would never be hers again.

She pushed back in and looked around. In the last few days she'd begun to try to see the merits of her new home and she had admitted to herself that Caristone wasn't all bad. Sure, it needed a bit of work, as most castles did, but she could see it as a beautiful place in time. It had good bones. At least that's what her husband had said when they first approached the lands and castle her father had given him.

Her husband. The words still seemed unfamiliar on her lips, and yet in many ways it seemed they'd always been. She wondered if that was how it was for most women forced to marry a perfect stranger. Three months prior, she knew nothing of him—the mammoth of a man with dark, brooding eyes and a brow that was forever pulled down to form a permanent V at the base of his forehead. He wasn't a bad looking man. Quite handsome, in fact, even in spite of the stormy shadow that seemed to encompass him.

She'd been told by one of the staff that he wasn't much older than her when he'd watched his father die on the battlefield. Her uncle, Edward of Woodstock—Prince of Wales, had knighted Hezekiah as his father's dying wish. He'd also promised Theodoricus Strahm that he'd see to his son's future.

And he had. On Edward's deathbed, he'd arranged that the two families be linked, giving Theodoricus' son lands and title and status. Not that he hadn't already earned status for himself, having risen as one of the greatest knights England had ever seen. And all in less than six years' time. The man was yet to see his thirtieth birthday.

Had her uncle Edward lived, God rest his soul, there was no telling what all Hezekiah Strahm might have achieved by his side. Known as The Storm, he fought with the fury and power of the mighty storm that brewed inside him—a power that radiated from him.

It had scared Ivetta at first, though she hadn't needed to worry. The man was the epitome of control. He'd shown that in his unwillingness to force himself upon her.

She looked down, her red hair falling forward to shield her face. It hid the shame that caused her cheeks to flame when she considered how honorable her husband had been. She'd been nothing but defiant.

Why, she thought? Sure, he'd taken her away from her home. At the age of eleven, upon her grandmother's death and per the woman's wishes, Ivetta had been given the position of Castellan of Woodstock Palace in Oxfordshire. Woodstock was all she'd ever known, the only thing she'd truly loved... except for her family.

She'd felt betrayed at first. Her grandfather, Edward III—King of England, had promised his dying queen, Philippa, that he would never use their beloved granddaughter as a pawn for gain for either himself or his country. A letter from him that had arrived while Hezekiah was away told her of her uncle's passing and apologized for the abruptness of her betrothal and subsequent marriage. He told her that he believed he was not long for this world either and that he had seen the union as a way to provide for her future. In his heart and upon the prince's word, he felt the knight known as The Storm was a worthy man who would do well by her, that he would take care of her.

Ivetta sighed. She was coming to believe that as well. It had taken her nearly three months to stop mourning for her past and who she had been. It was time to surrender to her new life and to the man she called husband. She hoped, in time, that she just might be able to learn to love him.

Hezekiah scanned the group that waited for them in the courtyard outside his keep. His scowl deepened with the realization that his wife wasn't among them. He slid from his horse, removing his helm and the aventail mail curtain that protected his neck. Thrusting them and his horse's reins at a nearby groomsman, he turned to bark orders to his second in command then wheeled away. His last words were that he was not to be disturbed. None of them knew of the unfinished business he had with his wife, otherwise, the command would not have been met with disguised snickers.

Ignoring all else, Hezekiah marched inside the keep nearly laying his wife out flat when they collided on the staircase just above the second-floor landing.

"My lord!" she breathed out as his hands closed around her upper arms and he lifted her to her feet. Her wide-opened green eyes bore into his as she stood before him. "My... my... I'm sorry I did not meet you. My shoe broke as I was coming down the stairs and I returned to my chamber to get another."

Hezekiah's mouth pulled down and she flinched making him frown harder. Was she afraid of him? He'd given her no reason to be so.

"Are you hurt?" he asked when she squirmed. He realized then that he had tightened his grip on her arms in the few seconds he'd been holding her. He forced himself to loosen his hold as well as to relax his expression. Slowly, she shook her head, her eyes never leaving his face.

"I..." She moved to place her palms against the armor that covered his chest.

He glanced down and could see the beating of her heart beneath the deep green material of her kirtle. As his eyes came back to hers, she caught her lower lip between her teeth for a second before she continued.

"I am pleased to see you well, my lord."

Through his thick armor, beneath the heavy layer of his padded tunic, Hezekiah could have sworn he felt the heat of her hands touching his heart. Simple words she'd spoken, but words he'd longed to hear even more than he'd realized.

Slowly, he leaned toward her, his mouth covering hers for only the second time since he'd married her. The other kisses had been chaste, ending quickly. This time she didn't resist, didn't pull away. Instead, she moved closer to him and his arms quickly encircled her, crushing her against him. One hand snaked up into her hair, his fingers entwining with the soft, red strands.

Hezekiah groaned, the tip of his tongue tracing her mouth, pressing between the crevice of her already slightly parted lips. Dear God, she tasted sweet, just as he'd known she would.

"My lord..." The sound of his page's voice interrupted and he growled, especially when she attempted to step away. He held her firmly against him as he looked over his shoulder and told the boy to be gone.

"But... your armor... who will help..."

"I will help him," Ivetta called, her voice shaky but loud enough for the page to have heard. She was thankful the boy quickly took his leave.

Hezekiah stared down at his wife wondering if she understood the full implication of her words. It was hard enough to keep his hands from roaming freely over her in that moment. Without the barrier of his armor, he feared his resolve would be too weak, that he'd take her on the spot.

Staring into her eyes, he prayed she knew and that it was him that lacked understanding.

"Come, my lord," she whispered, pushing away from him and reaching for his hand. When her fingers slipped into his, he realized she was shaking.

"Ivetta." He stood his ground, pulling her back against him. He nuzzled her neck and grazed the lobe of her ear with his teeth, provoking a soft sigh from her.

"Today, this moment, I am not a strong man, Ivetta," he whispered against her ear. "I'm battle-weary, too weak to fight against the fire you ignite within me."

She turned in his arms, pushing up to press her lips to his. "Then don't fight them," she said, her voice low and husky. She stared at him for a few seconds before she turned and led him up the stairs.

Inside his chamber, he pushed the door and threw the bolt, locking out the world. There'd be no more interruptions. Nothing, save an all-out war could stop him now. Even then, he might just let the walls fall down around them.

She watched as he removed the vambraces from his forearms and unbuckled the couters from his elbows. It wasn't until the rest of his arm coverings fell to the floor and he began to wrestle with the spaulders across his shoulders that she stepped forward, reaching for the buckles that held his breastplate in place. Hezekiah resisted touching her, instead allowed her to help, unfettered. He smiled. He was surprised at how easily she worked the worrisome buckles. Even his page often had a time with them since they were larger than most due to Hezekiah's size.

When she moved to his back, Hezekiah held tight to the front portion of the plate, lifting it from his body as soon as she had finished. He stepped away from her and pulled his hauberk over his head. With his mail gone, only his padded tunic hindered him from being able to feel her touch. He reached down to remove the armor from his legs, knowing the sooner he got it off, the sooner he could rid himself of the heavy upper fabric.

Ivetta watched with wide eyes as the last of Hezekiah's armor clanged to the floor along with his hose. She sucked in deeply when he pulled the padded tunic over his head and approached her wearing nothing but his knee-length braies. She'd told him she was ready, but the way she stared told him she'd never seen an unclothed man before. The thought of her innocence fueled his need and he pulled her to him to shield the blatant evidence of that desire. Linen braies were no match for his lust.

He forced himself to slow down, mustering every ounce of control he had. He wanted her, but he wanted to make their first coupling memorable for her more.

Standing before her, he held her face in his massive hands. "From the first time I saw you sitting and talking with your grandfather I harbored fantasies of having you by my side. I never dreamed they'd come true. Yet here you are and here am I." She nodded slowly and wetted her lips, his eyes riveting to her mouth. He ran the pads of his thumbs over their sweet shape before he continued. "This day you will become my wife in every possible way," he croaked out.

"From this day I ask only that you will promise to lay with me alone, forsaking all others, taking no mistresses to share in this sacred act between husband and wife. Will you promise me that in exchange for my undying love? Husband?"

Hezekiah had not been prepared for such a request, though he would have promised her the kingdom at that precise moment. And he would have found a way to give it to her.

He affirmed that he would, reminding her that a knight's word was as good as done. Then he pulled her close and kissed her, his hands gliding down to the belt she wore at her waist. With deft fingers he removed it before grasping the skirt of her kirtle. He pulled it up and over her head, managing to catch her chemise as well. When she attempted to fold her arms to cover her nakedness, he grasped her hands. He never wanted her to hide from him in any way.

Without a word, he scooped her up and turned, depositing her on the bed in a gentle manner that seemed impossible for a man his size. Seconds later, his braies were gone and he settled down beside her, pulling her close as his hands began to worship her body.

She was thin, so much so that he worried he might break her at first. But when he tried to pull back, she reached for him, quickly delighting herself with the power she held over him with the slightest stroke of her hands. Unsure he could wait another moment and knowing she was as ready as he could possibly make her, he pushed her to her back and positioned himself between her legs. The rest of his body covered hers as he pressed his manhood against her swollen core and slowly sheathed himself within her. They were both panting by the time he was fully engulfed by her, but it was her that began to move first, a smile of wonder spreading across her beautiful face.

Hezekiah's chest swelled with joy as her arms dropped to the mattress beneath them, allowing him to take complete control. He realized it was her way of fully surrendering herself to him. Ivetta. His wife. They were one. She had unlocked a piece of his stormy heart, allowing love to bloom in a garden of stone.

LESS THAN A year later, Hezekiah paced the corridor outside his wife's chamber. He was reminded of the time he'd waited to escort her from the king's chamber back to the Queen's Tower at Woodstock Palace. She'd been just sixteen then. It was the first time they'd ever spoken, the first time he'd gazed into her green eyes. He felt certain it was the day he'd fallen in love with her.

When the door opened, the midwife greeted him with a broad smile. Hezekiah was so overcome with emotion he couldn't find it in him to return it. His eyes were already riveted to the tiny bundle she held in her arms. He moved forward, gingerly taking it from her, tears in his eyes as he looked into the face of his firstborn child. He glanced from the babe to the woman.

"You have a fine, healthy son, my lord," she told him.

"A son." He sighed in relief. Not because he had a son, but because the lad was healthy. He looked up and past the door. "My wife?"

"Aye, my lord. She is well."

"I will see her," he said, not waiting for permission as he pushed his way past the woman and into the room.

Standing next to his wife's bed, he gazed down at her sleeping form. Even with her hair tousled, dried tears on her cheeks, and the remnants of perspiration beaded on her forehead and upper lip, he had never seen her look more beautiful. He lowered himself to the mattress, laying the baby beside her as he stared down at them both.

"Husband," she whispered as she stirred. "I have done well?" Her eyes fluttered but remained closed.

Hezekiah chuckled knowing she already knew the answer. "Aye, my love. You have."

"Karlous is a fine name, not too big for a wee babe," she offered, her eyes still closed.

Karlous Edward Theodoricus Strahm. They'd chosen the name when she'd first realized she was expecting, each agreeing that the babe should have his own name while also carrying the strength from the names of his ancestors.

Hezekiah touched the cheek of the sleeping lad before planting a kiss on his wife's forehead. She smiled and sighed as he rose knowing she needed her rest. He never told anyone, but he took his leave, heading straight to his own chamber where he wept like a baby, giving thanks for the path life had chosen for him.

May 1410

YEARS LATER, AS they waited for their grown children to amass back at Caristone Castle, Hezekiah was struck again by how much he loved his wife. They were connected, he and this woman who had come into his life as unwilling as a bride could be.

The alert that riders were approaching brought Ivetta to the railing of the balcony outside their chambers where he stood watching and waiting. She pushed a last pin into her hair and leaned forward to survey the bailey below before she pressed up to kiss his weathered cheek.

She settled her backside against the cool stone while Hezekiah studied her. She was still as beautiful to him as she'd been in her youth. If anything, the changes in her as she'd aged had made him love her all the more.

Her hair, as red as his was dark, had strands of grey streaking through it now. She remained thin enough, though her figure was softer than it used to be. He liked it. She'd been such a wisp in younger years that the first time he'd held her, he'd been fearful she'd break. She hadn't, of course. Instead, she'd met him with a fierceness he hadn't expected and had grown into a lover who took as much pleasure as she gave. She'd captured his stormy heart and he considered himself blessed beyond what he deserved, especially since she seemed happy most of the time.

That had been his one true fear after he'd taken her from her beloved Woodstock and resettled her in the northeast part of the country. He swallowed hard, thinking of how hard it must have been for her at times. He wondered how she'd put up with him.

Reaching for her, he pulled her against his solid form, his massive arms encircling her. She didn't squirm to get away as most women would have. She didn't giggle or shy back. Instead, she pressed herself more firmly to him and turned her face up to his. He chuckled at the challenge in her expression, knowing she knew as well as he the fires she ignited in him... the embers that had begun to smolder even before their love took hold. What they shared would never fade, not even with age.

"Ah, Ivetta." He smoothed roughened fingers over her soft cheek, caressing her lips with the pad of his thumb. "You have weathered the storm well, my love."

Ivetta chuckled, kissing his hand. "Aye, my lord. 'Tis a simple task." When he lifted a brow, she continued. "You see, The Storm and I, we are one. All it took was sweet surrender."

the end

A Love Full of Colors

A Love Full of Colors
Edward Buatois

Haven and I had known each other since childhood, among old-wealth families—dynasties, really—who claimed lineage beginning with the *Mayflower*. She was every man's fantasy of the unattainable woman, but she was mine and always had been mine: tall, and funny, and athletic, and blond.

We'd lost our virginity to each other, not actually on her sixteenth birthday as that would have been a rather public affair, but on my father's boat the weekend after. It was magical and frightening all at the same time, two teens discharging years' worth of pent-up hormones in a pantomime of romance under the stars, next to candles and a bottle of Perrier Jouet 2012.

Then it was official. We were a couple. Not that there had been any real doubt.

No one wondered where we were or where the boat was, despite that we told no one where we were going or how or why. They knew. That we would be together was never questioned.

By anyone, least of all me.

I believed I loved Haven.

And then...

I met Becka while waiting for a car repair. She was listening to a band called Crash Test, an indie band which was definitely an acquired taste in the same way Australians like Vegemite. Techno-grunge-goth; my friends described them like listening to Satan hacking up hairballs while crushing cans set to electronica.

I've literally never met anyone outside a concert who likes them, so Becka was kind of a Yeti.

She was from New York City on FMLA, taking care of her father. I guessed she was about twenty-eight. Bookish. Rimless glasses, no makeup. In utility clothes, she was all unpretentious non-fashion. Had a boyfriend, name of Todd.

Her mind was nimble. Unpredictable, supple, unexpected. She was a sprite moving between realms, picking at the gauzy film of the world and hinting at the color underneath.

I could have passed her on the sidewalk a hundred times and never noticed, yet there she was.

We didn't exchange numbers, because, why? As we parted, though, I left with the feeling I was acquainting with a stranger for the first time, and that stranger was me.

TWO WEEKS LATER, Saturday. Haven rented a room at le Cirque for a catered cocktail party and dinner for my birthday, a relatively intimate affair of twenty-five of my closest friends and their significant others.

Mingling after dinner in the anteroom over champagne and cake, Haven surprised me with four tickets to the Crash Test concert later that night.

I was so surprised I actually asked her who they were for.

She laughed, perfect teeth rimmed in Anastasia Beverly Hills lip gloss. "Why, you and me, of course."

I read the tickets again, to be sure I'd read them right and they weren't for something more Havenesque, like all-access VIP passes to the Winter Olympics. She liked hobnobbing with the skaters.

They weren't.

I fixed my eyes on hers as if expecting them to spontaneously grow hair. "But ... the one time you listened to them, you said they sound like cats being strangled to the sound of trash cans being banged together."

"Did I really? That doesn't sound like me, describing them that way." Then the corner of her lip curled with a giggle as she took a sip of champagne. "I must have been being kind."

I chuckled back, happy to have confirmed no hair was sprouting on her pretty green eyes, but nevertheless feeling trapped in some episode of *The Twilight Zone*. "You really don't have to do this."

She *tinked* her glass to mine. "Don't ever say I don't self-sacrifice. Who knows, I might like them if I see them in person."

"We'll see," I said doubtfully. "Who are the other two tickets for?"

"Mmm," she said and pushed the bit of champagne in her mouth down so she could speak. "Matt and Sophia. Actually, it was his idea. And she's going along to keep me sane—though possibly that's too late, come to think."

Ah, Matt. Now it makes sense. My eyes found his and he smiled from across the room, raising his snifter of Macallan 25 into the air.

Matt and I had discovered the band late one night when he was staying over and we had taken a break from *Call of Evil* to resolve an argument we were having about who'd done the soundtrack to the game. That involved a quick cut to YouTube. It ended up he was right, but in the right-hand bar, of course, there were videos to similar bands and there appeared to be a half-woman/half-demon using power tools to music.

We had to click on it and were captivated by Sincia Danta, a tattooed goddess who was half-naked, half-steel-armor and who, along with another female demoness, liked to create firework-like sparks running things like power sanders off the armor. She actually didn't sing much because clearly that wasn't her thing. But the male lead singer, Guy Tal, laid down tones that were hypnotic in a way they impacted on your brainstem, throbbed in with a world-ending techno beat that pounded nails of truth into your soul.

I can't describe it if you don't know what I'm talking about. Either you get it or you don't.

When the party wrapped up, Haven and I swung by the house to change before meeting Matt and Sophie at the Blue Note. One didn't go to that kind of event in cocktail party attire, goodness no.

I changed into black jeans, shit kickers, and a ripped band t-shirt, with black lipstick and black eyeliner —yes, I learned to do that, long ago. One does what one must do.

Haven costumed herself like a cheerleader's impression of a death metal band, like if the character from *Clueless* took Spinal Tap seriously as a guide for dress code. But, by God, it worked: Her main wear was black yoga pants and a black crop top that showed off her taut belly, with smoky eyes and pale blue contacts ... it all made her look unworldly.

Before we left, she did a line of coke, too.

I wished she wouldn't do that, but I gave her a pass on it this time. She was doing all this for me, after all. And it would dull the nerves, I told myself.

Once there, we found Matt and Sophie waiting at the head of the rope line, and for the cost of a bill, we were in.

The warm-up band, Death Knight, was ripping away at their guitars as we entered and my pulse immediately quickened. The dance floor was packed and we went upstairs to try to find a little more room and scope out the place. Matt found us a spot at the railing overlooking the dance floor.

Each concert was different, but this one was running like a rave, all sweeping lights, fluorescent paint, and glow sticks. Before long, Sophie and Haven huddled up the way girls do and I was left to my own thoughts for a while. I idly wondered where Becka was and what she was doing; if she was happy, and if her father was okay.

I imagined her down there, a part of the frenzy and yet somehow above it, a sylph making foam on the chaotic sea.

Death Knight finished their set to great applause. We took advantage of the lull in the crush to find a good spot near the stage. After twenty minutes, Crash Test's rig was ready.

The lights went down.

And by down, I mean all the way off. The place went silent as a sepulcher. Long seconds passed.

Haven half-spoke, half-whispered to me. "Do you think the—"

We all jumped with the sound and sparks of Sincia Danta and her friend, standing ten feet from each other and twenty feet from us, driving power sanders against their armor as they gyrated like twin exotic medusas.

Matt and I would have gladly turned to stone for them, and Matt had a shit-eating grin on his face that I'm sure mirrored mine. Haven, however, screamed. Her face was white with shock and she pressed her palms to her ears. Sophie wasn't much better.

By mid-song Haven and Sophie had recovered and got into it as much as they could, gamely following suit and dancing like debutantes at the prom, but it didn't last long. Three songs in, the girls' painted-on smiles showed signs of serious melt. In the brief quiet just after the third song, Sophie pulled

Haven in to say something in her ear, and Haven turned to me and gave me the signal they were going to the bathroom.

Matt and I followed them 'til we parted ways to head to the bar.

Twenty minutes later, I was getting worried and about to go check on them when Haven reappeared. She had an out-of-it Sophie in tow.

"What happened?" I asked as Matt took over holding Sophie up.

"She's sick," Haven said into my ear. "I think she's had a little too much fun. I'm sorry."

A sick feeling twisted my stomach, remembering the cocaine earlier. "Are you sure *you're* okay?"

"I'm fine," she said, missing or ignoring the accusation in my voice. "I'm going to take Sophie home." She gave me a deep kiss, the kind that was a promise for later. "I'll come back if I can." The partly reflective irises in her contacts made Haven's eyes seem to glow.

The band had just started up *Stygian Angel,* a "love" song about a Succubus who hollows guys out. Not a good juxtaposition.

"You take care of Sophie," I said flatly.

She did a double-take but said nothing, instead nodding curtly and taking the unoccupied spot next to Sophie. With one last glance at me, the three of them disappeared into the crowd.

Just like that, there I was, at a concert of my favorite band in the middle of a thousand ravers ... on my birthday, alone.

Just fucking balls-out great.

Deciding I needed air, I took the long way around the dance floor and was almost out when a dancer caught my eye. A girl dancing by herself.

She was good, too.

There are people who dance like they don't care, and people who dance like they *do* care, and then there are people who *become* the music, a thing of nature almost. People who develop a connection to it, like this girl: unpretentious, unafraid to be alone and just ... *being.*

I realized I was staring and nearly looked away, but I wasn't fast enough and our eyes met.

Becka.

It was Becka.

While she watched, I checked her out top to bottom. She looked different without the glasses! And gone were the utility clothes. In their place were a metallic grey satin tank top and a layered frilly pinkish-gray skirt. And

Doc Martens. Still no makeup, aside from the fluorescent green Ankh symbol dominating her left cheek.

It felt like discovering your mousy little sister is a serial killer but in a good way. A *very* good way.

"Carlton!" she exclaimed and ran over and hugged me. I didn't think we were at the hugging level. But I certainly didn't argue.

Her hair smelled of lavender.

When we pulled apart, I gave her another appreciative once-over. "Your outfit is perfect," I told her. I meant it.

"Would you believe, ten bucks?" She ruffled her skirt. "I found an awesome thrift store. They have the best stuff."

I had to laugh. Haven would have spent eight hundred dollars on a skirt like that, custom-made yesterday to look like it was made sixty years ago.

Becka leaned in conspiratorially. "I have to know; the eyeliner. You?"

I touched my finger to my face, just below my eye. "As a matter of fact, yes."

"Awesome," she said with a bright smile.

That smile seized my heart and stopped my mouth. I forced out the first thing I could think of. "The energy here is amazing, isn't it?"

"*Ugh*," she said, but it was enthusiastic, while looking around. "It's unbelievable. I *so* needed this."

Me too, I realized. All of it. *This.* "Want to dance?"

She shrugged. "Where's your girlfriend?"

Oops. "Excuse me?"

"Your girlfriend," she repeated, deadpan. "I saw you earlier, up by the stage. She's pretty."

"She went home." I couldn't think how to even begin, so I put the full history of the night on my face for her to read, to see if she'd get it.

She did. "Yeah, I thought she might bail. She didn't seem the type."

And that was the end of that. A song started up, and she began dancing. The song was *Love's Savage Spirit*, from the same album as *Stygian Angel*, about the girl who saves the guy from the Succubus with love. Becka's movements were sharp and feral in the first, battle, half of the song, but graceful and hypnotic in the mournful/triumphant part when, exhausted, she wins back his soul.

As the song closed its final several measures, Becka closed her eyes, almost standing still, and as I mirrored her, eyes closed, we must have drifted together because when we opened our eyes she was *right there* and she slowly looked up at me.

She didn't back away. My eyes dropped to her lips.

A few seconds passed, and I—

She stepped back and laughed, waving her hands as if to erase something. "That was wild! You're a pretty good dancer yourself. I was totally with you."

Bitter disappointment warred with apocalyptic relief. My brain stopped.

Again, I reached for the first thing that popped in there. "Want to grab a drink?"

She considered, then shook her head, with an indulgent smile. "No, I'm good. But I could use a walk, though."

I had forgotten that's where I was headed before I bumped into her. "Sounds good to me."

We exited a side door onto the sidewalk into the old garment district, where some old warehouses had been converted into trendy shops and clubs like the Blue Note. Others had been converted to cafes on the ground floor and the like, with living space above. We got a strange look from a couple walking a French bulldog.

I remembered my black lipstick and eyeliner. "We must look like refugees from Halloween out here."

She looked confused for a moment, then laughed. "I guess so. This would be a slow night in the West Village."

I chuckled, trying to imagine her in it. "I'd like to see it. I've never been."

Her face squinched up. "Do you mean you've never been to New York, or you've never been to the Village?"

"I meant, I've never been to New York."

"Ha! That's hard to believe."

My turn for the squinched-up face. "Why's it so hard to believe?"

She shrugged. "They say New York's in the blood. Whether you were born there or not, I think you're one of those."

"What makes you think so?"

"Just a feeling. You get a sixth sense for these kinds of things, I guess."

We continued walking for a while; it didn't matter where. Honestly, I got a little lost, seeing parts of the city I'd driven past on the highway and never given a second thought about.

Over an ice cream cone, I asked if she was sure she'd never been here at the corner of God Knows Where and Lost Beyond Hope.

"Girl Scout's honor, never been," she replied. "I love it, though, seeing new places. It's usually an adventure in waiting, and you just have to grab it."

I looked at her over my ice cream cone. "Don't you ever get afraid of breaking the rules? Or getting lost? Or getting hurt?"

"What's the fun in that?" she asked with a laugh. "Seriously, sure, you have to be careful. Don't be insane. But life's about pushing your limitations, finding out what's out there, what you can do. *Not* doing the expected. There's death there, *living death*. I really believe that. Death of your soul." She finished her cone. "Ready to get walking again?"

"Hold on there, speedy," I said as I wolfed down the last quarter of my cone. "I'm getting brain freeze."

But it wasn't the cone. I needed a second to recover.

Pounding nails of truth into my soul ... she said it so naturally and obviously, as if she were discussing the weather on her planet. For me, it was like falling through my closet and finding Narnia.

After that, for me Becka glowed like Galadriel. But I didn't want to seem like a besotted idiot so I kept that to myself.

We were *almost* to a piece of the city I recognized when Becka stopped mid-sentence to listen to something I swear only she could hear.

She gave a squeak of delight and, me following, ran across the street to a neatly painted tall iron fence and pressed her face against the bars, listening. A pale glow emanated from the other side of the bars that seemed to cast her face in candlelight.

Her breath caught. "Dracula!"

"What?"

"Dracula! Bela Lugosi's 1931 Dracula. Have you ever seen it?"

I chuckled, not sure what to do with her excitement. "No, I haven't."

She looked at her watch. "Well, now you will. Come on."

"What?"

"We *have* to go. Push me up."

"Becka, this is private property," I said in a harsh whisper.

"It's a local college doing theater on the lawn. It's public-*ish*. What are they gonna do, arrest us for eating popcorn? Come on."

I laughed, not able to help myself as I pushed her up in her layered skirt and Doc Martens. When she got to the top, she gave me a hand up.

All I can say is I'm glad it wasn't one of the spiked fences. She would have been okay because she was part squirrel, but I would have been a Carlton kebab.

She stage-whispered at me while we skulked through the bushes. "How could you not have seen Dracula? It's a classic."

"Um, I've never seen anything that was made before color."

She looked horrified. "Why?"

"I just ... why see something in black and white when you can see it in color? The production values are so much better."

"*God*," she said as we navigated to an open area more appropriate to walking normally, so we held hands like two college students out on a date. The sixty-foot-diagonal screen was ahead of us with Bela Lugosi's twenty-foot-tall head on it, being closely watched by three hundred people in lawn chairs.

"Yes, the production values were cheesy, but that's part of the fun," she continued. "And look at how they light his eyes, everything else is in shadow except his eyes. You don't see that in color films, the effect gets lost. Did you know they parodied that with Anjelica Huston's Morticia in the *Addams Family*?"

I'd noticed she was the only character in the 2011 movie who'd gotten that treatment, but I never really thought about why. "Really? They got it from this?"

"Yes!" she said like I was an idiot as we found a couple of empty chairs near the back. "I don't think there's a single scene in that movie where they didn't do it. Now shut up and watch."

It wasn't just that movie; Becka begged me to stay when it turned out it was a double-showing with Boris Karloff's *Frankenstein*. I was happy to. I didn't want the night to end.

After, we walked to a nearby pier overlooking the harbor and watched the sun rise. I watched the tendrils of Becka's brown hair flare in gold as it was pushed by the wind.

Everything seemed right when we got back to her car and I kissed her. She responded at first, kissing me back, but when I tried to pull her into my arms, something changed.

She pushed me away. "Carlton, I don't think this is a good idea."

I felt like I was standing at a precipice, over air and not stone, waiting to fall into the abyss. "Why not?"

"You're Carlton Reese," she said as if that explained everything.

Wait. "I don't remember telling you my last name."

She sighed. "How many people in this city do you think are named 'Carlton?' You're all over Google. Carlton Reese, from a family so old it's almost American royalty; a George Clooney look-alike literal jet-setter who was probably voted homecoming king with the hottest girl on the planet."

She took my hand, hyper-formally, and shook it. "I'm Becka Hamilton, vet tech for a tiny animal hospital in Brooklyn who lives with three roommates, two cats and one turtle in a New York City walkup. And you're not really interested in me."

That made no sense at all. "Why wouldn't I be interested in you?"

"I like you, Carlton. I really do. But I'm the weird girl."

"Excuse me?"

"The weird girl. You're bored with your Stepford girlfriend from the good family, and you're looking for something different." She searched my eyes. "Tell me I'm wrong."

That hit really close to home, and the blood drained from my face. *Is that me? Is she right? Is that what I was doing?*

No, I decided.

"It's not anything like that at all."

She sighed. "You're rich. You're beautiful. You can have any woman you want, and a supermodel girlfriend you're in love with." She laughed pityingly. "I'm different and different's attractive, but different becomes familiar and familiar leads to boredom. Trust me."

I sighed, frustrated. "You're lumping me in with God knows who or what, I don't care. I grew up with Haven and never questioned that, ever. Until you."

She bit her lip, and a tear appeared at the corner of her eye. But she didn't budge. I shook my head and realized that the best thing to do was let her go. That was the hardest thing I had ever done in my life.

"I shouldn't have kissed you … you have Todd and your life in New York. I have Haven, and I love her. But if you take anything from this, know this: You *are* special and unique. To me."

She crossed the few feet between us and hugged me.

She released me and I let her go, and she turned and got into her car. As she turned the ignition, I rapped on her window.

When she lowered it, I held out my business card.

"Carlton..." she said, pained.

"Throw it away when you get home. But take it now; this is my personal cell. If you need anything, let me know."

"Thank you," she said, and took the card. "For everything you said, it ... made me think."

"Back at you," I said seriously.

She sighed and gave a wistful smile. "Sorry I freaked out on you tonight. I don't think you deserved it, and ... for what it's worth, you're not what I expected, either."

HAVEN APOLOGIZED TO me, for ruining my birthday night. I didn't tell her it was one of the best things that ever happened to me. And besides, it was wrong of me to blame her for what happened. Sophie's a bit of a force of nature. I think it scared Haven, though. I haven't seen her take drugs of any kind since then.

Things weren't the same, though. Becka had peeled the gauze from the world, but without her, nothing had any color.

I tried to forget about it. It wasn't like I had a future with Becka. I tried to change my expectations, get back to the way I was, but it didn't work. I tried to change Haven, but that wasn't fair of me. She was happy the way she was. The problem was with me.

I did what I thought I would never do. I left Haven.

My parents' reactions were interesting.

My mother thought I had cold feet and a lack of commitment. She talked about what a great match Haven was, brought up the history of our families and what a great pedigree our children and grandchildren would have. That was something which used to fill me with pride and a sense of duty, but now it felt false and superficial and physically ill. When her arguments failed to persuade me, her real concern came out: that my actions were irresponsible and selfish. That this would bring a scandal that brought "humiliation on the family."

Family dinners were pleasant.

My father believed I had cold feet, too, but his solution was to man-to-man me over scotch whiskey and cigars, and tell me I just needed to get my literal *wanderlust* out and of course, the best solution to that was prostitutes. Or *ahem*, high-priced escorts. My problem, according to him, was I'd only ever been with Haven. I just needed to dock my schooner in more than one port. *He actually said that.* I'll never be able to unhear it, any of it, especially after he told me it didn't have to end with marriage, as long as discretion was applied and appearances were kept up, and he could teach me discretion.

I don't speak to him much anymore.

I did become my social circle's most eligible bachelor. After a suitable number of days (I think it was a week), the vultures circled. But I knew who they were. Some were even Haven's friends, even while she was *grieving*, for God's sake, and that was special.

They disgusted me.

Nevertheless, it didn't take long for me to start dating again. I tried the "being alone" thing, but that didn't work. Becka had opened my eyes to what it was like to be stimulated by someone; not to just be *alive,* but to *live.* I wanted to find out what that meant.

I was out to dinner with a pretty art student, Trina, who I'd met over Tinder (yes, Tinder). I was okay on finding out where it went. She was quick and engaging. On the decision of whether to take her back to my condo, I was leaning toward "yes" when my phone chimed.

I didn't recognize the number. I almost never picked up on those, but something told me I'd want to pick up this one. I excused myself from Trina's spirited discussion of the use of mixed media in modern art and engaged the call.

"This is Carlton," I said in that tooth-stiff way that is deserved by unknown numbers.

"Carlton? I'm so sorry to bother you," said a familiar voice.

"*Becka?* How—what's going on?"

She sounded like she'd been crying. "My father collapsed at home. I'm at Fairview Hospital and they're admitting him. I'm so sorry to lay this on you, I know it's not fair, but can you please come? I'm freaking out. I can't be alone."

I said, "I'll be right there. Hang tight," as I looked directly into Trina's eyes. Trina asked me what was wrong after I hung up, and I said my apologies, throwing a hundred dollar bill on the table and leaving. If Trina said anything after that, I don't remember.

I went straight up to the ICU waiting room. Becka embraced me without a word. This felt right, like she belonged there, even after everything that had happened and I closed my eyes with some tears of my own. I held her tight, running my fingers slowly through her soft hair. She'd changed to a pageboy cut, and she smelled of Chamomile.

"My father's dying, isn't he?" she said from somewhere near my chest.

"I don't know," I answered, not sure of what to say. "Whatever is happening, it's with the love and peace of knowing you were there to help him through it."

She looked up at me with watery eyes, her lips parted. I got that urge to kiss her again and shoved it down, down, down. It got me into big trouble last time. The nurse at the desk rescued me, telling us that her father was ready for visitors. Becka took my hand, her fingers entangled with mine, and we walked back together.

He was still frankly a handsome man. Mid-fifties, I guessed. Not even as old as my father. Just a sprite of gray at each temple. And he had laugh lines that brought a booming laugh to mind. I deeply regretted that I would never hear it.

I'm not a medical person, but the machines were keeping him alive. I knew what life looked like, and this wasn't it.

Becka let go of my hand to walk around and kiss him on the forehead.

The heart monitor beat its relentless metronome.

I sat in one of the nearby seats and listened as Becka, in soft tones, recounted to her father some of her favorite memories of him growing up. Taking her out for ice cream when Billy Masterson broke up with her at the age of eleven. Taking her to her first LaCrosse game and even when she sucked he never let her give up, cheering her on years later when, as Captain, she led them to the state championships. Proudly seeing her graduate college and knowing he'd see great things from her.

It turned out that was one of the things that really bothered her.

"I must be such a disappointment to him," she said wistfully.

"Why would you say that?" My incredulity was genuine.

She shrugged. "I'm twenty-eight and I still live with three other people. I feel like I've been an adult half my life and I'm still waiting for my life to start. Not exactly doing great things here."

"I think he'd want you to be happy no matter what you're doing. Not every victory has to be a great one, just a satisfying one. A fulfilling one."

She looked up at me and smiled, then put her head against my shoulder. "Dad would have liked you." She intertwined her fingers with mine again and kissed them. "I hope you don't mind. I'm only borrowing you."

It took me a few seconds to realize what she meant. "Haven and I aren't together anymore."

She sat up, her big brown eyes fixed on mine. "I'm so sorry! You guys seemed so happy."

"*She* was. I thought I was, too, until ... until a few months ago. I realized I was only going through the motions, that that life wasn't for me. I wanted more." It was really hard confessing this to her. "You can borrow me as long as you like. I'll stay until Todd gets here."

She gave a bitter chuckle and looked away. "Todd and I aren't together anymore."

Okay, reverse. "*What?* What happened?"

"Distance. Maybe. It was mutual." Her eyes flicked to mine and away again. "I wasn't sure you'd come."

"I don't want to be anywhere else."

She looked up at me and her lip quivered. "Are you sure?"

"The life I come from, it's all fake and I don't want it. You're the only real thing in it, and I want you. The greatest thing."

She gave a sob, and her hand tightened in mine. This time I kissed her with abandon and without fear. The world shrunk down to a single point where only the sensation of our lips on one another mattered, and I felt like I had finally found home.

♡

BECKA'S FATHER DIED a few days later. They say even people in comas can often hear what the people in the room are saying, and there's no doubt in my mind he knew Becka was there every minute until he passed, and I was there with her.

I never left her side, even after my family disinherited me and gave it to my weaselly little brother. But I was done with all of them before that ever happened. I still had a trust fund my grandfather had set up for me that was enough to buy a small building in Greenwich Village and convert it into an animal rescue and clinic Becka runs called the Wagmore Hotel. In five short years, it's become one of the most popular in the city and we're in talks to buy one of our competitors, so we're excited about that.

That's not all. We live in a beautiful loft with exposed brick and (barely) enough room for three dogs, a cat, and a hamster named Willie.

And Paul and Mazie, and a little mystery bundle on the way.

It's life and a love full of colors. And it's great.

the end

WHISPERS of Fate

WHISPERS OF FATE
JENNIFER DANIELS

PROLOGUE

I WOKE UP today without one bout of nerves. No jitters. No worries. Today I am getting married to an amazing man who is loyal, kind, hardworking, and best of all, he loves me. How did I get to be the lucky woman who landed this wonderful man?

As I lie in bed in my old bedroom at my parents' house, I was thinking about how my day would be. Mom knocked then peeked around the corner.

"Good morning, sweetheart. How did you sleep last night?"

Mom was so gentle and kind. She never yelled at me or my twin brother, Tyson. She always had a way of getting her point across. The tone of her voice changed a little and the look on her face became very stern.

"I slept like a rock. What time is it?"

"Seven o'clock, time for you to get up. The coffee is on. Would you like anything special for breakfast?"

Mom always made sure that breakfast, lunch, and dinner was prepared for us when we were kids. She worked from home as a seamstress and could create just about anything you wanted. She made my wedding dress, my beautiful ivory lace wedding dress. It was simple yet elegant: shallow neckline, scooped back, long sleeves. The fitted bodice and A-line skirt with the smallest of trains fit perfectly. It accentuated my tall, lithe frame.

"Just a cup of coffee and a bagel for me. Thanks, Mom."

I went straight to the shower and after dressed in a comfortable pair of blue satin pj's. I was going to do my own hair. As a cosmetologist, I saw no reason to go to another hairdresser. A simple French twist and a crystal hair clip to the side would work beautifully. My best friend, Molly, was my maid of honor and since she was in business with me, I knew she'd do her own hair, too.

I walked into the kitchen and saw Mom had my coffee and bagel on the table waiting for me. Dad was busy making breakfast for himself and Mom. Just as I sat down to eat, my brother Tyson flew through the door.

"There's my little sister." He came over to me and gave me a big kiss on the cheek.

"Tyson, you are four minutes older than me."

"That maybe the case, little sis, but I'm still older. I just stopped in to see how you are and to delivery this."

Tyson handed me a note and a tiny blue velvet box. I opened the card and read it.

"Hello, my love. Since I couldn't see you this morning I still wanted you to know I'm thinking about what a lucky man I am to be marrying you. I love you so much and will see you in a few hours. All my love, Logan."

I slowly opened the box to find the most beautiful pair of blue sapphire stud earrings and matching teardrop necklace. It was perfect for my something blue.

"Oh my God, Mom, look!" I handed my mom the box and saw her eyes mist over.

"You are one lucky lady, Tipper."

I knew just how lucky I was, thanks to Tyson, of all people. My brother followed in Dad's footsteps. He went to college, majoring in Criminal Justice and Logan, my soon-to-be husband, was his roommate. They were inseparable in college until Logan and I hung out one day and the rest for us is history.

Tyson and Logan went through the academy together, and I knew if Tyson approved of Logan and me, that Logan was a good guy. With Tyson and I being twins, we are close and have that twin thing between us. We just know when things are going on with each other *and* if someone was going to be good for the other.

I had a card for Logan and gave it to Tyson to pass along to Logan.

"So, how are your nerves? You seem good."

"I'm as cool as a cucumber. I'm ready to be Mrs. Logan McGraw. Now, you better get back to your post being the best man. Don't you have duties to tend to?"

Tyson laughed and grabbed a piece of Mom's toast as he was flying out the door and ran right into Molly. He dropped a kiss on her cheek and wiggled his eyebrows at her.

"Looking good, Molly." Tyson whistled at her and continued on his way.

Molly came in all ready in her light blue dress that mirrored my dress with no train. She did look beautiful. Molly was tall like me but with blond shoulder length hair.

Molly helped me with everything I needed help with, including getting into my dress. I looked out the picture window and admired the day. It was an overcast spring day, but still perfect for the wedding or I thought until I saw Tyson coming down the road in his patrol car.

"Mom, please tell me I'm not going to my wedding in the back of Tyson's squad car?" I yelled from the living room.

"What are you talking about?" Mom looked out the window and saw Tyson in his tuxedo, his face somber. She put her arm around me and my stomach dropped.

Tyson looked straight at me then walked through the front door.

"Tyson, there is no way I'm going to my wedding in the back of your squad car. Now, what are you doing here?" That's when the fake smile I had plastered on my face faded. I noticed Tyson's eyes were red and puffy. Something was going on.

"Tipper, you better have a seat."

That was the day my entire world stopped.

Chapter One

"Tipper, how's the schedule looking? Are we busy today?" Molly always liked a rundown of the day. She was very organized and OCD about her schedule.

"Along with the haircuts, you have a couple colors, and several manicures to do. As for me, I'm taking today off. What? Go ahead. Spit it out. I know you have something to say."

Molly looked deflated by my words. She took a deep breath before she spoke. She had always had a way of speaking as to not upset me. She was such a tender heart.

"Tipper, it's been two years Logan died. I know how much you loved him, but he wouldn't want you sitting around pining for him. He would want you to live your life, and I think you know that, too. Listen, I know how difficult his death has been for you. I was right there by you, but it's time for you to start living your best life."

I couldn't hold my tears any longer. Molly was right, but how was I supposed to do this? I still missed Logan so much. I swear at times I could smell him near me.

Molly lifted my chin, put her hands on my shoulders, and made me look her in the eyes. "I don't say this to hurt you. I hope you know that, but it needs to be said. Take today and promise me you will start to live again. Don't continue with your get up, go to work, return home, repeat routine. Promise me!" She shook me to make sure I was paying attention.

I wiped my tears and started to giggle. "I promise. I will try to do my best. That's all I can do right now, Molly."

"I will take that, it's better than nothing." She smiled and hugged me tightly.

We heard the door open and Tyson came walking in. After Logan's death, he suffered the loss, too. He'd lost his best friend. Tyson had become good friends with Molly over the past couple years, because she never left my side. That has led to much more for them. They have been together pretty much since then.

"Hey, little sis! How are you today?" He came in, kissed Molly, then hugged me.

"Probably I feel a lot like you do today. What's on your mind?" I always knew when he wanted to talk.

"Since Molly is going to hold down the fort today, I think we need to spend the day together. I have it all planned out. So, grab a jacket and let's go."

Chapter Two

Here we are at the cemetery, standing in front of Logan's grave. I bent down and rubbed where his name was engraved into the stone. Today was much like the day we lost him except it was a bit misty outside. I laid the flowers that I had gotten for him down and removed the old ones that I had put there last week. This was one of the places I visited the most, for it gives me peace.

"Ty, I miss him so much that somedays it takes my breath away. How do I go on? We had things planned out and stuff we wanted to do. It all seems like a bad dream I'm reliving day in and day out."

"Tip, it's a dream that you alone are holding on to. You don't need to ever forget him, just let him go. You know as well as I do, he is still hanging around. I still smell his tacky cologne every now and again. He will never leave you until he knows you are okay. And the way you have been, he knows you aren't."

Wow, I thought I was nuts about the whole smelling thing. Guess I was wrong. I'm not as crazy as I thought.

"Do you really think he is still here?" Just as I said that the wind picked up and then abruptly stopped. "I guess that answers my question."

Tyson wrapped his arm around me and gave me a squeeze. I placed my head on his shoulder and we just stood there in silence for a while.

"Tip, you're not the only one who needs to let go. I do, too, and I think Logan deserves to be at peace. Since neither of us said goodbye two years ago, I think we need to now."

Tyson and Logan were like brothers. They had gone through a lot together and that was something I had selfishly forgotten. Tyson spoke his peace one last time, and I could feel the tension leave his shoulders as he let everything out and let go. When it was my turn, Ty let me have my own time.

"Hi, baby. Everyone says it's time to say goodbye, to let you go. I don't know how to do that. But today I'm going to try, for you and for me."

The tears came and I let every word I had built up inside me go. I was on my knees, head down, snot and tears were everywhere. I swear I could smell him, the mix of spice and citrus with a smoky undertone, I loved it. Then I heard the little whispers.

"I will always be with you."

My head shot up and I looked around startled. Then the smell of him was gone along with the slight breeze that had blown by. I, too, felt that a slight weight had been lifted from me. It was time to live my best life. I would take it day by day.

Tyson and I left the cemetery and never spoke of what we did, we didn't have to. Being twins was so cool at times. We were so much alike yet so very different. We were both tall with dark brown hair and brown eyes. I was thin and lean. Tyson was muscular and strong.

After the cemetery, we grabbed a bite of lunch. It was nice spending the day with my brother, but I could tell he also had other things on his mind. He was hyped up form some reason.

"What's up with you? It looks like you are holding in a fart. Spit it out."

Ty took a big gulp of his soda and pulled out a box from his coat pocket and set it in front of me. I almost fell out of my seat.

"Holt shit, Ty! Are you going to propose to Molly?"

He looked around to make sure no one heard me. "Shh, keep it down and I would like to, but would you look at the ring and see if it's something she would like?"

Holy crap! My big brother wanted to be engaged to my best friend! Molly was going to pee herself. I picked up the little red velvet box and opened it. Staring up at me was the most gorgeous oval diamond flanked by two smaller ones. It was the most beautiful ring I'd seen.

"Jesus, Tyson, she is going to love it! You did an incredible job picking it out. When do you plan on proposing?"

"Tonight, I have everything planned out."

He told me about his plans but he wanted me to let Molly tell me herself so I was to act surprised. Yeah, right. Molly and I are best friends. Nothing is left un-talked about.

We finished our lunch and Tyson dropped me off at home. Since my shop was next to my house, I walked over to check in with Molly then hopped into my car and went to the mall. I decided I needed a shopping day and I spent the rest of the day alone.

It turned out to be a good day, which I hadn't expected it to be, until I went out and treated myself to dinner. I ordered my dinner and went to use the restroom. The floors had just been mopped and I slipped and fell, banging my head on the floor. Everything went black and the next thing I remember is waking up in an ambulance. WTF dude!

YOU KNOW WHEN you are walking up from being out cold and everything and everyone sounds so far away? I woke up to that and a very cute man staring down at me.

"Hey there, welcome back. Do you remember what happened to you?" The hot guy asked me.

I had to think about it for a minute. Not really all that sure, I tried to trace my steps to what I had done today when it came to me. "I was going to use the restroom and slipped and fell." My head was pounding and the man talking to me was blurry. Not to mention I now had a strange collar around my neck.

"My name is Aaron. I'm a paramedic and you have a nasty bump and cut on the back of your head. Leave the collar alone," he said, pushing my hands away from the brace. "The hospital will take it off once your neck x-ray is clear. Can you tell me your name and date of birth?"

I thought for a moment, it was hard to think with my head pounding so bad. I could hear my heartbeat in my ears and it hurt!

"Um, yeah, my name is Tipper Winters and my date of birth is May first of ninety-three. My head is pounding and the lights are killing me."

Aaron the paramedic covered my eyes with a washcloth after he flashed a light into them to check my pupils or I think that is what he said. He continued asking me all kinds of questions, took my blood pressure, and checked me all over.

I reached up to touch my head and felt something sticky in my hair. Mr. Paramedic man grabbed my hand and told me not to touch the cut. I felt like a child. Apparently I whacked it open when my head hit the floor.

"I'm not feeling so well, my stomach feels sick."

"We are pulling into the hospital now, Tipper. It will be a little bumpy for a minute once we pull the stretcher out of the ambulance. Keep your arms in and covered up. Here we go."

The next thing I knew the hospital staff was checking me out. I wanted to have someone call my mother but everything seemed so foggy.

"Tipper, is your brother Tyson?" I was shocked he knew my brother's name. I shook my head and everything spun. "I can call him if you like?"

"No, not my brother, he is busy tonight. Please, call my mother." That was all I got out before I vomited.

The doctor had given me something for pain and vomiting. I don't remember much more after that. When I awoke, my mom was sitting beside me. I had been placed in observation overnight and was in a room by myself.

"Hey, sweetheart, how are you feeling?" Mom stood over me, concern etched on her face.

"My head is killing me. Why did they keep me?"

"It seems you have a nasty concussion and a large laceration on the back of your head that needed stitches. You ended up with eighteen. Good news is, you're going to be okay."

I reached up and felt the back of my head and could feel the dried blood caked in my hair. Gross! Then I remembered the cute ambulance guy.

"Who called you to let you know? And did they have to shave my hair?"

"Yes, the Doctor had to cut your hair. It was a nasty cut Tipper and your hair will grow back. Molly can fix it all up for you once you are feeling better. As for who called me, it was some guy that Tyson works with every now and again. Very nice gentleman, his name was Aaron."

I had to concentrate on what she was saying because of the pain and brain fog. Then I remembered something right before I was given medication.

"Sweet Jesus, Mom! I think I may have thrown up on him. I was telling him to call you when I got sick. That's freaking wonderful, how embarrassing."

"For crying out loud, Tipper, that is his job and I'm sure it comes with the territory from time to time."

If she only knew how cute this guy was and the day I had already had. I needed to fall back to sleep and have a do over day.

The nurse came back to my room to check my head, vitals, and pain level. After the assessment, she returned with more nausea and pain medications. I needed it more than I'd realized. Once they both kicked in, my stomach calmed and my head throbbing dulled.

"Will I get to go home soon?" I figured it didn't hurt to ask the nurse.

"I would plan on staying until early to late afternoon. For now, rest when you can because we come in a lot to check on head injuries. I was the nurse keeping my eye on you through the night. I would ask you questions, and after you answered them, you fell right back to sleep. Your Mom told me about how your day usually goes on this date. It was already a lot to deal with, then you get a knock to the head. I'm sorry this had to be added to your day." The nurse reassured me that rest was the best and then left the room.

What could I say to that? I looked at mom and she grabbed my hand and gave it a shake.

"I love you, baby girl." Her voice cracked as she said those words.

"I love you too, Mom."

Chapter Three

I ENDED UP taking the week off from work. Having a concussion is a bitch along with the headache that follows. So, I slept as much as I possible could. Mom stayed with me for the first night. She would have liked to have stayed another night, but I really didn't need her. My shop was right next door, and if I needed anything Molly was right there. Tyson popped in and out, too. I hate when people hover over me. I was lying on my couch watching TV when all three of them came bounding through the front door.

"Um, hi! What's going on and why are you all here?" I was very annoyed.

"We came to check on you, Sis."

Enough is enough. I can't take it anymore. I sat up and went to the kitchen to pour myself some gingerale.

"Listen, I appreciate you all helping me out. But you're now beginning to hover and it's pissing me off. I'm okay. I need rest, peace, and quiet, all of which I'm trying have, but when you all are here in my business, you make it impossible for me to do that.

"So, this is how it's going to work for the rest of the week. Molly will check on me when she gets here in the morning. If I need anything she will help me out. Mom, please just call. I'm fine. I needed a break from life and this accident, so please let me have that. Now, all of you go home! I'm thankful for each of you, but I'm not a porcelain doll. I will be just fine. Now, get out…please."

I went back to the couch and Mom came over and kissed my head and understood she had been a bit much. "I'm sorry baby, I was just worried about you." She turned on her heel and before they all left, they waved at me.

I took a sip of my gingerale and laid down. It wasn't long before I was napping again. For the rest of the week Mom would call once a day to check on me and Molly or Tyson would come to see if there was anything I needed.

By Friday I was feeling much better. I had a stiff neck and a slight headache, but nothing like it was the first of the week. I was up at my normal time and sitting in my chair watching the morning news when Molly came by.

"Good morning. I saw the light on so I figured you were up."

"Good morning. Grab yourself a cup of coffee and have a seat. You're here rather early, what's up?"

Molly knew where everything was in the house and had no problem making herself at home.

"I figured by today you would be up and at it and feeling more like yourself. Also, I thought you may want your hair cut."

"Yes, please! I need it washed so badly. Mom cleaned it up as much as she could and I have been very careful not to get it wet, but I thought now that I could, you could help me?"

Molly came over to inspect my incision. "It looks really good, but a wash and cut will help. I might have to layer it some, but with it shorter it will fluff it up. Plus, I have a surprise for you."

That made me nervous and excited. "What do you have planned?" I looked at her with a wrinkled forehead.

"Oh relax, I took today off to spend with you. It was a busy week and I missed having your smiling face around." She was being sarcastic after my little rant the other day.

"I'm sorry, that was meant more for Mom and Tyson. They made me nervous and gave me a bigger headache than I already had. When you were all together you were feeding off each other's energy. Mom was so worried and watched my every move and, let's face it, Tyson is just loud."

It was then I realized I'd never acknowledge her and Tyson's engagement. I looked at her ring finger and there sat her beautiful new accessory.

"Oh my God, Molly! I have been a horrible BFF... Congratulation on your engagement." I got up from my chair and went over to my best friend, giving her a big hug. "I have been so self-absorbed I never even said anything. In my defense, I have had one hell of a headache. Please forgive me."

Molly squeezed me back then pulled away from me and swatted at the air. "There is no need to forgive anything. You had a frigging head injury; you get a free pass this time."

I grabbed for her left hand and held it up so I could see the beautiful stone my brother had picked for her. "It's beautiful, but I have to confess, he showed me the night I got hurt. That is why I didn't call him that night. I knew what he had planned and I didn't want to ruin your night. I'm sorry it has taken me so long to say anything."

"Don't sweat it. Now, go shower and let's get your hair taken care of. It looks horrid."

That was the end of that conversation and I did just what Molly told me to do. I loved how we could say anything to the other and not be offended.

She had to cut my long, straight hair and add layers to hide the unevenness of having a patch chopped out because of the stitches. I now had a cute above the shoulders, layered haircut.

"Sorry, Tipper, it had to be done. But you, my dear, needed a change in hair style. This cut really suits you." Molly curled it and gave me slight messy waves. It felt a lot healthier and lighter.

"I like it. You were right, I did need a change." Molly smiled and I could tell she was glad that I liked the cut.

"Let's go out and get some lunch, on me. Where would you liked to go? Anywhere you want."

I thought about it for a minute and decided my stomach was still a little touchy and I didn't want to eat much. "Let's go to the new coffee shop that just opened up around the block. I have been there a couple of times and they have really good food."

Because I was still having headaches, Molly drove. She pulled up in front of the new café. I'd heard so many good things about it, especially that the owners treated their customers very well, and the food was amazing.

I ordered an iced peppermint latte and a soft hot pretzel with icing. These things were huge and tasted so buttery. Molly ordered a chicken sandwich and a cup of cream of broccoli soup. We found a seat and waited for our order.

We were enjoying our lunch and talking about when she and Tyson were getting married. Molly asked me to be her maid of honor and, of course, there was no way I wouldn't be.

When we were kids, we had planned our wedding days, what we'd wear, and who would stand with us on our special day. Now that we were older, things had changed, but we were still just as excited.

The café door opened, but I didn't pay much attention to who had come in. Then I heard a man's voice say my name. It sounded familiar, but I was unsure of who it could be.

"Excuse me, sorry to bother you ladies, but are you Tipper Winters?"

I looked at this guy that apparently knew me but I didn't know him from Paul, or did I? Then it clicked. He was the paramedic that was on duty the night I fell. Holy shit! I want to hide.

"Yes, I'm Tipper." Oh God, kill me now. "Please tell me you are *not* the paramedic I vomited all over?"

Mr. Paramedic started laughing and shaking his head up and down, much to my embarrassment. "Sorry, but yes, I'm indeed that lucky paramedic. Let me properly introduce myself. I'm Aaron Connors."

He held out his hand to shake my own and oddly enough when our hands met, a warm feeling spread from the tip of my toes to the top of my head. Weird, I hadn't felt that feeling in so long that I had forgotten what it felt like to feel. Immediately I got butterflies and pulled my hand back.

"Hi, it's nice to meet you. This is my best friend, Molly." Aaron reached to shake her hand also.

"Pleasure! How are you feeling since your fall? I see you cut your hair, you had one hell of a gash on your head."

He noticed my hair cut, that was a first, not even Logan noticed when I got my hair cut. Must be because so much of it was taken off.

Logan... I missed him. I felt myself wanting to give in to my feeling when I felt a funny breeze again. I shook my head to get myself out of my daydream.

"I ended up with eighteen stiches in the back of my head and a nasty concussion... Not to mention the headache that came with it. I'm feeling better every day, though. Thanks for helping me out and calling my mother. I don't remember much about that day, only that I puked on you."

"It's goes with the job. I'm just glad you're feeling better. Duty calls, I must go to work. It was a pleasure to formally meet you, you too, Molly. I hope I see you around, Tipper."

Smiling, he turned and walked out of the café with his large cup of coffee and bag of food. I looked at Molly knowing just what she was going to say.

"Wow, Tipp! He was just flirting with you and, you just smiled at him."

Molly the hopeless romantic.

"Oh, please, he was not."

I knew he was flirting but there was no way I was going to give her the satisfaction I knew.

Molly grabbed the sides of her hair and with very large eyes, she wanted to get her point a crossed and damn near screamed. "Yes! he most certainly was!"

"Shhh... Molly. He was just being nice, that's all. I'm sure he does that to other people he has taken care of."

Molly wanted to shake me. "Tipper, we talked about this. You are supposed be putting yourself out there more. Stop being the unwilling participant."

She had a point there, but I was thinking about Logan and those memories don't easily go away. What did she want me to do, anyways, ask him out on a date? That was not going to happen. I dropped the subject because I was unwilling to talk about it anymore. So, Molly let it go also, once she realized I had shut the conversation down.

"What would you like to do now?"

I looked at Molly and suddenly was spent. "I'm sorry, Molly, but I'm beat."

"You have gotten a bit pale. You've done more today than you have in a week. No wonder you're tired. I'm going to order some chicken noodle soup for you to take home and you can eat it tonight after your nap. Tyson and I are going out for dinner. If you feel better, you're more than welcome to join us and save your soup for tomorrow."

"Thanks, Molly, but I think I'm going to get into some comfortable lounge pants and take a nap."

I was beat but I also wanted to be alone. It was the first time I had noticed anyone take an interest in me since Logan, and it was a weird feeling. I needed to process all of this.

Molly was true to her word and got me soup, a croissant and a tin of macaroons. I'm so glad that my best friend is now going to be my sister-in-law. She means the world to me. No one is better for my brother than Molly.

When we got to the house, she came in to make sure I had everything I needed, which I did, and she wouldn't leave until I was all snuggled onto the couch with my pillows, remote, and gingerale. Molly grabbed my big fluffy blanket and covered me up and out the door she went.

I never did turn on the television, I did however turn on my electric fireplace. The light glow from that put me right to sleep and I slept the entire day, got up to use the bathroom once, and fell back to sleep and slept the rest of the night.

I AWOKE THE next morning feeling pretty good and I had no headache. I thought I would go to the coffee shop and start my day with sunshine and a great cup of coffee. It was the first time I had driven in a week. I brought a book with me to read while I drank my coffee. I used to do this all the time. I was an avid reader but had gotten out of many habits since that one hellish day. I was all settled in and had totally lost track of time reading when I heard a familiar voice.

"Tipper, we meet again."

I looked up from my book to see Aaron standing in front of me.

"Good morning, Aaron. Are you following me?"

"What if I was?"

Aaron was an incredibly handsome man: tall, short dark brown hair, brown eyes, and buff as shit. He was very easy on the eyes. But I did give him a shocked look as he said that.

"Tipper, I'm just joking with you. May I?" Aaron pointed to the over-stuffed chair across from me.

"Please, have a seat." I place my bookmark into the page I was reading and realized how much I had read since I had been here.

"How's the head?"

I reached up and touched the back of my head to feel my stiches. The area was getting itchy. Although Molly said that the incision looked good, it was tender.

"I feel a bit more normal today. I'm still wanting to nap a lot, but I think it will get better every day."

There was a long pause before Aaron spoke.

"I'm good friends with your brother and I knew Logan well, also. He was a good man. I'm sorry you lost him so soon."

Wow, that shocked the shit out of me! Not many people would say much about Logan and here he was unafraid to broach the subject.

"Thank you. It's been very difficult."

"Not to bring up old wounds, and I don't know why I'm telling you this, but I feel I have to. I was on scene when Logan passed away. Technically, I'm not supposed to talk about it, but he didn't suffer. I wanted you to know that."

I didn't know what to say. I was surprised he said anything to me. But, for some reason it gave me peace knowing that he felt no pain. That had haunted my dreams since day one.

"I knew he'd been pronounced dead on the scene, but it's been a lingering thought. Thank you for telling me. It makes me feel loads better."

It really did. It felt like more weight was lift from my shoulders and I also felt that strange breeze again. It felt like Logan was with me, letting me know things would eventually be okay. It was almost as though he was waiting for me to move on.

"This might be too forward but, would you like to go out to dinner with me?"

My eyebrows rose up and I was shocked. Molly was spot on. I didn't know what to say.

Live and be brave.

"Um ... Sure, that would be nice."

Aaron smiled and took a sip of his coffee. "Would you be up for it tomorrow night? I know it hasn't been a good week for you."

I thought for a moment and decided that it would be perfect. No better time than right now. "I would love to. Can we possibly go early? Because by seven I'm pretty much done for the day. Head injuries suck."

Aaron chuckled at that. "Yes, they are nasty and can have after-effects, depending on the injury. Give it some time. How's four o'clock? We can do an early dinner."

"Perfect." I was scared shitless but it was only dinner, right?

"What are you up to now? Would you like to take a walk with me through the park?"

I needed to be brave, but this was crazy that I would feel comfortable enough to ask him that.

"It's a beautiful day for a stroll in the park. Sure, let me grab us a coffee to take with."

The park was directly across from the coffee shop and it followed a river. The town always kept it very well groomed. The flowers were all in bloom and made everything smell so sweet. People came here to jog, have picnics, or walk their dogs. It was a very happy atmosphere.

We walked, not really talking about anything of importance. But I needed to get a feel for this guy. He made me nervous but in a good way and that made me more nervous.

"There's a bench over there. Let's go and have a sit and drink our coffee. I also got us each a muffin. I hope you like chocolate chip."

Chocolate chip was my favorite! I had always had a sweet tooth and being thin, I was one who could eat but never gain weight. I would like to, though.

"Oh, that sounds great. I have a hint of an appetite today. Since hitting my head, my stomach has been off and I haven't been hungry."

We sat and ate our muffins and watched the swans swimming in the river with their little cygnets and the ducks with their ducklings. The little puff balls were so cute as they waddled after their moms.

"They are so cute! Look how puffy they all are. But for as cute as they look, swans can be nasty." I looked around and remembered how much I used to come here and how many things I had stopped doing.

"Do you come here a lot?"

"I used to. I have been at a stand-still for a while now." I looked at Aaron squinting as the sun was shining bright today. "But yes, I came here almost daily for my walk. It gave me clarity being here."

Aaron thought about what I had said. "What does it do for you now?"

I wasn't expecting that question, but it was a good one. Because I was doing the same thing right now, finding clarity of being with Aaron and things had never seemed clearer.

"Gives me just what I need." I sat quietly, picking at my muffin and watching the river. I realized even more by watching the river flowing that I needed to do the same and just let things flow.

"I'm really hungry. Would you like to go back with me to get lunch then come back here and have a picnic? They have tables we can sit at to eat."

I was proud and shocked that I asked Aaron to do that, but he was happy to do so. We went back to the café, ordered lunch and came back and ate. We talked about whatever came up. It was a nice, easy afternoon, nothing serious, just a get to know you moment. After lunch we went our separate ways, and I looked forward to dinner tomorrow night.

Chapter Four

IF THIS WAS only supposed to be dinner, why am I worrying so much about what I'm wearing? I changed three times already and settled on a pair of light pink capris and a white and pink floral shirt with flowing sleeves. I heard a car pull up and I looked out the window, and sure enough, stepping out of the car was Aaron. Sweet baby Jesus in a loin cloth! He looked damn fine! I went to look at myself once more before he knocked on the door.

Our eyes locked when we saw each other and that feeling came back in my stomach, the ones that made me feel giddy. Like I was a teenager again.

"You look beautiful." Aaron handed me a bouquet of different flowers in a variety of colors. They were so beautiful.

"Thank you so much. Please, come in while I put these in some water."

Aaron came in and looked around the living room.

"Your house is gorgeous."

I thought so myself. The interior of my home was mostly tongue and groove pine. I liked the country vibe.

"Thanks, are you ready?" Aaron opened the door for me and we walked out and I quickly turned around and locked the door.

We went to this cute restaurant that had an outdoor balcony where we sat and enjoyed our meal. It overlooked the lake and had hanging flower baskets of purple and white petunias. Clear fairy lights were strung around the balcony. It was very pretty. The waitress took our drink orders, Aaron ordered a beer and I ordered a fuzzy navel.

"I have never been here before. It's so pretty out here and the view is incredible."

Tonight, was the perfect night to have dinner outside. It was warm with the slightest of breezes, it felt so nice.

"I picked up a patient here once who also slipped and fell, but it was off the stairs of the kitchen."

Would this embarrassment ever go away? I put one hand under my chin and hung my head in mock shame. "Will I ever live that day down?"

Aaron reached over and placed his hand over my other hand that was lying on the table. I looked up at him cringing. "I know it was a terrible day and remainder of the week for you. But, it ended up being a great day for me."

Wow, that shocked me! "You must love the smell of vomit then."

Aaron burst out laughing just as the waitress came back with our drinks and menus.

"Here are your drinks and menus." She listed off the specials and left us so we could look over the menu. I wanted the grilled chicken marinated in their special seasoning and a baked potato. Aaron got a steak and potato.

"So, what made you want to become a paramedic?"

Aaron looked out over the water and back at me. "When I was eighteen, my Dad had a heart attack. I had to do CPR on him until the ambulance squad got there. The way the crew worked as a team, each doing their job and bringing Dad back to life. It was amazing. I found a college that taught a Medical Assistant course. There I could take phlebotomy and EKG along with it. I received my certificates for those then got my EMT and worked my way up to Paramedic. Since then, I have taken all kinds of classes for Emergency Response and pretty much anything you can think of. It's sure a far cry from my original major of criminal justice."

This guy was motivated. I could tell he loved his job and took pride in his work.

"What made you want to become a hairdresser?" When he said it like that it made me feel stupid compared to everything he had done. I wasn't a vain person by any means, I was actually down to earth.

"Well, when Molly and I were in high school we did everything together. We decided to go to the technical school for cosmetology and esthetician training. We've attended so many conventions to keep our skills up to date. I've always liked doing hair, even as a kid, and it just stuck with me."

My career choice seemed so crappy compared to Aaron's but, Molly and I did pretty good for ourselves. Our shop was always very busy. We stopped talking when our meals came, then chatted about family, friends and life in general. But there was something I needed to know.

"Aaron, I have a question and hopefully you can answer it for me?"

Aaron had a look of remorse on his face, and I knew this was something he shouldn't talk about.

"What did you mean about Logan not suffering? Aaron put his head down and then gave his chin a rub thinking about what to say.

"Look, Tipper, this is something I only brought up because I wanted you to know that I was there with Logan. I didn't mean to stir up old wounds. I didn't want you to find out later and wonder if I was being truthful. It's also something I'm not supposed to talk about due to HIPPA laws, and I will not speak of it again." Aaron was stern about this and I knew what he was trying to tell me. He wanted to be up front and honest with me.

"The impact of the crash was bad, I'm sure you went to the sight and saw the damage. At the speed that Logan hit the tree and the injuries he sustained... by the time we got there, he had already passed, and we arrived very quickly. So, what I was trying to tell you is that he died on impact. There wouldn't have been anyway to save him."

I knew that Logan's neck was broken and he had multiple internal injuries. We couldn't have an open casket due to those injuries.

"Thank you. I thought that was the case, but during the time I was inconsolable. I spent my wedding day in the hospital in shock and was given meds to make me relax and sleep. Through the entire time of the visitation and funeral, I was pretty much catatonic. I remember very little of that time and I'm thankful for that in an odd way. I realize you wanted to be straight with me, Aaron, and I appreciate that. Thank you."

In that moment, I smelled Logan's cologne around me. My eyes filled with tears as I was talking about the past but felt more at peace knowing that Aaron had been with him. I know this is something you shouldn't talk about when you're out to dinner with some other guy, but I needed to know. I felt lighter in that moment but poor Aaron looked like hell. It was time for me to break the ice and continue with whatever this was with Aaron and me.

"After we eat, why don't we grab another drink then walk along the waterfront? It looks like there is a path right there."

That seemed to get Aaron out of his funk. He gave me one hell of a sexy smile that made me react in a way I hadn't in a very long time. We followed the path and watched the different boats go by. I imagine some had spent the day on the lake and some were fishing. I noticed a lot of people were still swimming. What a beautiful evening.

We walked closer to the water so I could dip my feet in. The water was warm, it would be very fun to spend the day on the lake.

"If you would like, I have a boat we could go for a ride or spend the day on the water. I have skis, too, if you like to do that?"

"Me on skis? No way, but I do love to swim. That sounds like it would be fun."

Aaron smiled. "Tipper, I enjoy your company. I find you so refreshing compared to some women. You're very easy to talk with."

Aaron walked closer to me and looked at me like he knew everything about me. "I have wanted to kiss you from the first time I laid eyes on you."

I didn't stop him because in that moment I knew that was what I wanted, too. The next thing I knew my arms circled around his neck. As we pulled away, I felt his heat moved with him and I was disappointed. "I hope that was okay?"

"It was perfect. You are the first person I have let in since, well you know. I like the feelings I get from you."

Aaron still had his arms around my waist. I was so glad he hadn't let go. "Oh yeah? And what feelings are they?" He grabbed a piece of my hair and twirled it.

My cheeks instantly got red. "You give me butterflies in my stomach and I feel happy that I can be myself with you. You make me feel whole again, and that is a foot all of its own."

Aaron leaned in and kissed me again and I felt a warmth now growing even further down to my stomach. Oh my! We spent the rest of the evening making out on the beach until Aaron stopped us.

"Would you like to come over to my house? No pressure, but damn, woman, you're killing me here."

Did I want to go to his house and most likely end up having sex with him? I just shook my head and he stood and reached for my hand to help me up. He gave me another quick kiss and we were off.

Aaron lived in a log cabin down a dirt road with no neighbors. He came around to my side of the car to open the door for me.

"It's so beautiful back here."

I was nervous, I hadn't done this in so long. We walked into Aaron's house and he asked if I wanted a glass of wine, which I graciously took. Aaron came close to me and he took my wine glass and set it down on the counter and he kissed me, but Aaron being the man that he was wanted clarification.

"Are you sure you're ready?"

For once in my life I felt very bold. After a couple of sips of liquid courage, I grabbed the bottle off the counter.

"Lead the way."

Aaron needed no encouragement. He grabbed my hand and led me to his room.

Once we were in his room, I took a sip from the open bottle and put it down on the desk. I walked slowly, sexily to where he stood and kissed him passionately. My hands caressed his ripped chest and began to unbutton his shirt. When my hands reached bare skin, a sharp intake of breath revealed my surprise at how amazing those muscles felt.

I tossed his shirt to the floor and he did the same thing with mine. I shuddered when I noticed he was admiring my scantily covered breasts. I may be skinny but I have a nice bust.

Dipping his head, he kissed my breast through the bra and in an instant, the piece of lace was discarded. He sucked my nipple, then lightly skimmed his teeth across the swollen, sensitive tip.

I reached for his button and zipper. His erection pressed through his jeans into my abdomen. Damn this was hot! In no time flat, we were both naked on his bed.

Aaron passionately kissed me and worked his way down my neck, kneading my breast and pushing his knee between my legs. His hand found its way downward and his fingers into me.

"Oh, Tip, you are more than ready for me, so wet, so warm for me."

No one had ever said anything so hot to me before. Before I knew it, he replaced his fingers with his tongue. He was quite comfortable between my thighs.

I looked down at him to find he was looking right back at me. He spread my folds and watched me as he licked. This man had me moaning and squirming all over the bed with one lick... Fuck, I was in trouble.

He licked and nipped at me until I came. He found his way back to me, and when he kissed me I could taste myself on his lips. I was so turned on by this man. He positioned himself over me and entered me slowly. Once he was all the way in, Aaron waited for my body to adjust to him, then he started pumping in and out of me.

"You're so tight, yet wet for me. You have no idea what that is like for a guy. Do you realize how beautiful you are? I don't know if I will ever get enough of you."

He pumped harder and harder until we were both breathing heavily. I orgasmed first and he followed right after me, but as he let himself go, I followed again after him.

As we slowly regained our bearings, and while he was still inside of me, I could feel him getting hard again and we had another go at it.

We stopped long enough to talk about anything that came up. It was like we had to share everything with each other this very night because there wouldn't be another moment. We told each other our deepest, darkest secrets, embarrassing moments, and joyful times. You name it, we talked about it.

Aaron said he hadn't been with anyone in over a year after a break-up. But he was okay with how things turned out and held no bad feelings for the girl. It was bad timing for her and good timing for me, yet I was still jealous over a person I had never met.

He was leaning up on one arm with his head resting on his hand and I was lying flat on my back. He was rubbing my stomach over the sheets and just looking at me.

"Do you think that all of the shit we go through in life happens for a reason? It's something I often wonder about."

I thought about it for a minute before I answered.

"I think in a way, yes, but only to a certain extent. We also have our own choices in life that we must make. Like you and your ex. She started having feelings for someone else and told you before things went too far. And if Logan would have stayed and waited for my brother, maybe he would still be here or maybe I would have lost both of them. Maybe you would have caught your ex with the other guy. Maybe you wouldn't have been there when your dad had his heart attack. We make choices for the things we do. And I think most of the time, fate intervenes and other times it's just life."

Aaron continued to rub my stomach and I wondered what he was thinking. But I didn't have to wait long.

"All I know is that I'm glad you needed an ambulance. Not that I wanted you to get hurt but because I found you."

Was it possible to care so fast for one person after I had been pining for another for so long? I felt as if I was already falling for this guy and falling hard. That scared the shit out of me but tonight I was just going to enjoy the time I was having with this amazingly kind man.

I rolled on top of Aaron and rubbed my center against him. It didn't take him long to answer my call, and as I slid down his shaft, we rocked and rolled with each other all night long.

Chapter Five

We woke the next morning, both a touch tender from all of our loving making and body exploring. I was on my side and Aaron was spooned up against me. It felt so nice to be wrapped up in Aaron's arms. I have heard of people falling in love at first sight but was it really happening with me?

"Good morning, how did you sleep?" Aaron's voice deep from just waking up.

"Who slept?" I rolled over to look at him and we both laughed.

"Don't get freaked out by what I'm about to say, but I feel as though I have to say how I feel."

Oh god, what was he going to say to me?

He could see the concern in my face and he kissed my head. "Don't worry it's nothing bad, at least I don't think it is. Do you believe in love at first sight?"

Holy crap! It was like he literally plucked this thought from my own brain. That had never happened before.

"I was just thinking the same thing last night. I didn't but now I'm starting to think that I do. How is that possible?"

"Do you think that this is fate intervening with this thing between us or is it just happenstance?"

I stopped and thought about this one. I didn't have an answer to give Aaron. We let this conversation go for now.

We had things we needed to do today. We agreed to meet at Aaron's house at one o'clock. I wanted this to be just between us for now. If we stayed at my house, Molly and Tyson would be over and I didn't want to share Aaron just yet. I was greedy and wanted him all to myself.

Aaron dropped me off at home and I showered and readied for the day. I also put a small bag in the back of my car with just a few things I may need if I stayed again, including a change of clothes.

It looked like it was going to be another sunny day. I had put on a pot of coffee as Molly and Tyson stopped in for a bit to visit.

"So, what are you guys doing today?" I was curious if they had noticed I had been missing for several hours.

"We are looking at venues for the wedding. Do you want to come with us?"

"Thanks for the offer, but not today. I have a few errands I need run. You guys go and enjoy your day. Remember to not get upset with one another. When you see the place, you will just know."

Molly came over and hugged me. I knew she was worried about me, but for once I knew everything was going to be just fine. "I love you, Tipper."

"I love you, too, Molly, but I'm good. Stop worrying, I'm going to be just fine. Now, you two get out of here."

Once they were gone, I gave myself a once over and was ready. But there was one more thing I had to do and that was go to the cemetery.

I STOPPED AT the store and picked up a fresh bouquet of flowers to put on Logan's grave. I had been coming here weekly for the past two years. But today, I was ready to put that life behind me. I needed to, not only for everyone I was around but also for myself, and Logan.

I got out of the car and walked the small way to where his final resting place was. I wiped where his name was, it was a ritual I did every time I came to see him. I took the dead flowers that Tyson and I had put here just a few days ago and replaced them with the new ones I brought.

"Logan, I'm sure you know why I'm here. This is not my regular visit." That was when the breeze picked up and I smelled Logan's cologne. Ironically, I knew this would be my last time smelling that fragrance and I was at peace with that... Something I hadn't felt in a very long time.

"The last two years have been a complete nightmare for me, not that it's been pleasant for you, either. But as you know, I'm not living the life you would want me to live and I hate to do this because I know once I let go, your smell and you will go away. But again, that's not fair for either of us. Not to mention it's a very selfish thing on my part for keeping you here."

I had brought a red checkered blanket to sit on because I knew I might be here for a while. So, I laid it out and sat down.

"I met someone. I know you'd like him. His name is Aaron. He is a paramedic and he happened into my life like it was fated to be so."

After I said that, I stopped and thought about what Aaron had asked me and I had found my answer. How crazy was that? Of all the places to find my answers, it would have to be here. I had a sneaking suspicion that fate was having a bit of help from an amazing angel.

"He was actually there at your accident." There was that breeze again, lending validation that I wasn't crazy. You may already know that. He's a good, kind, and caring man. I don't know how I managed to fall in love with one amazing man, lose you, and be lucky enough to find another. What makes me deserving of that?"

That is when I heard him... Logan.

"Because you loved me so hard and so purely."

My breath caught as I heard Logan in my ear, just as a whisper. I looked around but I was the only one here.

"Logan, I loved you so much I lost myself and I'm sorry. I'm going to be okay. I know that now. It took me a while to find myself again. Please, always know how very much I loved you and still love you. There will always be a place for you in my heart. I have to know, do you approve of Aaron?"

Not that I needed his approval but it would mean so much that he would think he was a good fit for me. His scent was on the breeze again as I heard his beautiful voice.

"I approve, he's a good man."

I started to cry. I cried for Logan, his family, my family, me and Tyson. I cried for anyone who was blessed to have known Logan. I wiped my tears and pulled myself together.

"I will always love you Tipper Winters, but let your heart belong to someone else now. I can go now. Tell Tyson I loved him like a brother. After Tyson let me go, fate stepped in so you could let go."

Jennifer Daniels

I felt the breeze once more, filled my senses with Logan's cologne, and the sweet kiss he placed on my cheek.

"Goodbye, my love."

The breeze was gone. Logan's scent was gone. And, my heart was light and carefree. My fingers lingered on the spot that Logan had just kissed. For the first time in two years, other than last night, I felt joy. I quickly picked up my stuff and went to Aaron's house.

I QUICKLY EXITED my car and ran right into Aaron's arms. He was sitting on the deck waiting for me. I kissed him and he spun me around. A wide smile brightened his handsome face.

"What happened when you were gone? You're glowing."

"Well, after a shower and a shave… everywhere," I wagged my eyebrows up and down at him. "I went to the cemetery to chat with Logan. I know that sounds weird but I needed to say a proper goodbye. I told him about how I met a man and that you were there for him when he needed someone. And, I told him that I haven't known you very long but I am falling for you. I asked him how I got so lucky twice."

I kissed Aaron and when I looked at him he had a shocked look on his face.

"You asked me today if I thought this was fated and yes, I do. I think fate played a big part in our meeting with possibly a little help from a special angel. I said goodbye to my past and hello to my future. I only pray I'm lucky enough to have you as the man standing with me."

Aaron gently held onto the sides of my head and looked into my eyes with a love I had only seen once before.

"Did you just say that you loved me?" Out of everything I had said, that is what Aaron focused on. All I could do was laugh. "Yes, Aaron, in only a week, you have managed to squirm your way into my heart and you made it start beating again."

Aaron took the next few days off. After telling Molly and Tyson about Aaron, I also added onto my days off. Molly was totally cool with it and Tyson was stoked that I had met Aaron. They got along very well. Once that was taken care of, Aaron and I spent our days off, just the two of us, holed up in his cabin.

Eight Months Later

"Tipper, it's my wedding day. I need to get into the bathroom."

I had stayed with Molly the night before her wedding and Tyson stayed at Aaron's. Things had been going extremely well with Aaron and me. My family loved him and I got along great with his family. It was like we had known them all for years.

I opened the door to find Molly leaning against the door frame. "Molly, there are two bathrooms in this house. If you had to go, why didn't you use the other one?"

"Because I'm used to using this one. And it has a long mirror in it. How does my hair look?"

Molly had put her hair up in a loose but intricate bun with rhinestones scattered throughout her hair. It looked gorgeous and her make-up was flawless.

"Tipper, are you okay? You look terrible! Please don't tell me you have a stomach bug. I don't want to be sick on my honeymoon."

Shit, this was not the time for spilling secrets on someone else's day.

"I'm fine. And relax, getting married is as easy as pie." Molly spun around and glared at me.

"Yeah, sure. When you up and elope, it is."

After four months of being together, Aaron and I knew we were meant for each other and I didn't want to go through the whole wedding thing again. So, I bought a pretty white off the shoulder dress and Aaron wore a nice white dress shirt with a blue tie and gray dress pants and we flew to Vegas, just the two of us.

"Oh, stop it! And move out of the way." I ran to the toilet and was sick again for the fourth time this morning.

"You *are* sick. I love you, but Tipper, stay away from me." She was snipping at me as I had my head stuffed into the toilet. I stood up and threw some water on my face.

"Unless you have a flu baby brewing inside of you, you're safe. Believe me, you cannot catch this." That shut her up and left her mouth gaping open.

"We didn't tell you because you have been crazy with the wedding and stressed out. And this is supposed to be your day, but unfortunately for me, morning sickness has kicked into high gear."

Just then, Aaron came through the doors to undoubtedly check in on me. The last three months have been dandy at work. How I kept this from Molly this long was a miracle. Aaron peeked around the corner looking for me. I had moved into the cabin with him and sold my house to Tyson and Molly. There was no reason for me to keep the house.

"Hey. How are things going in here? Do you need anything?"

Molly came around the corner with her mouth still wide open and smacked Aaron on the back of the head. He just looked at me and knew our secret was out.

"I see you have learned your going to be an Auntie. Sorry for keeping this a secret. We wanted to make sure everything was safe."

That was all Aaron got out of his mouth before Molly turned into a proud and very excited Auntie and hugged him.

"Oh my God! Congratulations! I'm sorry for my reaction. I had no idea. Tyson is going to shit himself."

Aaron came over to me and handed me a can of gingerale. "We don't want to ruin your day. We will tell everyone sometime this week."

"Are you kidding me? We will be lucky if my matron of honor makes it through the ceremony without yacking. And look at her, she *is* a bit green."

Just like that I was running back to the bathroom with Aaron hot on my heels. My amazing husband got me a cold cloth for my neck and rubbed my back. Once I was done I leaned back against the cool tub.

"Why don't you take that medication the doctor gave you? By the time Molly is ready to walk down the aisle, you will be fine, I promise."

Molly had decided on a backyard wedding and there just happened to be a big back yard on this property. It made for an easy way of getting things ready. The backyard was decorated and the caterers came prepared. They ended up having just a smaller more intimate affair. I think it was something Tyson wouldn't budge on. In the end, Molly was fine with it. She was just happy to be marrying the man of her dreams.

"Well, babe, do you think you are done for a bit, or are you going to be sick on me again?"

I glared up at Aaron like I was mad, but there was no way I could ever be mad at this man. I loved him with every fiber of my being. I rubbed my tummy where our two precious bundles were snuggled up and Aaron covered my hand with his own.

"I think you're safe for a few minutes, my love. But you never know when fate is involved."

the end

ROOMMATES

Roommates
Laura Hern

Introduction
December 1, School of Mines and Technology, Rapid City, SD

THE SHOCK ON Lainey's face was obvious. She was stunned at the bombshell her college roommate, Amy Walker, had just dropped in her lap.

"I'm pregnant and moving out as soon as the semester is over," Amy stated happily.

"Wait. What? You're moving out?" Lainey stuttered.

"Yep. Bubba and I are so happy!"

What? Who is Bubba? Moving out? I'm stuck with the rental lease?

Lainey sat slowly in the old green recliner she had purchased at a flea market last semester. Her mind was running a mile a minute. She and Amy had agreed last summer to rent this house together to finish out their senior year at the School of Mines. The old, run down house on Quincy Street was nothing to write home about. But it was close to the campus and gave Lainey privacy she couldn't get in her old dorm room in Connolly Hall. They had agreed to split the rent and utilities and had signed a one year lease with the landlord.

"I know it's a shock," Amy began. "Bubba's dad is going to let him work in his Caterpillar dealership repairing engines and big stuff like that."

"But it's your senior year. You're so close to graduation. You're going to give that all up?"

"Oh, I didn't really like engineering anyway. Bubba's going to make loads of money and I can stay home and raise little Bubba babies. Isn't that just dreamy?" Amy excitedly giggled.

Lainey shook her head in disbelief. Images of her being forced to work double shifts at Spuds and Stuff and watching the world gather at the clock in the center of Rushmore Mall by Osco Drug made her shudder.

"We signed a year lease for this house," Lainey muttered. "I can't afford to pay for this by myself."

"Don't you worry about that," Amy casually responded as she read a text on her phone. "Bubba's dad has a friend whose son goes here. He's moving in this weekend."

Lainey was speechless... again. Her mouth was open, but no words came out. Her seal point Siamese cat, Angel, jumped in her lap and appeared to sneer in Amy's direction.

Amy finished texting, looked at Angel and smiled.

"And it gets better... he has the cutest little doggie you've ever seen. Angel will simply love him!"

Chapter One

IT WAS SNOWING heavily as Lainey left the Mechanical Engineering building and walked across the Quad toward the Surbeck Student Center. Amy's recent departure and the anticipation of sharing her space with some guy she had never met set her nerves on edge. She hadn't been able to concentrate or study for her last final in Fluid Mechanics as much as she wanted to. After grabbing a coffee at the Miners Shack, she headed over to the library to study a bit more.

Many of the students had already gone home for Christmas break. Lainey planned to stay in Rapid and work through the holidays. She could pick up extra shifts and sock money away for the graduation present she intended to give herself... A red Mercedes convertible. Her passion for convertibles began when her dad traded a bunch of old pipe valves for a 1967 yellow and black Chevy Camaro convertible. It was her first car and while it was a junker, she thought she was riding in style!

The previous owner had stripped the car down to rebuild it as a race car. Needless to say the work was shoddy and about half complete. When her dad parked the car in the driveway, Lainey couldn't wait to get behind the wheel and drag Main Street. She didn't notice the faded yellow paint job, the dents and dings, the crooked antenna on the driver's side, or the words *Hanky Panky* on a sticker on the door. Little did she know that the car would be the source of some of her most embarrassing memories.

It had bucket seats. The driver's side seat was a dingy black and white plaid fabric. The passenger seat was covered with what looked like orange shag carpet that had clumped in places. It was a 4-speed and the shifter in between the bucket seats was a tall, thick piece of metal covered half-way up from the floorboard with what looked like the bottom of a rubber toilet bowl plunger. The top was graced with a large chrome ball that had a smiley face carved or chiseled into it.

Lainey's inaugural trip down Main Street didn't go as she had planned. After spending more than ten minutes getting the car started, plugging in an Elton John 8-track tape in the used player her dad had installed where the radio should have been, and using both hands to crank down the rusted driver's side window, she was ready to show off her new wheels.

Main Street was about three miles from her house. She rested her left elbow on the open window door frame, keeping her hand on the steering wheel when she shifted gears and put her foot on the gas. Her tires squealed and she was in heaven. Until she looked in the rearview mirror to see the flashing red lights behind her. She pulled over. She had gone less than a mile.

Flustered, she forgot to hold the clutch in before she turned off the engine and the car lurched forward, jerking to stop. She heard a familiar voice coming from her open driver's window.

"Got a new car, Lainey?"

She sighed, rolled her eyes, and shrugged her shoulders.

"Hello, Lt. Garrett," Lainey answered sheepishly. He happened to be the chairman of the board of elders at her church and great friends with her parents.

"Were you planning on dragging Main?"

"Yes, sir," she sighed.

"Did you happen to hear anything odd as you were burning rubber when you took off?"

Lainey knew that she had the volume on the 8-track turned as high as it would go... and she figured he knew that too.

"No, sir."

"Elton was singing pretty loudly, wasn't he?"

She nodded her head yes.

"Please step out of the car. I want to show you something."

Lainey got out of the car and slowly followed the officer to the back of her car.

"See anything strange here?"

She swallowed hard and nodded yes.

"And what do you see?"

"I think it's the tailpipe."

"Is it supposed to be dragging the ground? Or smoking? Or throwing sparks as it digs holes in the pavement?"

Lainey had no idea that the tailpipe in question had been loosely attached to the car with a thin piece of chicken wire. Since her driveway was made of pea gravel, when she squealed her tires, the rocks thrown up knocked the pipe loose. It had been dragging behind her the entire time. The crooked carved line left behind in the hot pavement was evidence of that.

When Lt. Garrett had thoroughly embarrassed and scolded her, she slid behind the wheel, and headed home to face her dad. Before the officer could walk to his car, a loud, high pitched, screeching sound pierced the air. He slowly walked back to the Camaro.

Lainey was frantically pushing the middle of the racing steering wheel trying to stop the sound. She didn't even know the car *had* a horn. Nothing was happening. The sound continued to blare. Lt. Garrett got in the car and tried to turn it off. Nothing.

Lainey was mortified, sitting beside the road, police car lights flashing behind her, and horn blasting while her classmates drove past. Some were waving, some were laughing, and some drove past a few times. The dreadful horn sounded until her dad arrived and unplugged it from under the dashboard. It would be a long time before she'd live this down.

From that point on, she had decided to never again be embarrassed by a junkyard automobile. She'd save her money and as a reward for getting her college degree, she'd buy a red Mercedes convertible.

But now that plan might be in jeopardy. Facing the possibility of having to pay the full amount of rent for the remainder of the lease was weighing heavily on her, not to mention the fact that some strange guy was planning on moving in with her.

"I can't tell my dad a guy is moving in with me. He'll have a fit," Lainey said aloud as she walked to her favorite spot in the library. This little nook and table had become her home-away-from-home the last four years. She spent more time here than in her dorm room. The library workers knew her by name and referred to that spot as *Bonner's Cell*.

Lainey laid her backpack on the left corner of the small table and put her coffee cup on the right. It made it easy for her to grab different textbooks, pencils, and notebooks from the backpack and not spill her coffee. She had been known to spill a few drops here or there.

"How's the java today, Lainey? I thought the Shack would be closed for Christmas break," a familiar male voice teased.

Jess Martin was also a business management technology major. Since their freshman year, they had been in every core class together. He helped her through Statistics, she helped him with Communications and Writing. Lainey thought he might have had a little crush on her that first year and while he was nice, kind, and cute, she was determined to focus on getting her degree with no strings attached to anyone. She explained to him that she wasn't looking for a relationship in the kindest way possible. He was disappointed at first, but since that day, they had become good friends.

"I have the caffeine-addicts preferred service at the Shack. They wouldn't dare close until after my last final!"

The two chuckled. Lainey stood up to take off her old winter coat and immediately began struggling with the worn out zipper.

"I swear, the teeth on this zipper are as jagged as the smile on a pumpkin's face!" she complained.

She threw up her arms in frustration, knocking her beloved coffee cup into the air.

It was like watching in slow motion as Jess leaned forward to try to catch the flying beverage and instead, tackling some poor student who happened to be walking by. Jess and the unlucky student fell to the ground and the cup poured out its contents on them as if it were on purpose.

"Oh!" Lainey exclaimed. "I'm so sorry! Are you both okay?"

"I'm okay, but Darren might not be. He broke my fall," Jess replied, standing up and offering a hand to help.

"Thanks, but I'm fine," the guy said, motioning off Jess's hand. He stood up and looked down at the wet spots on his jeans. "Nice tackle. What's this wet stuff anyway?"

"It's my coffee," Lainey said. "I was trying to get my zipper unstuck and knocked my cup off the table. Here, let me clean it up." She riffled through her coat pockets, pulled out a couple of crumpled napkins, and started to pat the spots on Darren's jeans. He jerked back in surprise, taking the napkins out of her hand.

"Hey... what are you doing?" Darren sputtered uneasily. He glanced at Jess, then at Lainey who was obviously embarrassed.

"I'm sure you can wipe yourself... uhm... it's not like I felt your leg or... I mean, you can pat yourself dry... oh, golly," she sighed aloud, horrified at how ridiculous her words sounded.

"Lainey was trying to help, that's all," Jess laughed. "She's the queen of klutz when it comes to coffee."

Darren rolled his eyes and walked away. "See you, Jess."

Lainey looked at Jess who was still laughing.

"Stop grinning and giggling! He thinks I'm an idiot!"

"Nah, he probably thinks you're a first semester freshman who doesn't have a clue," Jess chuckled. "That was vintage Lainey for sure."

"Umph." Lainey glared at him. "Who was that guy? I haven't seen him around."

"His name is Darren Maynard. He's a mechanical engineering major and has the brains of an Einstein. He's a senior, too."

"No wonder he can't carry on a decent conversation. Those ME's can play with numbers, but the few I know aren't very good at socializing, unless it's beer chugging and wet tee shirt contests over at the Hall."

Jess laughed. "When's your exam?"

"Ten-thirty this morning," she responded, sitting down and reorganizing her table. "I've been so stressed about Amy moving out and how I'm going to pay the rent, I'm not as prepared as I should be."

"You got this. MacDonald's final is predictable. He takes questions from the previous exams, mostly those missed by the class, and rewords them. You'll do fine. He knows what a good student you are."

Lainey shrugged. "I sure hope so. I need this class and a good grade on my transcript."

"I'll call you later," Jess said as he winked at her. "I'm heading home this afternoon."

"Sounds good."

She studied for a solid hour, then headed back across the Quad to her class for the exam. She dreaded timed tests. She usually knew most of the answers, but would get flustered trying to watch the clock to make sure she hadn't spent more than one minute on each question.

She had a routine of reading the first question and the last question. If she knew the answers to those, her stress level went down. If not, she knew it would be a race against the clock. Luckily, she knew them both today.

Thank you, Lord! Help me remember what I know and pass this test!

She put the completed test on Prof. MacDonald's desk with a few minutes to spare.

"Finished early, Lainey?" He asked, looking up through his thick framed glasses that were perched on his nose.

"Just a couple of minutes early," she said smiling.

"Perhaps I didn't make it hard enough then." He teased.

"No, no, it was more than adequate! I hope you have a Merry Christmas, sir."

"You, too. Grades will be posted by end of the day."

Lainey nodded and walked out of the classroom. She liked Professor MacDonald and was sorry this was her last class with him. She hurried across campus to her car and found a note taped to the windshield. It was from Amy.

I'm all moved out and here is my new phone number. Your new roomie is moving in this evening. I'll miss you!

Lainey gave a huge sigh as she got in her car.

Already? I still don't know who this guy is?

She started the car and headed to the grocery store to purchase milk and cat food. She was in and out quickly and headed to her house. Her mind wasn't on driving or grocery shopping or Christmas. It was clearly focused on who this roommate was and how she was going to explain him to her dad.

As she pulled into her regular parking spot on the street in front of the house, she noticed the side door was open. She grabbed her backpack and grocery bag, locked her car, and headed for the open door. She was worried that Angel had gotten out.

Why would Amy leave the door open?

She hurried inside, putting her stuff on the counter, and closed the door.

"Angel? Angel kitty? Where are you, sweetie?" Lainey called out, searching for the Siamese cat.

She heard a loud growling coming from her bedroom and knew it was Angel's angry sound.

Lainey couldn't have been more surprised by what she found in her bedroom. Angel, back raised up, tail fluffed out wide, was clawing and growling at a small wire kennel that held something captive in it.

"Angel, stop. It's okay." She picked up the territorial feline. "What are you growling at?"

Bending down, Lainey could see a dog in the back of the metal kennel. It was cowering, shaking... and slobbering.

"What in the world? It's okay, little fella. Angel won't hurt you." She put the cat in the hallway, closed the bedroom door to keep her out for a minute, and opened the kennel to try and urge the dog out. He slowly inched forward, sniffing and whimpering, until she could pet him.

"You're okay," she said, picking him up while trying not to get his slobber all over herself. She grabbed a tissue to clean his face. He was a pudgy little tan and white bulldog with so many wrinkles around his mouth that made him look adorable. "Why, you're a little cutie!" She wiped his face off and he seemed to calm down a bit.

Angel had been scratching and meowing loudly at the closed door, trying to get in. Lainey, still holding the bulldog, opened the door. The cat ran inside, made a beeline to the open kennel door, and sneaked inside to see where the dog was hiding.

"He's not in there, Angel," Lainey said, watching the bulldog begin to pant. "What's your name, little fella?"

"His name is Brutus," a male voice boomed out, startling Lainey.

She turned to see who it was. Her mouth fell open and she almost dropped the dog.

"You? How did you get..." Lainey began, then suddenly realized what was happening.

"You're the new roommate, aren't you. And this is your dog," she said with resignation in her voice.

"You must be Amy's old roommate. And that cat must be yours," the guy replied, not amused. "Any plans to spill coffee on me in the next few minutes?"

Just as Lainey was about to speak, the cute little bulldog she was holding let out the loudest, stinkiest toot she had ever heard or smelled.

"Oh, my gosh!" Lainey yelled, quickly handing the dog to its owner and covering her nose. "That smells terrible!"

"He passes gas when he gets nervous," the guy grinned widely. "I'll take him outside for a minute."

He patted the dog. As he turned to take him outside, he said softly, but loud enough he was sure Lainey could hear. "Good boy, Brutus. Show her who's boss."

"Umph!" she exclaimed disgustedly. She turned to Angel who had gotten out of Brutus's kennel and was standing guard next to her leg. "He *thinks* he's the boss, does he? We'll just see about that!" She bent down, picked up Angel, and stormed back into the kitchen.

Chapter Two

Lainey, still holding her cat, stood facing the back door, waiting to confront her new roommate as soon as he brought Brutus back inside. Minutes passed. Still she waited. No signs of Brutus or his owner. Angel, tired of being held or bored of waiting for something to happen, jumped down and was lying in the green recliner in the front room.

Slowly, Lainey's anger subsided. She took off her coat, put away the milk she had bought, and sat down in her recliner to relax, moving the cat over to make room. Angel stretched and gave a short meow indicating her displeasure at being disturbed. Then settled down beside her.

Lainey had to think. What was his name again? Darwin? David? Darren? Jess had said he was a senior and very intelligent. All she knew was that he was arrogant and had a smelly dog that slobbered.

This isn't going to work. I'm going to tell him to move out as soon as I see him.

She glanced at the few bills lying on the wooden box crate sitting beside her recliner. She used it as an end table. The room didn't have lights on the ceiling and had only one window. Lainey had found a small, broken leg lamp in a garage sale. The original lampshade had been patched with some type of camouflage fabric and the shoe on the foot of the lamp had scratch marks on it. It looked like someone had tried to draw fishnet hose on the leg portion with a black marker and the lines were a bit crooked. But for a dollar, it provided 60 watts of light to work by.

She opened the bills for the rent and utilities, then sighed. At that moment, she heard barking and toenails scurrying across the linoleum floor in the kitchen. She got up and headed toward the sound. Angel jumped out of the recliner, raced ahead of her, and was hissing and meowing loudly when Lainey caught up.

She saw Brutus, his back to her, hungrily scarfing up Angel's dry cat food. He was grunting and throwing food all over the place.

"Brutus likes your cat's food," his owner said, looking pleased as he smiled at Lainey. "By the way, my name's Darren Maynard, in case you don't remember drenching me this morning in the library."

Angel was still hissing and crouching ready to pounce. Lainey looked at the dog, then at the cat, then at Darren.

"Kids, what can you do," he smirked, shrugging his shoulders.

"You can tell Brutus to stop eating Angel's food!" Lainey snarled back.

Darren grinned for a moment, looking straight at her. He paused, then said, "Brutus, that's enough." He reached over to shoo the dog away from the cat's food.

"I haven't unpacked his dish yet. He must like the taste of that, though!"

"It's salmon and chicken flavored... and made for cats," Lainey said, trying to remain calm. "We need to talk about this roommate business. I don't see how it's going to work out."

Darren was still smiling at her. She noticed that one side of his mouth raised up slightly higher than the other, creating a cute little dimple behind it. Suddenly, she felt goosebumps on her arms.

Stop it, Lainey! Concentrate on the issue, not that adorable dimple!

"You might be right," Darren replied. "Let's talk this over. How about we go over to the Hall? I'll buy you a burger."

"What about your dog?"

"I'll put him in his kennel and close the bedroom door. He'll be okay if your cat doesn't attack him again."

Lainey rolled her eyes.

"I'll buy my own burger, thank you."

"Suit yourself."

Darren picked up Brutus and, as they walked past Lainey toward the spare bedroom, she got another whiff of Brutus's unique gift of gas.

"Phew!" She gagged.

"Don't worry. He'll get used to you," Darren said chuckling.

The wall phone in the hallway rang and Lainey walked over to answer it, still choking on eau de toilette Brutus.

I sure wish I could afford a cell phone.

"Hello?"

"I'm guessing you've met Brutus, huh," Jess replied. She could tell he was trying not to laugh.

"Did you know about Darren being the new roommate?"

"Lainey, I swear I didn't until after I saw you at the library this morning. When I left you, I ran into Darren again. That's when he said he was moving into a place on Quincy."

She paused for a long moment.

"It's not going to work out," she stated flatly. "We're going to the Hall to get a burger and I'm going to tell him to find something else."

It was Jess's turn to be silent.

"Jess, did you hear me?"

"He's really a nice guy. You just didn't meet under the best of circumstances. Give him a chance."

"He's conceited and bossy, and his dog slobbers, big time!"

Jess laughed loudly. "You love animals."

"I didn't say the dog was bad, just... smelly. And he ate Angel's food. Do you know how expensive that dry food is?"

"The rent and utilities are expensive, too, aren't they?" He commented quietly.

She didn't respond.

"Lainey, it's only for a few months. There's no dorm rooms available on campus and you can't possibly pay all the bills by yourself."

She remained silent for a couple of minutes. Then, knowing Jess was right, she sighed heavily.

"I know, I know. But this guy is bossy and he has this goofy smile when he laughs," she grumbled.

"I've known you a long time. You can be a bit bossy at times, too."

She rolled her eyes and shrugged her shoulders.

"Can you come to the Hall, Jess? I'd feel more comfortable if you were there with me."

"I can't. Mom is expecting me at home and I'm leaving as soon as we hang up."

"Okay," she muttered dejectedly.

"Give him the benefit of the doubt, Lainey. He's a mechanical major. You'll hardly see him. It's only for one semester and it would solve a lot of problems."

Or create more problems...

"I'll try, but I'm not promising. Be careful driving home and tell your folks Merry Christmas for me."

"You bet. I'll be back in January. In the meantime, you've got my home phone number. Call me anytime."

Lainey said goodbye and hung up the phone. The cord on the wall phone had long ago been stretched out to the point it hung down to the floor. Angel liked to play with it, twisting and swatting at it. Today, it twisted in silence.

Darren walked out of the bedroom as Lainey was trying to untangle the cord.

"Are you ready to go? I'll drive if that's okay. I need to stop and fill it up on the way back."

"Sure. Let me grab my coat."

"I'll meet you at the car."

He started for the kitchen, then turned as though he forgot something.

"Got your attack cat squared away until we get back?" He teased, grinning once more.

"Very funny," she muttered. Her goosebumps were returning and she quickly put on her coat, not wanting to look at him directly. She felt her face flush.

Darn crooked smile and dimple... breathe Lainey. Remember, he's just a temporary roommate.

She walked out the back door, closed and locked it, then turned to see Darren standing in front of a brown and white Jeep waiting for her. When he saw her, he walked over to the passenger side door and opened it.

"Your taxi to the Hall, Ma'am," he said, motioning for her to get in.

She smiled instinctively, then tried to hide it as she sat down in the seat. He closed her door, walked over to the driver's side, got in, and started the engine.

"Did you buy the Jeep because it matched your dog or vice versa?" She regretted her sarcastic words as soon as they were out of her mouth.

Darren looked at her for a moment and said nothing. He backed out of the driveway, heading to the Hall.

His silence made her feel even more uncomfortable about her last comment. She looked down at her hands, squirmed a bit in the seat, then turned to face him.

"I'm sorry," she apologized. "You didn't deserve that. My mouth gets me into trouble sometimes."

He nodded but didn't answer. She looked back toward the street and they drove in silence toward the Hall. He parked in front of the sports bar and, before Lainey could open her door to get out, he spoke.

"Let me get the door for you. My mom taught me to be a gentleman."

He got out of the car and walked around to open the door for her. He extended his hand to help steady her.

"Be careful, it's icy," he said. "A guy fell here last week and broke his ankle."

She looked at him, took his hand, and smiled as she got out of the car.

"Thank you," she said as she looked into his face. She noticed his dark brown eyes and long black lashes that matched his slightly curly black hair. She stood admiring his features, still holding tightly to his hand. Their eyes met and she tingled all over.

"Do you want to go inside?" He asked, smiling at her. "Or you can keep standing here holding my hand, too." He winked.

"Oh, of course," she said awkwardly as she let go of his hand. "I'm starving all of a sudden."

The Hall Inn, or the Hall as students from SDSM&T referred to it, was a sports bar in a strip mall located down the street from the campus. The bar and grill opened in the 1960's and, in its glory days, was the place to eat, drink, and be merry.

As Rapid City grew, though, large shopping malls enticed traffic away from downtown and the once thriving hotspot had to depend on college aged customers to stay open.

Burgers, beer, pool tournaments, and, of course, wet tee shirt contests were the main activities these days. The run-down little tavern was now a dive with a sign above the entrance that simply read *Pool, Food, Beer.*

Darren opened the bar's front door for Lainey and the smell of stagnate smoke, greasy burgers, and spilled beer stung her nose. They walked slowly inside to look for a place to sit. The Hall had very dim lighting, except for the string of white Christmas lights that had been taped to the long bar on one side of the building. They found a table toward the back. Lainey sat down and heard one of the guys standing by the pool tables shout out.

"Hey, DM! We need a fourth for the pool tourney. You in?"

"No, thanks," Darren answered as he sat down across from her, noticing the frown on her face.

"Sorry about that," he said. "You don't come in here in very often, do you?"

"Not really. It smells like dirty socks all the time."

"But the greasy burgers are pretty good, and cheap!" He laughed.

"I'll give you that," she grinned. "My freshman year, the new business majors met here right after orientation. I've never seen as much beer consumed in an hour in my life."

Darren laughed loudly. "Or as much throwing up in the dorm afterward I bet!"

She nodded, laughing just as loudly. Their gazes met and for a moment, Lainey's heart pounded as if she couldn't catch her breath.

"We should talk about the roommate situation," she commented slowly, lowering her eyes from his gaze. She knew he was still looking at her face.

He took a deep breath and put his hands on the table. "I'm sorry if my arrival startled you. I thought you already knew about me and that you needed help paying the rent."

Usually she had a good sense of whether a person was telling the truth or not. She looked into his dark brown eyes.

He seems genuinely concerned. And he is handsome. Maybe Jess is right about him?

"We're closing early. What can I get for you?" The bartender snorted gruffly, obviously upset about having to wait tables in addition to his regular duties.

"Two burgers and two cokes," Darren replied. "Thanks for giving us the heads up."

The bartender nodded, then walked behind the bar to the open grill. He quickly plopped two burger patties on the grill top.

"I guess he's the chief, cook, and bottle washer, too," Lainey said smiling at Darren.

"He's a good guy. I'm surprised Amy didn't say anything about me to you."

"I didn't know she was moving out till earlier this week."

Darren looked down at the table and nodded.

"I see why you didn't have the welcome sign out for me this afternoon. I should have tried to contact you before moving in my stuff...and Brutus."

"It's okay," Lainey replied. "I've been known to speak before I think sometimes."

Darren grinned. Their eyes met once more. It was like they were in a trance. Even their breathing seemed to be in sync with each other.

"Two burgers and two cokes. You'll need to come and get 'em yourself today," shouted the bartender, bringing them both back to reality.

Darren walked over to the bar, picked up their order, and sat down. The two began to devour the burgers. They talked about classes, professors, and other generalities, but they avoided talking about the reason they were at the Hall in the first place.

"Sorry, kids, it's time to close. I've got your tickets," the bartender announced.

Darren and Lainey finished their cokes and walked over to the bar to pay.

"How much do we owe you?" Darren asked as he pulled out his wallet from his front pocket.

"Watching you two reminds me of when I brought my wife here years ago," the bartender smiled as he stood behind the bar with both hands on the counter. "We were poor college kids once, too. It's on the house. Merry Christmas."

Darren and Lainey looked at each other with wide eyes.

"Oh, we're..." Darren started to say, then looked at her as if to ask for help.

"That is so very kind of you, sir," Lainey continued. "Please, tell your wife Merry Christmas for us, won't you?"

"Sure. Now get going and don't tell your friends I'm a nice guy, okay?" the bartender replied. "I've got a reputation to uphold."

They smiled at each other.

"You bet," Darren said. "Merry Christmas and thank you."

Chapter Three

They left the Hall and were in the Jeep before either spoke.

"Thanks for helping me out," Darren said. "I didn't know what to say."

We look like a couple? Lainey grinned at the thought.

"No problem. I didn't want to hurt his feelings. He's really a sweet guy."

Darren drove to the corner gas station and filled up the car. Within a few minutes, they were back at the house on Quincy Street. He shut the car off and turned to face Lainey, who was looking straight ahead, more than likely dreading any conversation. Tension hung in the air like a heavy fog.

In silence, both got out and when Lainey reached the back door, she unlocked it. Once inside, they took off their shoes and coats and walked into the kitchen without saying a word.

Angel was sitting in the doorway to the front room as if guarding an entrance.

"I'd better let Brutus out," Darren said breaking the uncomfortable silence. He walked past Angel to the bedroom.

"Well, Angel, what are we going to do?" Lainey said softly as she picked up the cat. She walked over to the green recliner and sat down.

Brutus came waddling into the front room, wagging his tail and slobbering. He jumped up on the side of the recliner and Lainey reached down to pet him. Angel glared at the dog and dug her claws into Lainey's leg.

"Ouch! Hey, Angel," Lainey said as she winced. "Put your claws back in. He's not going to hurt you."

The cat stood up, stretched, and then turned her backside to face Lainey and Brutus.

"I guess the cat is still a bit upset that Brutus ate her food," Darren commented as he walked in front of the recliner where she sat.

"She hasn't ever had to share the house with other animals."

They looked at each other and grinned.

"I'd ask you to sit down, but Amy took her chair with her."

"I have a couple of chairs that will fit in here just fine," he said, watching for her reaction.

She said nothing. He noticed her smile was turning into a frown. He sat down on the floor beside the recliner and Brutus crawled up in his lap.

"What do you need to know about me?" Darren asked, hoping to lighten the obvious concern written all over her face.

Lainey looked at him, at Brutus, and then closed her eyes for a second.

What do I say? I can't afford not to have a roommate but...

"I'm not an ogre, you know, and Brutus is really a lovable wimp," Darren offered.

She laughed.

"I can see that. Jess said you were a nice guy. It's just..." she paused. "You *are* a guy."

A cute little crooked grin appeared on Darren's face. "Well, I can't argue that point."

"These past few years, I've worked really hard to stay focused on graduating and I'm so close to achieving that."

"Agreed. I've studied hard, too, and worked full time. It's been tough, but we only have a semester left!"

"Where do you work?"

"I'm a night janitor at the hospital. They've been good at adjusting my work hours to fit my class schedule."

"I work in the mall at Spuds and Stuff, but only part time. I'm a person who needs to spend a lot of time studying."

He nodded. "I'm surprised our paths haven't crossed before now."

"I live in the library when I'm not in class or working," she grinned. "We probably have passed each other around campus and didn't know it."

"I worked in the Miner's Shack my freshman year. Who knows, maybe I brewed your coffee."

They laughed. Then the conversation turned more serious once more.

"I didn't expect a male roommate."

Darren looked down at Brutus, sleeping on his lap. "I didn't expect to be sharing a house with a girl my senior year either. It's a bit ironic."

"Ironic? How?"

He looked at her and opened his mouth to say something, then stopped. He glanced around the room before looking at her again. He took a deep breath.

"I dated a girl last semester," he said awkwardly. "She wanted me to move in with her at the beginning of this fall semester and I said no."

Lainey blinked, realizing that her mouth was slightly open. She closed it, hoping he hadn't noticed the shock on her face.

A girlfriend, huh.

"Oh, sorry that didn't work out."

"I wasn't ready to be serious with anyone. I have plans and dreams after graduation. I don't want anything to spoil that."

She nodded in agreement.

"I think Jess had a crush on me my freshman year. I told him the same thing. Luckily, we are still friends."

"Yea, he told me that."

"Oh," she stammered. "How do you know Jess?"

"We went to high school together in Lead. We both played trumpet in band."

"You grew up in Lead?"

"No, Deadwood. The high school is in Lead."

"What do you want to do after you graduate?"

"I want to travel the world. Maybe work overseas for a while. I've been interviewing with oil companies and hope to have an offer from at least one after the new year," his eyes sparkled as he answered. "What about you?"

"I want to travel, too. I thought I would work in a business tech department somewhere, but I had an interview with a research company that sounds really interesting."

She raised her hands behind her head and said, "The first thing I am going to do is buy a red Mercedes convertible!"

Darren's eyes opened wide in surprise.

"Wow. Why a red Mercedes?"

"It's a long story concerning my first car. It was an old 1967 Camaro that would constantly break down at the most embarrassing moments. I promised myself that I'd buy a Mercedes as a reward for graduating." She sat forward in the recliner with a determined look in her eyes.

"Why red?" Darren asked, leaning his head to the left to make more room for the snoring dog in his lap.

"It's my favorite color," she grinned. "It's a color of power."

"They're expensive cars," he cautioned.

"I can't afford a new one, but even used ones will last along time. Can't you drive them for three hundred thousand miles or so?"

Angel decided to make her presence known by standing up in Lainey's lap, stretching and yawning. She jumped down, sauntered over to the sleeping Brutus and slapped the little bulldog across the nose with her claws out. Then promptly ran into the kitchen.

The unsuspecting little dog jumped a foot straight in the air and began whimpering loudly. He tried to climb up Darren's shirt and hide his hurting nose in his collar.

"Angel! Bad kitty!" Lainey scolded. She jumped out of the chair to see if the little guy was bleeding.

"Poor little Brutus," she said as she picked up the crying dog from Darren's lap. "It's okay, let's see your nose."

Brutus snuggled up to Lainey. His entire body was shaking. She began walking around the room, talking and comforting the injured pup. She looked at Darren, who was still sitting on the floor in front of the green recliner with a confused look on his face. Brutus began panting happily and he once again released his unique scent into the air. Lainey cringed and quickly walked over to Darren and handed the dog back to him.

"That's just the worst smell," she chuckled. "And I think he was grinning at me when he did it!"

"He's okay," Darren laughed. "You love animals, don't you?"

She grinned. "Guilty as charged. Siamese cats can be a bit bossy and temperamental."

He put Brutus down and stood up. He was at least six feet tall and slender. His red plaid, long sleeve shirt had a pocket on the right side that held a mechanical pencil and one black pen. His jeans were faded from wear and fit him to a tee.

Lainey's face began to flush and her whole body started to tingle. He saw her looking him over from head to toe and smiled.

"I'm in a pickle here, Lainey. I gave up my dorm room and have no other place to go right now. A couple of my friends are waiting for me to call them to bring over the little bit of furniture I have. Can we work something out?" He was standing close to her, his brown eyes searching hers for an answer.

She put her hands on her hips and let out a big breath.

How can I say no to those eyes?

"Okay. But we're not dating or anything," she said, trying to sound more confident than she felt. "We each pay half the rent and utilities and buy our own food. Agreed?"

"You bet. Sound's like a plan." He put his hand out and they shook hands.

"By the way, why did you put Brutus's kennel in my room?"

"I thought the stuffed Smurf sitting on your bed would keep him company," he replied, laughing as he walked toward the kitchen. "I'll call the guys to bring my stuff. It won't take long."

"The Smurf's name is Joe and he never smarts off!" She grinned, calling after him. "And don't snoop around in my room!"

For the next few hours, Darren and two of his friends moved in a dingy couch covered with a faded floral print, a wooden rocking chair, a hanging lamp, a twin bed and a few boxes of clothes.

Lainey stayed in her bedroom and acted as referee between Angel and Brutus. The dog would slowly inch over to the cat, sniffing and drooling. The cat would wait till he was within paws reach, then ever so casually, swat at him and growl. Brutus would let out a wimpier, falling on his stomach as if something had pulled his legs straight out from under him. Then he would slowly get up and the entire scenario repeated over and over again.

"If you will just leave her alone, she'll stop growling at you," she said, shaking her head.

"Are the kiddos getting along any better?" Darren asked as he walked into her room. "All I've got left is to unpack my clothes. Where do you put the wet towel container?"

Lainey blinked for a second before asking, "My what?"

"The wet towel container. You know, where do you put your dirty towels?"

"Oh! You mean the towel hamper," she laughed. "The bathroom is so small, I just keep a plastic laundry basket beside my bed."

"In my dorm room, I had hooks across my bed loft and hung them there. Guess I'll need to run to Walmart tomorrow for a couple of things. Come on, Brutus, you've bothered her enough for today."

He turned to walk into the front room and Brutus happily followed behind him.

It had been a long day and Lainey was exhausted. "Maybe a hot shower will help me relax," she said to Angel. "You stay in here and behave." She opened the drawer to get her pj's out. She hadn't really thought what it meant to share a house with a guy until she walked into the bathroom. The small room had a shower in the corner with the commode next to it.

On the sink, next to her toothbrush cup, was a clear plastic zipper bag. Inside, was a pack of disposable razors, a fold-up toothbrush, and travel size toothpaste.

She checked to make sure the bathroom door was locked and showered quickly. She dried off, put on her pj's, and spent more time than normal brushing her teeth. The loud crashing sound startled her, causing her to poke the back of her mouth with the toothbrush.

"Ouch," she muttered, trying to spit out the toothpaste. She opened the door to see a wide-eyed cat run past her.

Lainey hurried into the front room to see Darren, picking up the now shoeless leg lamp off the floor.

"I'm sorry," he apologized. "I was getting some water from the kitchen and the next thing I knew, Angel was chasing Brutus and he ran into the crate." He stood there, leg lamp in one hand, the broken off black shoe in the other. "I think I can fix it with electrical tape."

She raised up her hands, shrugged her shoulders, and shook her head.

"Now, what can I use for light in here?"

"Venus gives off plenty of light," he said, putting the pieces of the lamp in the green recliner. "Watch this!" He walked over to the corner of the room and picked up the hanging lamp he had moved in earlier. "Give me a hand and we'll get Venus warmed up."

She moved closer to where he was standing.

"Can you hold the cord while I hang the lamp on the hook?"

She took the gold colored chain link that surrounded a gold colored electric cord.

"What is this?" she asked, looking at the pitted chains.

"It's the power cord for the lamp," he replied, stretching to hang up the bronze lamp on the ceiling hook he had installed.

"Why do you call it Venus?"

"You'll see. Give me a little more cord."

She handed him more of the nine foot cord and watched as he carefully wrapped the cord around the hook, making sure it hung in a loop before cascading to the floor.

"Plug it in, okay?"

She nodded. She searched for the nearest electric plug and did as he had told her. When she turned back around, he was admiring the lamp.

Lainey looked at the lamp. It was a bronze color with four pillars connecting the base and the top. A pedestal seemed to be suspended in the middle. The statue of a woman pouring a vase was standing on it.

"There's no light. Do you need a bulb or something?"

He turned to her and smiled. "Nope. It needs to warm up. Keep watching."

She moved closer to the lamp to examine it. The top and bottom had roman type leaves on it, and crisscrossed between the pillars were plastic wires. She was raising her hand to touch the plastic wire when lights began to glow from them. She jerked her hand back in surprise.

As she watched, liquid started dripping down each of the lighted wires and she could hear a scratchy sound coming from the lamp. The same liquid dripped from the vase the statue was holding. She looked over at Darren.

"Venus is an oil lamp that hung in my grandmother's house for years. Hear that sound? It's a calming waterfall," he said beaming with pride. "Isn't it great?"

She looked again at the lamp and smiled. "I've never seen anything like it."

Chapter Four

THE NEXT WEEK passed by quickly with the most exciting news being the twelve inches of snow that was forecast to fall before Christmas Eve. Lainey worked extra shifts at the mall and Darren worked long hours at the hospital. The only times the new roommates interacted was in the kitchen, feeding their pets, or in the front room consoling Brutus after an unexpected Angel ambush. She wouldn't admit it to anyone, but she liked having Darren around.

"One week till Christmas," Lainey told herself, driving up to the bank to deposit her most recent paycheck. She liked saving the extra cash, but the long hours standing on her feet serving grumpy customers with crying kids was wearing her patience thin.

She left the bank, stopped to splurge on a coffee from Starbucks, and drove to the house. As she pulled in front to park, another car pulled in behind her flashing its bright lights on and off. She looked in the rearview mirror, not recognizing the car.

Who is that? Are they in trouble?

Before Lainey could get completely out of her car, a tall girl wearing a white satin colored coat with a black fur collar was standing at the back of her car.

"So, *you* are the new female in his life, huh?" The girl snarled.

"I'm sorry, but have we met?"

"I doubt seriously that we run in the same circles," the girl replied smugly. "I'm here to see Darren. He's my personal mechanic."

Judging by the sly grin on your face, I'd say he's more personal than a mechanic.

"He must still be at work. Maybe you can catch him there?"

The girl rolled her eyes. "Why he is still pushing a mop around that place, I don't know. My daddy has a great job waiting for him."

Lainey smiled and shrugged her shoulders.

The haughty girl sighed. "Well, let him know that Mandy needs him right away…and," she paused to lick her lips. "It's urgent."

The girl turned, got back into her Lexus, and drove off. Lainey locked her car and went inside.

"Well, Angel," she said aloud as she put cat food in the dish. "Mandy says it's urgent." She needed to shake off the jealous feelings that were running rampant all over her. She changed her clothes, washed the few dishes in the sink, and cleaned out the litter box.

She was in her room looking up her grades and class schedule for the next semester when Darren came home. She could hear him talking to Brutus, then both went outside. When she was sure he was back inside, she walked into the front room to give him the message.

"Hey, Lainey," he said, turning on the Venus lamp and sitting down in the wooden rocking chair. "How's work going?"

"Fine." She sat down in her green recliner. "There was a message waiting for you when I got home this afternoon."

"Oh? Was it the school?"

She shook her head no.

"The girl said it was *urgent*."

"Ah," he nodded, rocking back and forth in the chair. "You must have met Mandy."

"Yep."

Darren nodded, calculating his next words carefully.

"What is urgent this time?"

"She said you're her personal mechanic…and it was urgent."

The sarcasm in her voice gave away her true feelings and she knew. She tried to regroup without him noticing.

"I think it has to do with her car."

He nodded and leaned forward in the chair.

"I have no feelings for her," he began as he rested his elbows on his knees. "I'm good at repairing cars and fixed hers a few times. That's all it is."

Lainey nodded, wondering if she should ask about the job Mandy mentioned. She thought better of it.

"She's very pretty," she commented instead.

"She's nice, but spoiled. I'll give her a call later." After a couple of minutes of awkward silence between them, Darren got up from the chair and asked, "If you're not working tomorrow, want to come to the hospital with me? It's their annual employee Christmas breakfast. They make the best bacon and egg bake you'll ever taste!"

"I'm working in the morning. Another double shift," she lied, knowing she didn't have to be at work until after noon.

The disappointment shown on his face. "I understand. Well, I'll catch you later," he said and walked into his bedroom.

She tossed and turned all night. Visions of Mandy wearing nothing but a skimpy white fur coat and Darren standing next to her wearing nothing but boxer shorts with big red hearts all over them kept waking her up. Why hadn't she accepted his invitation to breakfast? She liked him, didn't she?

The next morning, Lainey purposely waited in her room until she knew her roommate had left for the hospital. Her counterpart at work had called in sick, so she dressed and drove to the mall around nine. She tried to follow her normal routine, but couldn't seem to concentrate. The mall hours had been extended for the holiday rush and she was exhausted when she closed the doors at 9 p.m.

It had been snowing hard for several hours and more than six inches had accumulated in the parking lot and on her car. She kept her ice scraper brush in the trunk and headed to the back of the car to get it out. She opened the trunk and leaned in to pick up the scraper. Suddenly, she felt pain in her legs and her head being slammed into the lid of the trunk.

"Do you know anyone else who needs to be called?" The ER nurse asked Darren.

"No, I've called our friend, Jess, and he will call her folks. When can I talk to her?" He'd been pacing around the waiting room for more than an hour.

"I'm sorry I can't let you back to see her yet. I can tell you, though, she's going to be okay."

He nodded and began pacing once more. After a few minutes, he saw Mandy hurrying through the ER front doors. She walked up to him, hugged him, and kissed him on the cheek.

"I don't know what happened," she gushed in an attempt to be sincere. "One minute I was leaving the mall to head over to Cindy's and the next minute, my radio stopped working. I only looked down for a second."

He pushed her away from him and searched her face for any signs of real concern.

"After all, if she had told you to call me, my radio would have been fixed, and I wouldn't have had to look down," she added arrogantly.

"You're blaming her for this?"

"No, but I did tell her it was urgent." She blinked her eyes and tried to hug him again.

He stared at her in disbelief. "You could have killed her."

She shrugged. "I wasn't going that fast and my car slid on the ice in the parking lot. She wasn't seriously hurt anyway."

Darren's temper raged and his ears turned bright red. Before he could stop himself, he shouted out angrily. "She's the kindest person and wouldn't hurt anyone. You, on the other hand, are a spoiled rich kid who I wouldn't spit on if you were on fire. You don't belong here. Get out or I'll make sure you're thrown out!"

Mandy, stunned at his outburst, started to cry. "Well! After all we've meant to each other and you dare to talk to *me* that way?" She spouted indignantly.

"Don't kid yourself. There's nothing between us. Please, just leave."

The few tears she was trying to shed dried up instantly, like sand in the hot desert.

"You're not good enough for me anyway. Keep your cheap girlfriend and your janitor job!" She threw back her head, turned, and walked out of the waiting room.

Another hour passed. Darren had stopped pacing and fallen asleep in one of the waiting room chairs. He woke up when a nurse called his name.

"Darren, she says it's okay for you to come back. She's in Room 4."

He jumped up, hurried past the reception desk, through the double doors, and pushed back the privacy curtain where Lainey lay.

Lainey gave a half grin when she saw him.

Darren walked into the room and stood by the bed. There was an IV pole on each side of the bed along with several monitors that were beeping or dinging as they checked her vitals.

"I've been so worried about you."

"I'm fine," she said weakly. "They said a car ran into me in the mall parking lot," she paused. "I have a terrible headache."

"You took a pretty hard blow when your head hit the trunk." He leaned over to get a better look at the bandage that now graced the part line in her brown hair. "Doc said it took twenty-five stitches to sew up the wound."

She grimaced. "Dad always said I was hard-headed."

He laughed. "He was right!"

"My right knee is throbbing. Did I fall on it or something?"

Darren swallowed hard. "Your knee was pushed into the bumper of your car. It looks like you have a fractured knee cap and maybe some ligament injuries."

She turned her head slowly and looked directly into his eyes.

"They are going to do surgery on it, aren't they?"

He smiled. "I think so."

"What about my car? Was it badly damaged?"

"It's not driveable, Lainey."

She frowned and a deep crease appeared between her eyebrows.

"I'm going to miss this semester, aren't I?"

He looked down and picked up her hand.

"I don't know. But, whatever happens, I'm here to make sure you get through this...and you will graduate."

It broke his heart when he saw tears start to roll down her cheeks.

"Try and get some sleep. I'm going to sit right here," his voice cracked a bit.

Lainey awoke, head pounding, and tried to sit up.

"Oh, my whole body hurts," she groaned.

Darren woke up when he heard her voice. He leaned forward and took her hand.

"Good to see your eyes open," he said gently. "Can I get you anything?"

"How long have you been here?"

"You've been sleeping for a couple of hours. The hospital let me off work to stay with you."

"What time is it? What day is it?"

"It's Saturday morning, December twenty-first," he replied and squeezed her hand.

"I've got to call work," she moaned quietly. "They'll need someone to cover for me."

Darren grinned. "Already taken care of. Old Brownstone said not to worry about working, just get better."

"Does my dad know what happened? He shouldn't try to come here. Who'll take care of Mom?"

"Jess called your Dad," he began somberly. "He told him that we would take good care of you." He paused, trying to hide the sadness in his face and eyes. "I didn't know your mom had been sick."

Jess had told Darren about her mom's long battle with cancer and of the terminal diagnosis she had been given only a week ago.

"Mom has pancreatic cancer," Lainey said sadly. "Dad retired early to stay home with her. He sits with her through the treatments, holds her head when the nausea hits..." she bit her lip to keep from crying. "They are soul mates. He can't leave her now."

Darren nodded and smiled. "He knows you are in good hands." They looked at each other. She nodded.

"There is some good news," he began trying to lift her spirits. "The doctor came by and..." he stopped, raising his eyebrows as if to coax her to ask him to finish.

"Is he a cute doctor?" She grinned, knowing what he had wanted her to say.

Darren rolled his eyes. "He's too old for you," he chuckled.

"Well, what is the good news?"

"The damage to the ligaments in your knee is not as extensive as they first thought."

She opened her mouth to speak, then rolled her eyes instead.

"So, I still have to have surgery?"

"Yes, but the recovery shouldn't be as long."

"When? Can it wait till after this semester?"

He shook his head. "Tomorrow morning."

She stared at the large bandage and ice pack that surrounded her right knee.

"I've spent thousands of hours studying, lived on peanut butter and jelly on crackers, and waited on so many crabby customers. To come so close to finishing… now," she said softly as her voice trailed off.

"Now, you'll need to learn to walk on crutches across the Quad, that's all," he said gently as he picked up her hand and kissed it.

Chapter Five
Christmas Eve, Rapid City, SD

Snow was lightly falling when Darren drove in front of the patient release doors to pick up Lainey. Her surgery had gone well and she was chomping at the bit to escape the confines of her hospital room.

"Your private limo awaits," Darren grinned as he helped her into the back seat. "It'll be easier to keep your leg straight. Lean against the door and stretch out."

She grimaced as she scooted across the backseat and tried to get settled. "Whew. I can't believe how tired I am just getting into the car."

Darren looked in the rearview mirror and grinned. "You're going to be sore for a while, but at least the nurses put a nice, red bandage on your stitches. Looks good with your hair," he grinned.

"Ha, ha," she said, touching her head, "don't make me laugh. It makes my head hurt."

It wasn't long before she realized they were not heading in the direction of the rent house on Quincy.

Maybe he's going to the store?

It wasn't until she saw him turn on to I-90 that she spoke up.

"Where are you going?"

"Why? Are you in a hurry to get somewhere?"

"No, but I thought we were going home. Angel probably doesn't know what happened to me."

"Angel is fine. So is Brutus." She could see his big brown eyes looking at her in the rearview mirror. She crossed her arms and stuck out her bottom lip to tease him.

"Okay, don't pout," he shrugged. "I thought you needed a little Maynard family Christmas cheer."

He saw the surprised look on her face and it made him smile.

"We're going to your folks house for Christmas? They don't even know me. I don't want to intrude on your family."

"Relax, Mom and Dad know all about you," he answered. "After raising three boys, Mom is looking forward to having another female in the house for a few days."

She smiled. "I won't be of much help. Sure I won't be in the way?"

"Nah. She's taken quite the liking to Angel, too."

Lainey's eyes grew wide. "Angel is at your house?"

He nodded, grinning. "Still terrorizing Brutus, as usual."

"I don't know what to say," she began, struggling to find the right words.

"That's a first!"

They laughed out loud.

"Before we get to the house, I want to show you something. Think you are up to it?" He asked.

"Sure, as long as I don't have to walk too far."

"I'll get you as close as possible."

The two drove in silence, heading down the interstate towards Deadwood. She looked up to see him taking Exit 30.

"Isn't this the exit to Sturgis?"

"Yes, it is. It's not much farther."

Anxiously, she watched as he drove, turning down street after street, finally stopping in front of a big metal building.

He turned off the car, hopped out, and opened the back door to help Lainey out, holding her up till she was somewhat steady on her crutches.

"Let me help you inside," he said.

He put his hand around her waist and she tingled all over. They stopped in front of a metal door. Darren took keys from his pocket and opened it.

"Let me help you inside, then I'll turn on the lights."

She hobbled through the door and stood blinking, trying to get her eyes to adjust to the dark.

"Don't move. It takes a minute for the lights to come on." She could hear his footsteps across the cement floor. Then she heard a click and a humming sound and dim lights from the ceiling became visible. He walked back to stand by her as the dim light grew brighter and brighter. She looked at the old cars and parts that were scattered around the building.

"Is this a car body shop?" she asked.

"The college rents this place for students to work on their project cars," he answered. "Part of our graduation requirement is to build a vehicle and make it run. We come here, trade parts, and put our book learning to good use."

"Wow. I didn't realize you had to build an entire car for your senior project."

He nodded. "Mine is over there," he motioned to the back of the building. "Close your eyes and I'll help you walk over to see it."

"Close my eyes? I'm the klutz who spilled coffee on you, remember?"

"My jeans are still stained," he joked. "I'll guide you."

They walked slowly to the back of the building.

"Okay, open your eyes," he said, keeping his hand around her waist.

Her mouth dropped open as she stared at an old, grey Mercedes.

"You're building a convertible? A Mercedes convertible?"

"Not exactly building it," he smiled, "just repairing and restoring it."

She couldn't take her eyes off the car.

"Years ago, a girl was killed when she drove this car into a tree during a snow storm. Her dad was so broken-hearted, he parked the car in his garage and let it sit."

"Almost like a shrine to his daughter, I guess," Lainey said slowly.

"Something like that."

"How did you find it?"

Darren let go of her waist and walked around the car, rubbing his hand along the sides.

"I traded for it."

She looked him squarely in the eyes.

"What did you trade?"

He moved a little bit closer to her. Her heart was beating and she felt her face flush.

"I traded the Dodge Dart I had been rebuilding for this one." He gazed intently into her eyes. "I'm going to paint it red."

She parted her lips. "Red?"

He smiled down at her, pulled her close, and whispered, "I think you'll look great in red."

the end

the NIGHTINGALE

The Nightingale
Andi Lawrencovna

There was, once, many times many years ago, a young woman who had a most beautiful sister. They had a father who was very fond of them, and wishing no ill ever befell them, he built a tower deep in the woods with only one door and only one key, and he locked his girls inside. The walls were stone and unmovable. No matter their screams or the pounding of their fists, the girls could not escape. He wept with them, but for their safety, he would not be moved to let them free.

At first, when they were still young, they did not want to flee.

The tower held everything they could ever need or desire. Paints for the walls. Books for their minds. A basket of food that never went empty and sated the hunger in their bellies each day. One girl plucked at instruments, a musician through and through with the voice of a nightingale. The other was frail and beautiful and she pined for stories of princes and jewels and adventure far beyond her humble home.

It was not long before the eldest, the beauty, could feel nothing but bitterness for the father who trapped her there.

She longed to be set free by whatever means necessary.

During the days she would sit atop the windowsill, high in the sky, staring over the tops of the trees surrounding their prison. If she jumped…but the trees were not close enough, and she had no wings with which to fly.

The tower was not as stifling for her sister who sang and played her instruments. The beauty plotted for freedom, while the singer sought only her next tune.

"Liala, come here, come and sing for me." Faraday extended her pale hand, strands of her silver-blond hair blowing around her face with the breeze from the window where she sat.

Truthfully, Lia could not argue for or against her sister's beauty. They were so different in nature and temperament. Faraday brought sunshine to their darkened walls. The rainy days were made more beautiful by a smile from her lips.

Lia longed to have that same kind of beauty, but she understood too that having beauty without any to appreciate it was a curse like no other.

She was content with her cymbals and her harp as company.

Faraday never would be.

Unlike her sister, Liala's hair was mousy brown and full of curls – unruly curls that refused to be combed into any semblance of order. As a child, she'd had a fever and the redness had never left her cheeks, staining her skin in freckles that blotched over her nose and forehead, and, if she were to ever look into a mirror, over her chest as well. She was not lithe and willowy like her sister, instead she curved and rolled. Her feet were large, and her fingers callused.

Faraday fretted at the faintest mark or perceived cut that might mar her skin.

Where Faraday raced to find every thud and knock she thought she heard, Lia shrugged off the sound and continued to sit dreamily before her instruments thinking up new tunes, knowing no one had come. Liala wore plain colors and patterns, simple, unembellished gowns, while Faraday insisted upon dresses filled with flounces and pleats with pieces of glass sewn into the hems to catch the light like diamonds.

A princess.

And her tutor…

That was what Lia laughed at in her head.

But they were sisters, and each other's only companion, and she loved Faraday dearly despite their differences.

If their father refused to let them go, then so be it.

Lia was content in her tower.

"What would you like me to sing, Faraday?" her voice was dulcet and pure. "Something romantic or about adventure? A dashing young prince, perhaps?"

Faraday did not take her gaze from the view outside the window, a finger twirling idly in her hair as she thought or mused or dreamed of life outside far below. "I should like, I think, to hear of princes from far off lands rescuing damsels in high towers."

There was no song like that to Lia's knowledge, but part of the game was making them up.

"Let's see," she thought, for a moment, and then began to sing.

Her voice filled the small tower room, reaching high into nooks and crannies. It danced on waves of notes, each more perfect than the last, a song about a handsome youth traveling alone down a road until he saw, from the corner of his eye, a glint of silver flying high above his head.

He caught at the fly-away hair, drew it close to his face to catch the scent on the strand.

It was a scent that spoke of high climbs and soaring trees.

The scent was so alluring that he could not get the smell out of his head, his nose following the path that would lead him to the vixen whose hair he'd caught.

A beautiful vixen, he was sure, but where could she have come from?

Lia's voice spun the song into a spell, the forest surrounding their little tower growing silent to listen to the words.

Would the prince find his maiden? Was she worthy to be found if he did?

The branches in the trees waved in the wind, trying to come closer, trying to catch the words to her song before any brother-creature might hear them so they could claim to be first...

"Hello? Hello up there?"

Lia's voice caught in her throat.

Faraday jumped so high in surprise she nearly fell from her window perch to the ground.

She slipped to her knees beside the windowsill and hung her head from the opening, leaning as far out as she dared to see. A hand reached back, and Lia grasped for it, holding her sister who leaned further abroad.

"Hello?" Faraday shouted back.

Lia tried to see over her sister's head, but the angle was wrong and all she spied from the opening were the tops of trees, motionless, despite the breeze, waiting to see what happened in the tower they guarded.

Better than any song, Lia thought she heard the branches whisper.

A blush climbed over her patterned skin, knowing dreams were never as good as reality.

"Oh, maiden fair! Come down from there. I would greet thee."

Faraday's fingers clenched around Lia's, the shock of pain spiraling through Liala's arm as her fingers ground together.

"Sweet prince, alas, I cannot. I am held high in this tower unable to descend."

Well now, that wasn't quite true! They could descend quite easily, the stairs well preserved after all.

They just could not leave...

But Lia kept the words to herself.

"But there must be a way! I cannot leave without looking upon your face. It would break my heart in two!"

The compliment caused another squeezing of Lia's hand.

She desperately wanted to pull her sister back from the window so she could sneak a peek of their visitor, but it was Faraday's dream to be rescued, not hers, and so she kept her sister from falling out the opening instead of trying to trade places.

"My father locked me here. Only he has the key. There is no other way to free me."

"When does your father come?"

"Each morn when the sun rises, and each night as it sets."

The excitement in Faraday's voice was punctuated with the kicking of her tiny feet on the stone floor of their room.

A moment of apprehension filled Lia.

If the man, prince, groom, whatever he was, confronted their father, what would happen to the man? Either man. She didn't want her father injured, nor did she want this stranger who was so fresh and new hurt either.

"I will wait for him then, and I will free you from your prison!"

But what would freedom mean?

For twenty years or more they had known no other life than their tower. The thought of leaving it was at once terrifying, and a bit exhilarating.

Faraday squealed with delight and the man below laughed at her reaction. "You are my hero, fair sir. Might I have a name to call you by?"

"Cabal, my lady. And you, might I not know your name as well?"

"I am the Princess Faraday. But you may call me Fara."

Lia frowned at her sister's reply.

"Fara" hated nicknames, eschewed every one that Lia had ever tried to give her sister.

And neither she nor Lia were princesses by any stretch of the imagination, though the story sounded better to claim to be thus than anything else.

"I shall free you, Princess. On my oath!"

To which Faraday pressed her free palm to her lips and blew a kiss to the prince down below.

THE HOURS PASSED slowly, prince and princess yelling to one another from their resting places, speaking of dreams and wishes and their lives spent wandering or trapped, respectively.

Not once was Lia mentioned.

She busied herself instead with sweeping the lingering cobwebs from the corners of their tower room. They had taken amiss to housekeeping when it was clear no one would ever come to visit them here.

She swept the bedroom, and the parlor, the room that held her instruments, and the room with old paints, drying from disuse. That her dress was mussed with dirt and her hair hung heavy with dust meant little to her. It was as it was meant to be.

When the sun began its descent, Faraday scrambled from her place at the window and pulled at Lia's arm to drag them into their dressing room.

A simple tunic dress would never suit to meet a suitor, after all!

So Lia helped her sister change into a gown of white-gold silk.

And when the stays were pulled tight and the corset laced to within an inch of its life, Faraday giggled with glee and flounced from the chamber, pulling the door closed tight behind her.

Lia shook her head, not surprised that her sister might have left her behind.

She twisted the handle in her fingers and pulled, only to find her way locked.

The door had never locked before.

She twisted harder, thinking that, in Faraday's excitement, she'd slammed the door and jammed it, but the wood would not budge, and Lia could not leave the space.

Like the walls of the tower, the wood was thick, and no amount of pounding could be heard outside her room.

Years spent resigning herself to solitude fled until all she knew was the fear of being locked away forever, the fear that had so petrified Faraday her whole life.

"Please don't leave me here," she cried, but no one listened.

If her father came, surely he would notice she was missing and find her.

But she did not know what Faraday's prince intended against her father, and she feared what would become of them all.

Through the small slat of a window in the room, Lia watched the last rays of light fade from the sky and darkness consume the world. She stared at that gash carved into the stone until the sun rose again and night became day.

No one came for her.

The room grew cold without a fire to heat the stones.

She had no bed to rest her head upon, and Faraday's fancy frills served only to scratch at her skin when she laid on them to try and sleep.

Her tears wet her rags, and her voice broke with a sob.

Lia lost track of days, until she knew only that she would end hers here in this place, never knowing what it was to walk the world beyond its walls.

Weak with hunger and thirst, she forced herself to stand and stumble to the window.

She could see the sky, bright and blue, up above.

No tree could reach as high.

"Oh sweet clouds, so white and pure, send me a drop of water to wet my tongue."

Send me a storm to batter apart these stones.

Send me a savior to free me.

She sang a tuneless dirge, a last farewell.

Her voice, cracked and frail, called out into the woods a song of goodbye.

Lia did not expect an answer. She especially did not expect an answer in the form of a nightingale winging its way through the tiny opening and perching itself on the top edge of the mirror in the room.

It cocked its tiny head towards her, brown feathers lying flat and sure along its back.

Her lips split in a small smile, offering friendship to the tiny creature, though only for a moment or two more.

"I will help you, maiden, to shed these walls."

What was more shocking: a bird that could speak, or that the small beastie could set her free?

Her eyes widened but before she could respond, the nightingale took to the air and swooped close over Lia's head.

She ducked in fear, never having been assaulted by a bird before.

A pluck, and a yap, and she uncrossed her arms from over her head to watch the nightingale swallow a strand of her brown hair.

"But what—"

The world around her began to shrink.

No, she began to shrink, but she begged her senses to be wrong, that she be faint instead of magically transformed. Stone floors came up to catch her and she reached out her hands to stop her fall only to shriek in fear when she realized she had no fingers to catch herself with, and where skin had been now feathers formed.

Her shriek became a squawk, and then a caw, then a chirp.

Small taloned toes replaced her feet.

She was human no more.

"But now you are free."

THE NIGHTINGALE FLEW far from the tower that was her home. It took her a day to understand the use of her wings, and an hour more before she could catch the winds that took her into the air to glide away.

No one remained at the tower. Not her father, not her sister, nor the prince come to save Faraday.

She was alone and it was without choice.

Her wings carried her into the forest where she found a branch to rest upon.

The leaves where so much darker here, deep within the wood. Light did not shine upon the ground in great waves but was dappled from the branches overhead. Like a great curtain, the trees shaded the world and cast it in silence beneath the canopy.

She shuffled on her branch, chirped once to hear the sound.

The shaking of the leaves from the wind stilled to listen.

Her tiny head twisted left then right.

All round her was quiet and waiting.

She drew in a deep breath, her chest expanding with air, and then she began to sing.

A nightingale sings at dawn's break across the sky. At night to catch a mate. She sang to sing, not caring of the time of day, following only the sorrow in her heart, a keening dirge for all she'd lost and all that had been taken from her. What was this form she was cast within? This being she did not know? Gone was the girl of dress and cowl, to feathered wing held low.

The branches of the trees dipped low in mourning. Below, where the grass stood straight and tall, the stalks drooped and curled in upon themselves. Dew formed as flowers' tears, and she sang on.

A rustling of leaves and twigs beat in counterpoint to her tune.

As Faraday's savior came from out the woods, so now a man strode through them.

His gaze roamed over the lowest branches, but she was so engrossed in her song that she did not see him staring at her.

Her voice grew hoarse with the force of her tune, fading though the words would not stop.

From below, the mellow strains from a lute rose to bolster her song.

Where hers was one of sorrow and regret, the lute wove in notes of hope, of pleasure.

Slowly, not daring to intrude, still following the song of the nightingale's lead, the lute began to change the melody to offer light through the darkness.

When her voice faded to whispers in the wood, the lute continued on to bring the song to a close.

She looked down and caught the eye of the man, instrument held in hand, staring up at her.

"Your voice is like none other, Lady Nightingale. It has been the greatest of honors to play with you this day." He bowed low to her, the lute swept out to his side, his knee bending to the dirt in homage of her skill.

Her feathers rustled. Her wings twitched.

There was a mulberry bush butted up against the trunk of an oak tree. The leafy shrub offered a sound perch for her small body to rest upon, and so she spread her wings and spiraled from her post in the branches to a place eye level with the man.

He opened his emerald eyes to watch her fly.

A light came to his face when he realized she was not flying away but towards, and she nearly floundered when he put his instrument on the ground, stepped hastily to a pack she'd not noticed before and drew from its innards a waterskin and bowl.

"You must be parched. Here. It's fresh. From the stream just yonder." He spoke quickly, a fear that she might fly away underlying his words.

The bowl in his hands sloshed when he reached out to her. A drop of water wet her beak, landed on her wing.

His face blanched.

"Oh gods, I'm so sor—"

She spread her feathers, shook to dash the water away, resettled her wings across her back.

"Please don't leave."

A tip of her head to the side, then she looked down at the bowl he'd let drop, its water pouring out onto the ground. She looked back at him, at the skin of water.

"Oh, oh, I'm sorry. Here," and he poured her another drink.

It was cool and refreshing, wetting her in a delicious wave of liquid salvation. She dipped her beak again and again into the bowl until temptation grew too much and she hopped into the container and splashed her wings in the wet to cool off.

He shifted his grip on the copper to hold it steady for her.

She chirped and there was pleasure in the sound. Her wings fluttered, spraying droplets everywhere. If a beak could affect a smile, then she smiled.

"You are amazing, lady. I have never met a nightingale like you."

"But I'm not a nightingale."

He blinked uncomprehendingly at her.

"I'm," she floundered, unsure what to say since she didn't know what the truth was herself. "I was a girl. I lived in a tower with my sister, but she left me...she left me there, alone. I was going to die there."

And instead I turned into a bird.

She knew how absurd it sounded, stopped the words from leaving her mouth.

He looked at her, this stranger, considering her words to the facts.

For some reason, he didn't call her crazy, which was crazy in itself. He stared at her, considering at her wings and the bird's feet she stood upon.

She'd looked in the mirror.

She knew that all semblance of the woman she'd been was hidden within the body of the bird; there was nothing of her true self that he could see with his eyes.

"That was part of your song, no? That's why you're so sad."

"Yes."

He reached out, as though to touch her, and she hopped back in the bowl, hit the side and nearly tumbled from her place, her wings spreading in automatic reaction, not knowing if she should fly away or remain.

His lips parted, the pink flushing his cheeks again. "I'm sorry. I didn't mean anything by it." He extended his hand, palm out.

She tentatively hopped onto it.

He didn't threaten to close his fingers around and cage her. "You are extraordinary, and your song is," he shrugged, the motion raising her with the movement of his palm. "Your song is enchanting, much as you are enchanted, I think?"

The nightingale who came to her had said nothing of enchantment, and yet, what else could it be?

A bird cannot shrug as a human can.

The pause in lieu of a gesture was understood regardless.

"I would help you lift your curse, but I am traveling to the castle. The king has chosen a bride and I am going to perform at the wedding." There was true regret in his words, a longing to stay that the world demanded he deny. She saw it in the strain around his mouth, the harsh line of his lips. "I have heard she is a beautiful queen, but cold. A beauty, it is said, but no love."

"Then why go?"

The minstrel looked at his lute lying forgotten at his side. "Because it is my job, and I love to sing, and sometimes song can bring love where frozen hearts abide."

She'd always thought the same, but then she'd had nothing else to wile away her time, and music was the only love she'd had besides her sister.

The nightingale nodded in agreement with the minstrel. "What is your name, sir?"

"Philomel, my lady. And you?"

The answer was on the tip of her tongue, yet she couldn't speak it. Her throat tightened and her air caught with even the thought of trying. All she could say was: "Nightingale will suffice."

His eyes widened at having witnessed her struggle, but then he bowed his head in understanding. "Part of the spell, I would imagine, that keeps you in this form."

Her bird-head tipped to the side to stare at him.

She'd lived a life apart, granted, but still, even she did not believe in magic...until that magic was an undisputed fact she was faced with.

"A talking bird who sings with the voice of an angel can only be magic."

Never before had she seen a smile like that directed at her. She'd heard it in Faraday's suitor's voice, the man outside the window who destroyed the nightingale's peace.

To see it in truth, was something astonishing. The warmth of the curve of lips, eyes bright with emotion, the beginning of caring shining forth from within a kind soul. He looked at her like she never thought a man would look at her, and she was not a woman who could accept it anymore.

That knowledge didn't stop the speeding patter of her heart race that much faster in her breast. Her wings fluttered, ruffled, then shook and then settled.

If she were still human, she would be blushing. As it was, she could not stop the chirp-cackle that escaped, undignified, from her beak.

He chuckled at her response, and she shook, not sure she was ready to be laughed at by a stranger.

"You seem so human, even as you look like a bird." He laughed again and shook his head. "Amazing."

She settled.

The laughter not at her but at life, her tragic, terrifying life.

"The castle. And the king. You said you were to perform at his wedding?"

"A surprise bride, I'm told. And I go where there is money to make the playing worthwhile, when playing is the only way to earn a coin for bread and wine."

She'd not thought of food. Her stomach not aching for the same though the mention of bread made hunger flare brightly.

Could she have sang to make her way in the world? The tower was always filled with whatever she needed, she'd never had to think of the same before now.

"You sing for a living."

His eyes darted to his instrument, his smile shifting to a more joking expression, joyful for his art. "And play."

"And play," she responded in kind, eyes following his to the strings she would never have a chance to pluck without fingers to ply upon them. "Your lute is quite fine. I never had one so nice, made do with what my father brought me to play."

"How did you learn?"

Small, short chirps burst from her beak. A bird's imitation of a laugh. "I never *learned* as you learned. I guessed, and I played, and what came out sounding nicely I repeated again and again."

"You do not know your scales?"

"What's a scale?"

"Notes? Clefs?"

She shook her head: "No."

His smile brightened and he seemed to look around him, for what, she didn't know.

After a moment, he took the bowl back in both hands and gently lowered it and her to the ground. She watched from far below as he stood and went rooting back in his pack for a bundle of papers which he laid on the ground before her and then picked up his lute.

"Here, I can show you."

"I have no fingers, Sir Singer."

"But would you like to learn?"

If she were human, she would have bitten her lip in indecision. "Do you not have to be on your way to the queen?"

It was not sadness that dimmed his smile, but something else, something darker, no, deeper. "I think, if it is not too impertinent to say the same, that I would rather spend my time with you. And I have until tomorrow to make myself known. For a moment, I can steal a little time for myself."

He looked at her the way she imagined Faraday's prince looked at Faraday.

It was a look meant for lovers, or two who might someday fall to the same, not of a man to an enchanted bird.

"What are you?" she asked, for surely no human would pass up a chance at meeting royalty for a bird in a forest, magic or no.

The soft smile returned to his lips, his eyes meeting her without any hint of a lie in his stare. "A minstrel," he said. "The Minstrel Philomel. But everyone just calls me Phil."

A lifetime passed between them, sitting and standing there on the dirt in the middle of a forest she had no name for, and he'd been wandering through without concern when he heard her song. He taught her the different notes on a scale. She watched his fingers pluck out the same on his lute. The instrument was meant for hard use, and he told her to follow with her beak, and she tried, truly, but the test was too much. It was easier, instead, to use her beak to hold down the strings and pluck at the same with her toes, her wings fluttering to hold her aloft just above the wires so the notes burst out strong and true.

Her song was beautiful, even if she didn't sing, but that would never do, he said, and took away the instrument so that she could use her voice while he played. His fingers made the notes soar, but not as high as her song did, her wings a weak thing compared to the purity of her tone.

"Would you come with me? To the wedding. Sing with me for the queen?"

"I'm just a nightingale, Phil."

"A nightingale can change the world, if her voice is strong enough to be heard. She can change a life, if she tries."

"Whose life am I supposed to change?"

He extended his hand for her to hop onto his palm. "Should we go find out?"

THE COURT OF the Queen.

She wasn't even crowned yet, but already the people of the country were calling it the Court of the Queen. Everyone crowded the streets the day she rode to the castle on the prince's horse and saw her face, arresting in its beauty. Hair of gilt, skin of porcelain, she was delicate and dainty and all who saw her fell madly in love.

How could they not?

Beauty was, after all, the greatest gift.

They reached the steps of the palace where the prince dismounted first and then assisted his bride-to-be from the saddle.

He carried the head of the wizard who had trapped the fair maiden in her tower in one hand and took her arm in the other to escort her to where his father waited at the top of the steps.

She bowed her head demurely while he strode forward to present his bounty to the king.

A wave of the lord's hand was all it took for her to rise and meet the man's gaze.

The man – a king…better by far than a prince who ruled nothing until his father's end.

And she was the fairest in the land.

"I ask your blessing to marry the Lady Faraday," the prince begged with a smile, expecting his father's generous reply.

"No." He replied, his gaze caught on the sapphire stare matching his own. "I have been without a queen too long and shall take this maiden as my own."

A king was far better than a prince could ever be, and she graciously accepted the arm extended towards her that brought her to the monarch's side to be crowned beside him.

"We must hold a celebration of my nuptials!"

And while the prince wept, the people smiled and danced with joy for they too would celebrate with their liege that the fairest lady in the land was theirs to stay.

"I would have jewels sewn into my gown and lace for my veil."
"Of course, your majesty."
"And the best minstrels to sing me down the aisle."
"Yes, my lady."
"How do I look?"
"Beautiful, my queen."

THE NIGHTINGALE SAT on Phil's shoulder.

Townsfolk stared at them as they passed, some laughing at the man wearing a bird as an accessory, others whispering that it was magic that kept the creature there without a tether around its foot.

The man raised a hand and the bird pecked at the seed he offered it.

How quaint.

"Is there an inn near the castle? I'm to sing at the feast and would like to rest before the evening's festivities."

The nightingale chirped agreeably, fluttering her wings in gentle commiseration.

The fishmonger's wife smiled at the tiny bird's antics, unable to deny the sweet creature of the man who carried her an answer. Her usually gruff and cruel voice mellowed in her response, "Down the street and two to the left. *The Honorable Cat*, it's called. You can't miss it, a big tabby on the sign."

"The Honorable...*Cat*?"

A chittering sound came from the nightingale.

The minstrel laughed in response. "I don't suppose there's a house less inclined to dining on my friend around, is there?"

THE HONORABLE CAT did indeed boast an orange tabby on its signage hung over a pole at the front door. It was neither a palace nor a hostel, but somewhere in between, in good repair, but not a rich establishment. From outside, the sound of men laughing in the tavern and hollering about could be heard. Firelight lit the tiny pub, illuminating the people inside, capering and enjoying themselves.

Though she could not eat the food, she could smell it, and it smelled divine.

"Roasted pork loin, if I had to guess. One of my favorite foods of its form."

There was chicken and venison that her father put in his basket each night, but she couldn't remember if she'd had pork loin before. If she had a mouth still, it would slather at the desire to taste the food. Instead, she kept to chirping, hiding her voice until the ceremony when Phil invited her to sing.

What a spectacle we'll cause!

She wasn't sure a spectacle was what she was after, but his excitement filled her, and she allowed herself to be uplifted by it.

A burly man with a red and white splotched beard opened the door before Phil could knock.

"What have we here? Mary! Mary, come and see! This one's got a bird on his shoulder."

"A bird, exactly, my faithful companion."

She looked to catch a glimpse of Phil's smile though her stare could not be fully turned from the view inside the tavern.

So many people gathered in one place, bustling around. Women wore dresses similar to those that she'd worn ages ago. Men dressed in trous and tights and paunchy split skirts with jackets that clutched too tightly to their stomachs. A boy-child ran around covered in soot, a pail in his hand overflowing with black dust, a bucket in the other near empty of wood for the fire.

"You'll be needing a room then, for the week I gather, considering all the events her majesty's planned for her coronation?"

"Just the night should be fine. We'll only be here for tomorrow."

"To sing for the bonny-miss's wedding then? She'll be a right beautiful queen. Saw her when she rode through the city with the princeling. Platinum hair hanging in silken waves down her back. Never seen one so pretty before."

"So I've heard tale. But beauty is such a small thing in our world, I'd rather—"

"Not for a king, mind!" The burly man laughed at his interruption.

Not that it mattered to the nightingale.

A woman with platinum hair?

Her feet tightened on Phil's shoulder. She twisted around, hiding herself in his darkly tangled hair so that none would see her face and the tears she cried.

The world was wide, that she could not deny, but how many maidens of beauty untold with hair a rich platinum could there be? How far could Faraday have travelled from their tower home in so few days between them? Who else could the maiden be?

Abandoned to death by the sister she loved…and for what?

A castle was just another gilded cage.

Even she who had never sought to leave could see the same.

It was lunacy to marry a man she didn't know, one who hadn't even been there to rescue her!

Her wings rustled his dark tresses.

Who was she to speak of freedom when she had the chance to flee herself and would not spread her wings to fly?

Her minstrel sang for the coin it paid and the safety that coin provided.

But her sister…her Sister!

"What a beautiful bird."

"A nightingale, lady, not a bird at all. And wait until you hear her sing."

How could she sing now, with her heart remembering only the pain of her loss? Tears threatened to stifle her voice, but she could not cry here.

Phil walked forward, and she pressed her small body against the side of his throat, nesting where it was safe and secure, hidden from sight by the stranger she inexplicably trusted with her life. For all she did not know him, she knew enough to say with certainty that he would not cage her, would only ever do what he could to help her fly.

Hadn't he said as much?

Had he wings, they could soar together.

His hands came and gently cupped around her form, drawing her from the nest of his hair, holding her in his palms before his face. He stared at her, and she knew he saw the beaded tears in her gaze.

No words were spoken. Compassion kept him silent.

He did not need her to speak her truths aloud to be able to guess at them.

"We need not sing tomorrow."

But they did.

Singing was his life, and it had always been hers too. Her song would herald truths tomorrow, and perhaps her sister would remember the nightingale she'd forgotten.

"I will be able to. How many chances does one have to sing before a king, after all?" The joke fell flat in her bird voice.

He did not dignify it by offering a laugh with her.

Three fingers ran from the crown of her head to her tail feathers, soft, comforting in their touch.

She closed her eyes, unable to look at the pensive expression on his face, far too caring for her own peace of mind, offering things she could no longer hope for, if she'd ever thought to hope for them before in her life.

"It is not about being able, my lady, but being well. This has hurt you, learning who it is who is to become queen. I will not ask this of you. You need not suffer it."

"I would have her see me. What I have become. As I would see what she has in turn."

He bent his head forward, and she moved to match it, the crest of her feathers tickling at his brow in the only touch they were allowed.

If he were a bird, he would fly with her; if she were human, she would run to him.

"Thank you, Philomel, for your kindness."

"Kindness, yes. It is how we all should treat each other, with kindness and love."

How she wished it was more than just decency that moved his emotions, more than a good, clear conscious that demanded his actions.

She stretched her wings and took flight from his hands.

The warm air of the room, heated by the fire, created a thermal for her to rise on. Enclosed and inescapable, she did not fear this place as a prison, confident that if she asked, he would open the window for her to flee.

A beam overhead served as a safe perch to rest upon.

She watched him settle his satchel on the ground, uncover his lute and fiddle with the strings until cords notes were tuned.

His fingers were sure turning the knobs. He stretched his hands before plucking out chords on the instrument, the precursor to a song she'd not yet heard him play. The melody was slow and dark. Though she'd never flown a stormy sky, the tune conjured the same in her mind. Nights spent watching lighting dance from cloud to cloud while rain fell against the windowpane, distorting the world beyond into a fantasy come to life. His melody danced in the downpour, skipped through puddles. Almost she could feel the droplets alighting on her skin and feathers. The storm spun about her in a great wind, yet she was not afraid to fly so high with so little control. A single, solitary note played against the melody, a line to follow back to earth and the safety of the man waiting to catch her below.

The song drifted to a close, the pattering of a spring shower fading to the dawning light.

Her eyes opened and she looked down from her perch to the minstrel staring up at her.

He offered a small smile at the bow of her head in gratitude. "Sweet dreams, Lady Nightingale."

"And to you, Lord Philomel. It is my honor to accompany you."

Wherever fate led him, she found she would follow.

THE SUN HID behind clouds the next morning. Nobles claimed it was ashamed to be pitted against the beauty of the queen, and so the sun dared not show its face when Faraday was crowned. If the rain came in the afternoon, it would be because the sun wept to never match the lady's elegance, so certain they were that her beauty was great than anything else in their world.

They rode in silk clad carriages to the castle where grooms took their horses to be stabled for the day. The gowns and doublets were brightly colored silks and velvets, the most expensive they could buy, all to try and catch the queen's eye as she had caught theirs.

The walls were decorated in satins of deepest burgundy and darkest blue.

Liveried servants waited at the bend of each corridor to pass flutes of sparkling drink to the guests for their delight.

The nightingale and Phil were forced through the back passages to reach the throne room unseen by the wealthier patrons of the day. They were hurried and pressed to be silent. Once, they were even shoved into an alcove so that the nobles who passed them would not be sullied by common filth – a working man and a pest.

When they reached the throne room, men and women were already standing at the walls, waiting for the ceremony to begin.

They were forced to scoot behind the lords and ladies like mice scurrying from a cat.

The dais was arranged with one grand chair and a second of lesser beauty placed slightly behind it. The cushions here were covered in golden fabric, bejeweled with the image of a rose, stuffed so full that they looked like clouds waiting for their king and queen to sit upon them. Silks hung in banners from the ceiling and twined around the pillars. There were no flowers, for the queen disdained the same, the jewel that she would wear as her crown would be decoration enough.

Unlike the royals, Philomel's stool had no covering, bare wood more suited for a dairy maid before a cow than a minstrel about to sing for a king.

Phil settled himself on his seat, and the nightingale flew to the sill of the high stained-glass window overhead.

The arched ceiling would carry her song throughout the hall.

Peasant and noble would hear her tune; none would be able to miss it.

The king entered and the room grew silent, parting from the middle to make an aisle for him to walk down to reach his throne. As one, the noble-folk turned to the far end to wait for his queen to enter.

The great doors opened wide.

The nightingale's chest expanded on an inhale.

Golden light filled the entrance and Faraday stepped into the hall.

The nightingale exhaled on a single, solemn note, long and pure and unwavering.

All heads turned towards the crisp, clear voice coming from the rafters. All heads, including the queen's and the king's and the prince's whose mouth fell open in shock, his eyes darting to the woman whose song he thought he'd saved, whose face was pale and eyes horror filled.

The nightingale sang the next note, and like magic, Faraday's foot stepped forward, her body forced towards the dais and the king waiting there. Her eyes could not leave the small bird holding so still not even a feather fluttered high overhead, only the song she sang mattering.

Notes turned into words, the dirge telling the tale of sisters beloved and betrayed. One who shown with beauty like the sun, the other who sang like a nightingale to the dawn.

The nightingale sang of a sister's wish for freedom from the tower that caged her. She sang of a song that became a call to a noble heart wandering near. Of a promise of salvation and the fluttering souls of dreams finally coming true.

Her song told of the savior who came, but sought only one sister, and the other left behind without reason. Left to die, forgotten.

A sister's love betrayed.

For what? For what? To become a queen who—

"Kill it! Somebody kill it!" Faraday screamed. "Make it stop!"

A fan went sailing through the air, torn from a noblewoman's hand by her husband who heard the order of the queen and sought to stop the bird from singing.

The nightingale leapt from her perch on the windowsill and rose into the rafters of the hall. She flew around the pillars, between the arches that formed the aisles and nave of the great room. A moment of rest was all she could spare, her feet clutching at the harsh stone beams before she took to the air once more.

All the while singing.

Singing.

Where was their father? Who loved them so? Where was the tower to protect them from foe? How can it protect thee when the betrayer lies within? What safety is left when a new life must begin?

She beat her wings to raise her higher, high into the sky, nearly to the top of the great hall, far from the reach of fans, and books, and rocks…

It clipped her wing.

The sharp stone struck her mid-downbeat and the shock of it tore through her body, paralyzing her midflight.

Her feathers refused to answer to her call, pulled tight to her body for protection that wouldn't matter when the ground rose up to meet her from below.

She caught Faraday's eyes, her sister smiling madly as the nightingale tumbled through the air.

What had she done to deserve that reaction?

She would never have tried to take Faraday's prince.

A hand batted at her. She was tossed forward, bumped against a head, then a shoulder, jostled by a knee. The ground was the least shattering of her collisions. The foot that rose above her would be the worst.

Wood and strings broke in a crack of sound that deafened the hall.

The remains of the lute shattered around her fallen form before the minstrel reached and picked her up, his instrument abandoned in saving her.

Philomel cradled her in his hands, close to his chest.

The crowd parted around them. Men and women held their breath.

She gasped in his hands. Her chest ached with every inhale. Her wings would not open with a thought. She'd thought to die alone would be the worst, but this was an agony all new.

A small part of her had hoped that her sister would hear the song and deny it, call for the nightingale to come home, that it was all a misunderstanding, the nightingale mistaken.

But Faraday demanded the nightingale's death.

That truth was worse than the song she'd sung.

Knights pushed through the crowd to surround the minstrel and his bounty. They made a path so that the queen-to-be could step into the circle, so that the king had an unimpeded view from where he sat in his throne, watching the proceedings, face impassive, eyes filled with a greed the nightingale could not understand.

Her small head turned from the man to the prince at his father's side, the boy looking at Faraday and to the bird, confusion in his eyes.

"How could you do this to me? How could you ruin this for me like you ruin everything in my life!"

Faraday reached to grab the bird from the minstrel's hands. Philomel tried to turn away only to be caught by the soldiers surrounding him, holding him still for their lady's demands.

He brought the nightingale to his breast, tried to shelter her there.

The queen motioned with her hand, and his arms were pulled apart, the poor bird trying to spread her wings to fly before she fell to the ground once more.

"I am the beautiful one. I am to be queen. Not you. You and your stupid song!"

"Wait!"

Faraday paused, her heeled foot raised over the bird panting on the ground.

The king stood. He walked down the steps of his dais and moved to stand beside his queen-to-be. "Who is this bird you hate so much, my darling? What has she done to you?"

There was no caring in the king's voice. He was amused by this show, nothing more. Intrigued, perhaps, but not about the uncrowned-queen. For the woman he would call wife, he felt nothing.

But for the nightingale...

"No one. She is nothing to me."

He bent forward, the crowd gasping at the act of a king bending down before a nightingale of all things. His hand hovered over the tiny creature. "Such a captivating bird. Have you ever heard a song like this before?"

The words were spoken to himself, thought given voice, not seeking an answer.

"I have heard it. Sung from a tower. The tower I rescued the princess from."

Faraday choked in a breath. The nightingale stuttered in the king's hands.

"But, son, you told me the lady fair had the voice of an angel that called you there."

The prince stepped forward, in his eyes a gleam that was cruel as Faraday's denouncement when she chose his father over him. "I thought she did. But she refused to sing for me again. And when asked, said nary another soul lived in the tower but herself."

"She lied."

"Apparently so."

"Then who is this?"

"A nightingale, nothing more." Faraday clutched the king's wrists, "She's just a bird. A silly bird."

"An enchanted bird."

Both king and queen-to-be turned their heads towards the minstrel in their midst. The prince placed one hand on his sword but did not pull the blade free.

"What do you mean, minstrel? What enchantment is this?"

Faraday's fingers tightened about the king's wrists. "Nothing. No enchantment, my king."

"Be silent, witch!" One hand clutched at the weeping nightingale. The other the king used to strike his bride. "Another word, and I'll have your head."

The mob did not like this, but the guards drew their swords, loyalty to king trumping beauty of the queen.

The king turned to the minstrel. "An enchanted bird?"

"How else could she sing like that? Legend says the nightingale king will come to those whose song calls him to be set free."

The nightingale picked up her head to stare at the minstrel spewing his story.

"All songbirds caged are under his care."

"But she is not a songbird, is she?"

"There is a way to find out."

The nightingale did not have the strength to ask what Phil was doing. What purpose could his lies have in saving her? He should run before her sister regained control of the king, or before the king took Phil at his word and demanded the magic be revealed and Philomel was left standing unable to appease the king.

"How?"

Do not answer, Phil!

"The one who trapped the songbird must release her."

Faraday laughed, sharp and cold. "The bird is free. Free to die just like any other creature too weak to survive on its own." She lunged forward but the prince pulled her away from bird and father.

"How?" the king asked again.

"A drop of heart's blood offered freely."

"I will not die for her!"

"For who, my dear?"

The beauty paled at being so called out. "No...no one, my king."

He smiled his cold, cruel smile. Beauty only went skin deep in this one. Not that he much cared, he knew the worth of beauty. He knew the worth too of magic, and in the end, magic meant more to a king than a pretty bride. "You lie."

The bird dropped to the floor, forgotten for the moment while he dealt with his bride-to-be, the only one who could unsummon that magic that bound her sister to the nightingale's form. "Guards, take her!"

"Let not the king hurt me!" Faraday cried in response.

To prove his worth, the prince drew his sword to defend the queen.

And Philomel lunged to save the nightingale lying silent on the floor.

THE HALL ERUPTED in shouts and screams. Ladies ran for corners where fighting men could not strike them. Men drew blades and clashed steel against steel to defend the cries of the queen. Guards battled back instinct to obey their king.

Rain let loose in a deluge outside the walls, blanketing the world in a steady downpour. Thunder crashed and lighting struck in blinding lines across the sky.

"Kill that bird!" "Stop the queen."

The calls sounded above the din.

The nightingale drew as deep a breath as she could.

The minstrel, trying to hide in the melee, forgot about the queen.

She who stole the bird from his hand...and squeezed.

"This kingdom is mine!" Faraday shouted at her sister.

The king sidestepped his son's attack, exposing the queen holding the nightingale behind him.

Mid-lunge, the prince could not stop; his blade pierced deep into Faraday's breast.

The hall went silent.

Philomel caught the uncrowned-queen, her gasping breaths the only sound to be heard, and lowered her to the ground, her head in his lap. Her hand hung limply at her side, the nightingale gasping with as much struggle as the bride. Phil reached over his burden and unclenched the woman's fingers from the bird. He gently lifted the poor creature to the lady's breast, the red of heart's blood staining the brown feathers of the nightingale.

Before him, standing with his sword still raised, the prince stared down at minstrel and woman and the blood slowly staining the ground.

The king, looking at the room around him caught in a paroxysm of horror and sorrow, laughed. "I suppose there shall be no wedding today." *And no magic either*, not with the queen dead and the nightingale dying. He sighed, "What a shame," then shrugged.

He snapped his fingers, and it was as if the world woke. The nobles pulled from their haze. Soldiers straightened to attention, sheathing swords. Women wept, but none would dare look at the tableau at the king's feet, the sunlight goddess devoid of shine, and the nightingale whose voice was silent.

"A wretch in a tower and an enchanted bird," the king chuckled. "At least it's not a boring day, and at least neither of us will be wed to this madness."

He wrapped an arm around his son and dragged the boy from the throne room. His guards followed in his wake. The nobles quickly after.

All that remained was the beating rain, and the minstrel sitting vigil.

"HEART'S BLOOD, OFFERED willingly, to set the enchantment free. Heart's blood, once offered with love, will let your true-self be."

The wire was thin and sharp. It laid on the ground among the tattered pieces of the lute.

"Some are not deserving of our love. And some need to be set free from cages of their own making to learn to fly."

A small, soft thrust, and the wire pierced the breast of the nightingale.

A small, round drop of blood beaded on the white hued breast feathers before sliding down to fall upon the white gown of the beauty.

Philomel placed Faraday's head on the cool stone flooring, moved Liala to rest beside her sister.

The Nightingale King stepped back, his hands folded before him, and watched brown feathers melt away to warm flesh, and cool flesh grow warm with a fresh breath and rustling wings.

Lia blinked.

Her arm was numb where she laid upon it, her fingers stiff. The crinolines beneath her head scratched at her cheek. She was cold from the stone flooring under her back.

Still in her tower, waiting for her end.

"Or perhaps a new beginning. For both a you. A chance to learn from the other's perspective, to be free, truly free, by your own choices."

Beside her, the fabrics rustled, a brown head popped from beneath the white, the nightingale hopping out of the cloths.

"Sister?"

"Let her go, Liala. She is free from the beauty that bound her; she can find a life to love that does not require she love only herself now."

Lia turned to stare at Phil standing over her.

"And you are free to love yourself, in the way she kept you from before."

"I loved her."

"Yes, and she ignored it for her own gains."

"I loved myself."

"Not enough to fight to be free." Phil bent down and extended his hand. The calloused fingers were warm in her own, gentle in pulling her to her feet. "I come to those who are caged and help them learn to fly. To the song in their heart or the song they sing, I come. I heard you, but what I offer can only be granted to those willing to accept it and learn to take their freedom for their own."

Lia wrapped her arms around herself, seeing the man before her for the first time with her own true eyes.

He was tall and thin, his hair brown and uninspiring. His eyes blazed with spirit though, and, when a ray of light broke through the clouds outside, she caught the glint of gold encircling his head. "Who are you?"

He smiled, the kind smile she remembered from the wood, the man who helped her and who set her free. "I told you. The Minstrel Philomel. The Nightingale King. And I should like to show you how to fly without wings, to sing with you, if you would have me. Your song truly is enchanting, Liala."

"You know my name."

"Yes. And you know mine."

The nightingale chirped, flitting around on fabrics of her old self.

"Will she be all right?"

"She will learn to fly as high as you." He extended his hand towards her. "Let me show you how."

the end

Two hearts

Two Hearts
M.M. Roethig

It felt like yesterday when the large king-sized bed was overflowing with bodies. The image was clear in her mind and she could see it all playing out before her.

The family dog lay at the foot of the bed trying his hardest to bite debris flying through the air. One pillow had broken and feathers were swirling everywhere. Laughter filled the room— the night was perfect. Earlier that evening John and Mary were lying in bed chatting about their week when their three adolescent children ambushed them and an epic pillow fight broke out. All three children had run into the room, jumped on the bed, and attacked. Not to be one to let a good fight go, John immediately grabbed his own pillow and the fight, quite literally, exploded.

If Mary closed her eyes tight enough, she could still hear the laughter, the banter, and genuine joy from all those years ago. It was a snippet in time, intertwined with many other small moments, that made up the fabric of her life. She loved her life. But what was once a fond yesterday felt a lifetime away.

With her children all grown and embarking on their own lives, the family dog long laid to rest under the large oak in their back yard, and years of experience, heartache, joy, laughter—life— behind her, she tried to pinpoint where her and John had gone wrong. She came up empty.

John, on another business trip, had yet to call and she lay alone in bed, waiting and wondering what the next stages of life would bring. Their master room, once cluttered with all the essentials of life with children, felt empty and lonely now. The children's toys and clothes that once littered the area were replaced by perfectly arranged modern decor. It was still a homey and comfortable room, just different. Currently, the only light in the room came from a television that Mary long stopped watching. It cast an eerie glow through the room that left her feeling empty.

As Mary snuggled deeper into her blanket and stared blankly at the screen, her thoughts roamed. She and John were happy, their marriage was full adventure, once upon a time. They'd never lacked for anything to do, vacations to plan and enjoy, sporting events to watch, or children to entertain back then. In reality they should have more time now to do things together because the kids were grown. However, something was different. Something had changed between them and she wasn't sure anymore where their marriage was actually headed. More recent than not she found herself in a battle of words and hurt feelings with the man she loved with all her heart. A man she'd loved for over thirty years. Her life wasn't turning out to be the fairy tale she'd always dreamt of.

The sad fact was, she really couldn't even put her finger on when things had changed, let alone how they changed. When John traveled, she yearned to have him home. But the moment he walked in the door there was as if a rift that followed him and the divide between them widened. *Is this what years of marriage does to a couple? Two hearts once beat as one now beat separately and alone? Was it ever really true love then?*

Mary sighed. She'd wondered once or twice if they ever really were compatible or if they'd only weathered the storms of life for the sake of the kids. Now that the kids were gone, did they have anything left?

The phone rang and she exhaled before picking it up and swiping right to answer. John's face popped up on the screen. He was lying in bed at the hotel miles away. The room was bright with lights directly above his face and she noticed he was wearing his white undershirt, which meant he'd been at the hotel a while. The noise from the television played in the background and Mary recognized the commercial playing. He must've called during the commercial break to his favorite show. She sat up in bed and flipped the bedside lamp on, illuminating her face on her darkened screen.

"Hey sweetheart," he said. "Sorry I didn't call sooner. I've had a lot going on all day and so much work after dinner. I'm just now getting a break. How was your day?"

"It was the same as usual. I was able to get a lot of my projects done and Amanda brought Brooke to visit a bit today. He missed his Papa though." Amanda was one of their closest children. They lived only forty-five minutes away and often brought their grandson to visit.

"I called him earlier to talk," John replied. Mary nodded. That was usually the case. John always made a point to call the children and grandchildren, and it usually happened before he finally called her. She continued, "I finished painting the closet today though, so that's nice. It looks much better. Bigger, fresh, and clean."

"Oh ya? Glad it turned out. Was it a lot of work?"

"It always is," she said. "How was your day? You said you were pretty busy, which I'm guessing is why you're just now calling me for the day."

John exhaled and closed his eyes. "It's been pretty busy, yes. I haven't really sat down to relax since seven this morning. We did get everything figured out though, so ya. I'm sorry I didn't call earlier. It's been a bit crazy today and I wanted to get it all done so I could come home tomorrow."

"I get it," she said, trying to be supportive and feeling as if she'd fallen short when he gave her that sad smile. His hair was ruffled and standing on end so she knew he'd been running his hands through his hair. A trait he had when he was overly tired.

"What time is your flight tomorrow?" she asked.

"I land around ten so I should be home close to lunch."

"That's even earlier than what you put on the calendar, isn't it?"

Mary watched as he nodded and yawned. She really didn't mind when he traveled. It was part of his job and he was good at what he did. He'd traveled for years and each year with each promotion, the travel increased. It was harder when the children were younger, but now that she was the only one at home it wasn't as difficult, just lonely. It wasn't the travel that made her sad, not really. It was the tiny arguments, the little verbal jabs they each hurled at each other, that made her sad. Especially when they happened right before he flew out for the week.

"I was able to change my flight to come home first thing tomorrow, so that will be good. We can spend the day finishing the projects around the house."

Mary nodded and let out a slow exhale. She didn't want to tell him that most of the projects were finished now. She'd already worked on them all week by herself.

"We can also finish the talk we started before I left," John said. "I didn't like leaving that way."

"I didn't like it either," she admitted.

"So tomorrow let's fix it and start over?" he asked. Another slow exhale escaped her lungs and she nodded. That seemed to always be the answer. Argue, ignore, start over, repeat. A constant cycle that repeated weekly, sometimes even daily. They'd been able to always weather any storm in the past, but those storms were coming more frequently these days.

"Sure," she answered.

"Mary, I am really trying here." John closed his eyes and dropped his head further back into the pillows.

"I do know that," she said. "I am too, believe it or not." He opened his eyes to look at her.

"So, let's go to lunch tomorrow when I get home." John gave her a pleading look and she knew what he wanted. She nodded and he visibly relaxed.

"Sounds good," she said as she laid back against the pillows. Exhaustion overtaking her.

"You look good, by the way." John smiled. It was a sad smile, much like how she felt. He always said that, but she didn't always believe him.

"Thank you."

"I'll see you tomorrow?" he asked. It was a loaded question. Mostly because when he left earlier in the week she'd told him she may not be there when he came back. The memory of their fight still fresh in both their minds, it would appear.

"I will be here," she promised. "I'll see you tomorrow. Have a good night. And John?" She waited until he looked at her directly in her eyes on the screen. "I do love you."

John paused, just slightly. "I love you too."

Are you sure? She wondered silently. She didn't ask. He didn't say anything more. The screen flashed and he was gone.

Mary dropped the phone beside her on the bed and looked blankly at the television screen. Pulling the covers back up to her chin, she reached for the lamp by the side of her bed, and flipped it off. The room dropped into the eerie glow of the television once again and she lay there blankly watching the screen. *What are we going to do?*

That was a real question. *Did he love her the way he did once? Was this divide just a temporary obstacle in their journey or had he already moved on?* Mary knew he still cared, that he loved her as much as she loved him. The question was, is that enough?

Did she love him like she once did? Had she been the one that changed?

Sitting up abruptly, Mary had to get some thoughts out on paper. It helped her think.

Flipping the light back on and pulling out her journal, she turned to the last entry and dated the opposite blank page.

Dear Diary, do I say that anymore? I used to say that when I was twelve, it's become a habit by now. But I've changed, much like everything else in my life. Is my life just a comfortable habit? One that I've lived for so long that I don't know if there's meaning anymore? It almost feels as if that's the case. Are John and I just a habit?

So, not Dear Diary. Hello? Greetings? Whatever! What can I say but I feel as if my life is not what I wanted it to be. Is the love of my life still the love of my life? Is he the love of someone else's life? No, I know he isn't. I don't know why my mind goes there so quickly. He works hard for me, for our family even though our children are grown. He cares, I see it in his eyes. He's a good man, he truly is. I don't really have any reason to feel like he's not still in love with me, but I can't explain this rift. We've had so many years together. You can't weather those many years just for the children. We almost divorced years ago, but we worked it out. It was hard work, but we did it and we were stronger.

So that leads to the major question, what happened and why now? How did we get here? How did I get here? Is it me? Our hearts used to beat so strongly for each other, it was intense and insane. Now, we're just two hearts beating a lonely cadence alone. I don't like it, not at all. I love him, I do. Is that enough?

Mary closed her journal and dropped it next to her phone on John's side of the bed. When he traveled, she never pulled his covers back. It was a strange feeling to have the whole bed unmade if she was the only one in it. Grabbing the remote, she punched the power button, dropping the room into total darkness. Lying back, pulling the covers to her chin she rolled on her side and prayed for another dreamless night.

JOHN PULLED INTO the driveway as he hit the garage button to open the large door. He waited until the door reached the top before slowly rolling through the opening and coming to a stop. He wondered how the rest of the day was going to go as he recalled what was said before he left. The day started out like any other, then quickly went downhill with many things said he hoped neither one believed. They were both guilty of SWA, or speaking while angry. Early on in their marriage they vowed to take a step back and calm down when they argued so they didn't say things they didn't mean just because they were angry. Lately, that vow wasn't exactly being followed. In fact, it was almost the opposite.

John put his truck in park, turned off the engine, and got out before he realized Mary was waiting for him at the door leading into the house. She stood on the stairs propping the door open, watching as he unloaded his bags and made his way to her. He mounted the first step and was eye to eye with her when she threw her arms round his neck and buried her nose close to his ear. He snaked one arm around her waist and they inhaled simultaneously. She held him for several seconds before letting go and stepping back. He didn't know what that meant. *Was everything back to normal as if their last four days never happened?*

"How was the flight?" she asked as she reached for his shoulder bag.

"Bumpy," he replied. "I'm a bit sick to my stomach, actually."

"Oh, that sucks. I'm sorry to hear that."

John followed her inside and down the hallway to their bedroom, wheeling his bag behind him. She dropped his shoulder bag on the bed as he hoisted his suitcase next to it. Unzipping the main pocket, he pulled all his dirty clothes from inside and dropped them on the floor next to him. He grabbed his toiletries bag and headed for the bathroom while Mary scooped the clothes from the floor and followed. She dropped the bundle into a basket overflowing in the corner of their closet while John placed the toiletries in the drawer in their master bathroom. He'd be leaving again in a few days so there wasn't much need to unpack his bathroom bag. It was easier to keep it stocked and put away than unpacking all together. That way it was ready to go the next trip.

"Work this week was good," he repeated to his reflection in the mirror knowing she was half listening. There once was a time they could talk about anything. More recently, it felt as if her eyes would glass over each time he mentioned his work, which he realized he mentioned a lot more lately. She listened, but she didn't *really* hear him. It made him wonder why. "We fixed the tank that's been leaking and the city signed off on it, so we're back up and running. That was a nightmare."

"Sounds like it," Mary said as she leaned into the doorframe. "I'm glad it is finally done then. That's been hanging over your head for a while."

John nodded and turned to her. Looking at the woman before him he marveled at how easily and gracefully she'd aged. She colored her hair, most women did, but her skin was still as flawless today as it was thirty years ago when he'd first met her. She was much older now and sported several scars from her vast array of surgeries. She'd put on weight, in fact she'd battled with weight most of their married life, but she was still as beautiful as ever. She limped now, her hips were constantly sore and some days it was hard for her to get around, but in his eyes, she was aging beautifully. He looked in the mirror and noticed his own middle had grown larger and softer with age. It was part of life.

"What do you say we go grab some lunch. Where would you like to go?"

"I'd like to go someplace with soft chairs, other than that I don't care." She pushed away from the wall and he noticed for the first time her limp was more defined than it had been days before.

"Your hips bothering you," he stated more than asked. When Mary nodded and walked passed him, he wondered how much she'd done around the house to make it worse.

The closet. She mentioned the closet and he forgot to notice it. Quickly stepping into the master closet and looking around, he understood why she limped. He'd been in Texas a few short days and she'd completely redone the entire room. She'd filled any holes in the walls, rearranging the shelving, and decluttered, and painted. No wonder she was struggling to walk. It seemed as if she always took on too much when he was gone, mostly because she knew he really didn't want to spend his time off working on her projects. He always had so much on his mind that her projects usually took a back seat.

John walked from their bedroom and watched as she tried to put on her shoes without wincing. She was one tough woman, one who didn't complain about her physical ailments. Half the time he didn't realize she was in pain, or that much pain anyway.

"Would it be better if we ordered delivery? Or I could go pick up something and we can eat here?" John asked. He was tired and flying always took it out of him, but this was his wife she was more exhausted than he ever could be. He needed to make it easier on her, with an exhausted sigh, she dropped her shoe and smiled up at him.

"Yes, please," she said. "Before you leave though, if you carry the laundry basket into the laundry room, I will start a load while you're gone."

John held out his hands and helped her stand when she reached for him. "Don't worry about laundry. I'll do it when I get back. Why don't you relax on the couch, maybe take a little nap while I'm gone? I'll take care of it."

"Are you sure?" she asked.

"I'm sure. I'll be right back."

John watched her limp her way into the living room before grabbing his jacket and heading back to his truck. It was moments like this that helped remind him how much he admired her strength. He wondered again why they seemed to argue so much recently. Mostly he wondered if they wanted to stop it, or if it was too late to fix whatever seemed to be broken. He didn't want it to be too late.

MARY SAT ON the couch and waited for John to return. He really was a good man. He worked hard, even though she teased him about his traveling. He was smart too. So smart that she had a hard time keeping up when he talked technical to her. She tried to follow, but she never understood when he talked about his projects. They all sounded intense and in-depth, she just didn't know the lingo or the particulars of what he did. However, for as smart as he was, his common sense wasn't so dialed in. She'd just laugh and shake her head when he'd do something so utterly funny, like cleaning the fish tanks with Pine-sol. He'd always said, *"Common sense ain't so common."*

She sat on the couch and pushed the button to recline. Grabbing a near-by blanket, she snuggled down into the cushions and had no trouble falling asleep.

Mary woke when John gently shook her leg, calling her name in soft tones. "Mary. Mary, lunch is here."

Sitting up, she accepted the lunch he offered, Mongolian. One of their favorite lunches was sharing a plate of Mongolian. It had been forever since they'd actually taken the time to sit and have a lunch together, both were so busy all the time. The smells made her mouth water and her memories flow.

One memory from years ago played out like a movie as she took the plate from him. All the children were in school and she'd been having one of *those days*. She didn't know why exactly, she was just down. Her body ached, not painfully, but just ached from her insides out and she was simply uncomfortable. With zero motivation to do anything she sat on the couch under a blanket and flipped through the channels looking for something to occupy her mind. It was that moment when John walked in unannounced and surprised her with lunch. Mongolian, much like he'd done today. John took a few hours off work to spend his lunch time with her and her day changed drastically.

John was a master of flavors and lunch was always delicious. But what made this memory so special was the extra time they spent *after* eating. Two hours later he'd gone back to work she was ready to take on what remained of the day.

Blinking to clear her thoughts, she looked at the plate John had just handed her. He'd loaded her plate with water chestnuts, baby corns, and fake lobster meat, which she loved. He'd removed all the pineapple from her dish and taken them for himself. This was a dance they'd perfected over the year. *The dance* was what John and Mary referred to as their carefully constructed movements in their marriage they'd perfected over time, much like a couple on a dance floor. Their steps fall together seamlessly as they move gracefully through the movements.

Similarly, their Mongolian lunches, this was all part of the dance. He knew what she liked, she knew what he liked. John danced his way through this moment by taking what he knew she didn't like and dishing up everything she did. *The Dance.* It took years to perfect it and most days they were flawless in their execution. Lately, they'd been stumbling through the moves.

Taking a bite, she wiped her mouth and turned toward him. "This is good, dear."

"Thanks, I tried different flavors this time. I like it."

They ate quietly, each passing glances to each other but neither saying a word as they ate. The silence was deafening.

After several moments, Mary placed her plate next to John, turned to face him, and leaning her head against the couch watching him.

"What?" he asked when he noticed.

"I think we have some things to talk about."

Sighing, John dropped his fork onto his plate, placed it next to hers before turning to face her. "I was wondering if you were going to mention this."

"Well, don't you think we should figure out what's going on?" she asked.

"I don't know anymore," he replied. "I don't even know what we're trying to figure out." John raised his hands in exasperation and shook his head.

She couldn't hide the hurt she felt. She knew he saw it in her eyes when his face fell in response. "I'm sorry. I shouldn't have said that," he said as he rubbed his hands over his face.

"Don't you feel something's changed? Something's happened between us," she exclaimed. "Do you even want to be married anymore?"

she asked. Mary didn't know where the words came from, they weren't planned. She regretted asking when he paused for so long.

"You don't have anything to say?" she asked when he remained quiet.

"I don't know what to say," he replied.

Mary felt the breath leave her chest as her stomach dropped. "Really?" she whispered.

"I don't want to hurt you, Mary. I do love you. It's just..." he trailed off.

"Do you have someone else?" she cut him off. Mary immediately stood and stepped away.

"No," he said. His voice strong and clear. "I would never do that to you, you know that."

"There's many things I thought I knew, but I find I don't always have it figured out."

John turned toward her and reached for her hands. She didn't fight him, but she still wouldn't look at him. "Mary, it's just I always seem to hurt you when we talk. Neither one of us can talk without hurting someone. I don't know what to say anymore."

He was right, partially. It made her sad.

"What happened to us?" she asked. The tears started falling now. "Is this what happens to marriages once the kids have grown and gone? We have nothing left anymore?"

"Mary," he said and she pulled her hands away. She felt the first tear trace down her cheek and she swiped it on her shoulder. He tried again. "Mary..."

"What are we going to do then?" she cut him off again. "Call it a day? Is that what you want, John?"

With a heavy sigh he sat back against the cushions and dropped her shoulders. "I don't know, Mary. It's all coming at me so fast right now, I can't think. Maybe we need to call it a day."

"You're right," she said as she stood and stepped for the hallway. "Maybe we gave the best years to each other and now that ship has sailed. Maybe our hearts used to beat as one, but now we're two people, two separate lives, and we need to stop fooling ourselves."

She turned to walk away ignoring him when he called after her. He didn't follow, she hoped he would follow, but she was alone. She heard his loud sigh. It was resignation. She made it around the corner before the remaining tears fell. She went into their room and laid on the bed. They really were through. She was desperate when she'd asked if they should call it quits and said the words she didn't mean. *Should we call it a day?* His response wasn't what she wanted.

JOHN WATCHED HER go until she was around the corner before the emotions in him welled to bursting. He wanted her to turn back, to talk to him and work it out, but he was so confused he couldn't think so he let her go. He'd learned years ago that he'd never win a word fight with his wife. She missed her calling and should've been a lawyer for as good as she could argue. As it was, he let her go. Past experience proved when she walked away, she needed time. He vowed to give it to her even though he longed to go after her and hold her until she realized how much he loved her. Instinctively he knew that's what she needed. He didn't move.

He heard the click of the door and his heart dropped to his stomach as her words played back in his head. *Our hearts used to beat as one but now we're two people living two separate lives.* She'd even asked if he has someone else. He didn't know where her feelings were or why she even thought he'd have someone else, but their recent arguments must've hurt her more than he realized. He knew she loved him and he loved her and he just assumed stress was getting in the way. Stress, work—his attentions were divided a lot with his new role at work. Was he not giving her what she needed? Apparently, there was more to it.

As the minutes ticked by, John stared blankly at the screen. Happier times invaded his thoughts. Remembering one particular moment when they'd taken their children to a baseball game and Mary was like a little kid watching, singing, dancing, and teaching their children it was okay to let loose and have fun. He remembered sharing peanuts, fried funnel cakes, and the ballparks famous cheddar sausage with grilled onions and cream cheese. He loved spending time at the ball field with Mary and the children. They didn't do much of that anymore. He wondered why.

More recently, he began to realize it seemed they had so little in common it was hard to find things to talk about.

John got up, his appetite now gone, and went to the kitchen to clean up their discarded lunch. Placing the leftovers in the refrigerator, he loaded the remaining dishes into the dishwasher and started the cycle. He stood there for several minutes listening to the sound of the water swirling around inside as more memories flooded him. How many times had they stood at that sink, or one like it, and talked while they did the dishes. Intimate talks that turned to jokes, then laughter, and finally kissing. He missed the kissing.

John pushed from the counter and made his way to the office. Originally the space had been set up for crafts and hobbies, but when he started working from home, he effectively kicked her out and taken over. She didn't complain, though. She'd just moved her projects to a different area to allow him space to work.

John sat in the large overstuff office chair and moved the mouse to wake the screen. Up popped a smiling vacation picture of their recent trip to Mexico. That was two years ago, right after their youngest had graduated high school and moved away to college. This was their first *empty nester* vacation and it had been perfect. They'd been happy there, at least according to the picture looking back at him. He remembered the night beach walks, the making out under the palm trees, the day excursions. He missed that simpler time. They'd come back more connected than when they first left, but here they were divided again.

With more questions than answers, John had renewed determination to find out when exactly things between him and Mary changed and what he could do to fix it.

John opened the digital photo file on the computer and pulled up the folder containing their life's memories, another project Mary took on to assure they always had their pictures. He started several years back when the pictures were full of children, sports, pets, events, and happy holiday moments. He smiled when he saw the picture of his older children dying Easter Eggs as he remembered the way they'd all laughed. His heart skipped a beat when he scrolled to a picture of his wife. Still the same face staring back at him. They were happy then.

John spent an hour looking through their photos, smiling and reminiscing all the fun times they'd shared. Movies, sporting events, concerts, graduations, dances—it was all there. All the love a couple could muster was visible in every picture. The young John and Mary were so in love, you could feel it on the screen with each digital snapshot.

As the time went by and the pictures became more recent, there were fewer and fewer pictures of them together. There were plenty of John on work trips visiting places he'd never seen before, or Mary walking the dog or hiking in the mountains. There were pictures of them at movies with friends or at dinners with co-workers. However, rarely were there pictures of them together anymore.

John exhaled.

He dropped his head into his hand, pinching the bridge of his nose as he thought. They'd grown apart when the kids left and they no longer had a common reason to be around each other unless they were with friends. The question now was, what would they do about it because that wasn't how he wanted his marriage to be.

John heard Mary clear her throat and he turned to see her watching him from the doorway of the office. She had a bag slung over her shoulder, her eyes were red and swollen. She'd been crying and he hadn't even bothered to check on her.

"I have a few things I need to take care of this afternoon. I don't know when I'll be back," she said. He noticed her bag wasn't her normal purse, but a large duffle bag packed full. Panic threatened to overtake him and he stood.

"Are you just running errands or are you leaving somewhere?' he asked and his voice cracked.

"I think I might find a hotel for the night, I need some time to think." Mary took a step backward and he followed quickly behind her as she turned and headed for the door.

"Please don't leave, not right now. We need to talk more."

"Honestly, John. I don't think I can. Emotionally I'm raw. Physically I'm exhausted. I need time to think. I need time that's not here."

"Please don't go," he pleaded. He felt the pressure of his heart hammering against his chest.

"I'm sorry, I just can't right now. I'll let you know where I'm at."

John reached for her but she stepped away, hands in the air.

"I do love you," she said and then quickly walked out the door. He stood frozen wondering if he should go after her or just let her go to give her the time she needed. He'd given her time an hour ago and here she was, marching out the door with a packed bag. His heart sank as he watched her drive away, wondering if his life was driving away with her.

MARY DROVE FOR only a few minutes before she pulled over to the side of the road. Putting her car in park, she laid her head back against the seat and closed her eyes. She didn't cry, not because she didn't want to but because she willed her tears to stay put. She needed to think without the overwhelming emotions. Especially since she spent the last hour crying anyway. It didn't help.

In all their years together, never had she felt so distant from John. They'd been through death of parents, death of friends, moves to new homes and states, fights with their children, new grandchildren, getting new pets, losing old pets—life. They'd been through it all and with each obstacle they'd faced, they'd come out stronger than they were before.

And they'd never run away from anything before. She'd never run away, until today. That's what she was doing. Running away.

A song came on her radio that gave her pause. She'd heard it so many times before it played over in her head on repeat. The song was right. If we have a strong foundation, the rest didn't matter. Any storm could come and shake the house, but the if foundation was strong and the house couldn't be broken. Double meaning. If their relationship has a strong foundation, they couldn't be broken either.

Shaking her head, she silently wondered what she'd done. Instead of asking John what he meant when he said he wasn't sure, or giving him the time to think as he asked, she'd jumped head long into self-doubt. It was easy to pack a bag after that and walking out the door was to hurt him more than anything. And that's what she'd done. She hurt the man she loved more than anything.

Taking a deep calming breath, Mary put her car into drive with new determination and headed for home.

She found John sitting on the couch. His elbows propped on his knees and his head was resting in his hands. The same song she'd been listening to was playing over the speaker when she walked in. *How fitting,* she thought as she silently rounded the corner. He was starting at the floor and looked up at her with relief in his eyes, immediately standing and going to her.

"I wasn't sure if you'd be back," he said as he embraced her so fully she was surrounded by the strength of him.

"I didn't know myself," she admitted. "But I realized we can't fix *whatever* this is if I run." She snaked her arms around his middle, expanded through years and aging, and rested her head on his strong, comforting shoulder. He wasn't the model on some romance novel cover, but he was hers and she loved him for all he was.

"I don't like this feeling, Mary. I don't know what's going on, but I don't like it."

With a deep sigh and shuttered breath, she agreed. "I don't either."

John leaned away as he looked into her eyes. She saw the love that still burned deep for her and instantly felt the tears begin to fall. John pulled her closer and started swaying in time to the music. Apparently, he'd felt a connection to the song as much as she did. She leaned her head on his chest, right over his heart so she could feel it beating steady and strong.

"Tell me what's going on," he whispered in her ear. She didn't know where to start because she didn't understand herself.

"I honestly don't know. Something's happened between us. We're not the same people we once were. There was a time when we had so many things in common and we always had fun together. Even when life wasn't perfect, we always found the joy. We don't anymore. Do we?"

"No," he agreed. "We haven't had much fun lately, have we. That's partly my fault. This travel is hard and I get tired when I'm home. I want to catch up on shows, relax, and gear up for the next round of travel. I don't put much stock in what's important to you, and I need to."

"It's not just you. Sometimes even the littlest things bother me more than they ever did before. It all just feels...different."

"I agree. It's different. I am gone, but it's for work, not fun," he said as they continued to sway. "I don't enjoy traveling all the time. It's hard being away from you and then it's hard being home. Everything keeps moving on without me when I'm gone. It's hard."

"I do know that. I know it's hard on you and life doesn't stop when you're gone. It's hard here too because I do it all by myself." Now they were talking she couldn't stop the words from flowing. "I know it's not easy for you, I do. It's just not easy for me either. But we've always done so well in the past."

"So why did you leave just now? Why did you pack a bag and walk out?" he asked. His voice soft and questioning.

"I left because you said you weren't sure you wanted to be married anymore."

"When?" he asked incredulously. "I wouldn't say that. I didn't say that."

"You did! I asked if you wanted to just call it a day and you said, *Maybe we should*. Those were your exact words."

"I was talking about *today*. I was talking about our discussion. I'd just gotten home and we started talking about things and I had zero idea what was going on. Then you start asking me if we've given each other the best of ourselves and I agreed we needed to call it a day and step back, *from the conversation*, Mary. Not the marriage. Never the marriage."

"I left and you didn't follow," she stated as she smacked his chest and turned away. "Why didn't you come after me and explain then?"

"I didn't know you took it that way *and* you always ask me to give you space."

Mary let out a deep sigh and closed her eyes. Dropping her head into her hands, she pinched the bridge of her nose. "What are we going to do?" she asked as she shook her head. All these theatrics over a misunderstood phrase.

"First, let's start over."

"John," Mary asked as she turned and looked him deep in his eyes. "Do you still love me?"

Without hesitation he answered, "Yes, Without a doubt, yes. If I had a chance to do this all over again, I would in a heartbeat." He started to reach for her but she stayed him with an outstretched hand.

"I'm old, John. I've gained weight. I look as if I've been peppered with a shotgun with all the surgeries and stretch marks I've gained through the years. I can't walk all that well anymore, and I have zero idea what you talk about when you tell me about your job. Zero idea. I try, I really do, but I just don't understand anything you do. You deserve someone smart, someone young who can keep up with you, someone who understands you when you talk. Why are you with me?" Mary rambled on. When she asked the final question, she put her hands on her hips and waited.

John pulled her into his arms again, holding her close as he began swaying to the music once more. The chorus was playing and they listened to the words as they danced. Finally, John replied. "Mary, you're more beautiful to me now than ever. I don't care about your weight, your scars, or how well you walk. I love you for you and that means all of you the way you are now and will be. I'm no spring chicken myself. I get winded walking around the block. I'm old and slowing down and not as active and I once was. You're not walking much slower than me anymore these days, and that's fine. I like walking next to you. As for work, it doesn't matter to me. I don't want someone to talk to technical to me all the time. I'd never have a break from all the stress. I need someone to help me understand the difference between *Revered Pewter* and *Grey*. Heaven knows I can't even match my clothes without asking you for help. I need someone to give me the pineapple out of their Mongolian or off their pizza and take my nasty imitation crab meat. I need someone to laugh when I match blue and black socks. I need you."

"Don't you want someone smart to talk to, someone on your level? Don't you want someone you don't have to worry about falling over walking in the grocery store?" she asked, mainly just to hear him tell her how much he loved her, again.

His answer was simple. "No." He looked into her eyes as he spoke next. "I married you for life, I married you forever. You are my one true love, my soul mate, my second half. I can't function without you in my life, Mary. I hope you see that. Your weight, doesn't matter. Your hair can be grey or brown, I don't care. You can limp next to me the rest of my life. I want you there."

"What about all the things we used to do? I feel as if we were once two hearts beating as one. Now I feel as if we are two hearts going our separate ways." Mary stopped swaying with him and stepped away. He didn't pull her back, but he didn't step away either. "We had one purpose, common goals, and so much to work toward. What do we have now?"

"I'll tell you what we have. We have three amazing children who grew up with the love of both parents to guide them through life. They still have two pretty awesome parents, if you ask me. We have a comfortable home that always looks great and is welcoming to everyone that enters, and that's because of you. We have grandchildren who love to see their *Nana and Papa* and live for moments together. We have a life time of memories and we still have more to make. We haven't changed our goals, maybe we've changed the path, but we've never changed our goal." John pulled her close once again and she didn't fight him. Placing his fingers under her chin, he gently lifted her gaze to look at him.

"Our goal is to grow old together, no matter how we do it. You said we were two hearts beating as one, once. I say we've always been two hearts beating *in sync*. We have always been two separate people, but that's what makes us, *us*. We have so much in common that most times we beat in sync, but not as one. Never as one. If we beat as one, one of us would be drown out and dominated by the other. I don't want you to be drown out, I don't want you to be the same as me. I want you to be you."

John placed a kiss on her forehead. "Be the woman who buys kitchen gadgets that annoy me because you love them and they're cute." John kissed her nose. "Be the woman that starts a new project at the spur of the moment so I can complain while I secretly enjoy watching you work." He leaned down and kissed her cheek. "Be the woman who dances to music while cleaning the house, even though I hate the song, because I love watching you dance." He kissed her other cheek. "Be the grandma who makes cookies in the afternoon even though I have no self-control and eat them all when you're done."

John cupped her face and captured her lips with his, kissing her deeply. He stole her breath as they swayed in time to the song playing once more. When he finally lifted his head, he smiled down at her, rubbing her swollen lip with his thumb. "Mary, just be you."

Mary smiled and looked at him searching for any kind of regret he may harbor. She found none.

"Two hearts beating in sync. I like that," she said. "This song was playing in my car when I decided to come back."

John dropped a kiss to her lips and smiled. "Was it?" he asked.

Mary nodded before she continued. "We're much like this song, don't you think?"

With a smirk on his face, he nodded. "It speaks to me, that's for sure."

"As long as we have a good foundation, nothing can bring us down."

"What do you say about making sure we have things to do together each week? We used to do a lot, but we don't anymore," he said.

"I'd like that," Mary replied as she laid her head back on his shoulder. "We could take turns each weekend coming up with something we'd each like to do. I might have projects."

"That's a great idea," he said as he dropped a kiss to the top of her head.

"Mine might be projects," she smirked and looked into his eyes.

He chuckled. "I'd be disappointed if you didn't." He dropped another kiss to her forehead and spoke again, this time to the gadget playing music on the counter. "Alexa, stop music."

Taking her hand in his he started leading her down the hallway toward the master bedroom. "What do you say we start this weekend with making sure our two hearts have a solid *foundation*?"

With a smile that vanished all her previous heartache she replied. "I'd love too!"

the end

About the Authors

GINA ARDITO is the award-winning author of contemporary, historical, and paranormal romance, currently published by Montlake Romance and independently. In 2012, she launched her freelance editing business, Excellence in Editing, and now has a stable of award-winning clients, as well. She's hosted workshops around the world for writing conferences, author organization chapter meetings, and library events. To her everlasting shame, despite all her accomplishments, she'll never be more famous than her dog, who starred in commercials for 2015's Puppy Bowl.

WWW.GINAARDITO.COM

Editor and internationally known author, GRACE AUGUSTINE, was raised in Montana. Her hobbies include music, acrylic painting, container planting, and old romantic movies. She resides in Iowa and is the mother of two adult sons and an adorable feline.

WWW.GRACEAUGUSTINE.WEEBLY.COM

CJ BATY loves a good mystery, hot sexy guys, the mountains, and a happily ever after. When she decided to try her hand in the book world, it only made sense to combine those things. She firmly believes that love is love in all of its shapes and forms. Her books contain broken spirits that need to be mended and a mystery, often a murder, which needs to be solved, so those spirits can find love. She calls southwest Ohio home, but her heart lives in the hills of Tennessee.

WWW.CJBATY.COM

LINDA BOULANGER has always been a hopeless romantic, which spills over into her eclectic mix of published books, numerous story singles, and short stories in a few group anthologies. She spends her "free time" designing book covers for others through Tell~Tale Book Covers and TreasureLine Designs, all from her desk just north of Tulsa, Oklahoma.

WWW.LINDABOULANGERBOOKS.COM

EDWARD BUATOIS is an eclectic reader and writer who enjoys many different genres including romance, thriller, sci-fi, and fantasy. He particularly enjoys writing urban fantasy, though he's been getting more involved with romance lately. And there is usually a fantastical element to surprise.

WWW.EDWARDBUATOIS.COM

JENNIFER DANIELS lives in Upstate, NY with her husband and son. She enjoys spending time with her family, fishing, camping, kayaking, and being on the water. Jennifer is a former nurse and for several years was very active with her local volunteer fire and rescue department. She is a paranormal/fantasy junkie, loves to read most things in those genres and is a binge-watching Hallmark Channel fan.

Writing was never on her radar until her son shared with her that he wanted to write a book. So, together they began and that was when

Jennifer decided to give it a try on her own. And that was how the Opalla Series was born.

AUTHORJENNIFERDANI.WIXSITE.COM

LAURA HERN is a native Texan and grew up reading murder and romance mysteries. She currently lives in Minnesota and is the author of the Lainey Maynard Mystery series. You can connect with Laura on her author Facebook page, Twitter, and her website.

WWW.LAURAHERN.COM

ANDI LAWRENCOVNA lives in a small town in Northeast Ohio where she was born and raised. After finishing her education, she decided that it was time to let a little fantasy rule her life for a while. *The NeverLands* were born out of a frustration with happily-ever-afters, and a burning desire for the same.

WWW.ANDILAWRENCOVNA.COM

M.M. ROETHIG is a happily-ever-after author who swoons for a good romance. From the time she was a little girl she was spinning tales for anyone who would listen. When she's not making up stories, she's spending time with family. M.M. Roethig lives in Colorado with her husband and son, close to one of her daughters and grandson. She loves movies, books, dancing, music, baseball, and traveling when possible.

WWW.MMROETHIG.COM